LOST
LIKE
ME

LOST
LIKE
ME

A BLUE WATER MYSTERY

Ivanka Fear

LEVEL
BEST BOOKS

First published by Level Best Books 2024

This novel is entirely a work of fiction. The names, characters and incidents portrayed in it are the work of the author's imagination. Any resemblance to actual persons, living or dead, events or localities is entirely coincidental.

Ivanka Fear asserts the moral right to be identified as the author of this work.

Author Photo Credit: Amanda Belec, Instagram @thirteen13designsnphotography

First edition

ISBN: 978-1-68512-589-9

Cover art by Level Best Designs

This book was professionally typeset on Reedsy. Find out more at reedsy.com

For my husband, Brian, my best friend without whom I'd be lost
You light up my life and keep the fire burning.
And
To our family
With all my love.

Praise for Lost Like Me

"*Lost Like Me* is a complex mystery intertwining themes of love and betrayal with a search for a missing woman. This smart mystery will keep you guessing until the final chapters when all the plot lines are resolved."—Gary Gerlacher, author of *Last Patient of the Night* and *Faulty Bloodline*

"*Lost Like Me* by Ivanka Fear grips the reader from the very first page. It's a clever mystery, full of twists and turns, complicated characters with hidden pasts, and non-stop suspense. The story begins as an investigation into the disappearance of a young woman told from a variety of perspectives, and then escalates into a full-blown revelation of secrets that the reader never sees coming."—Suzanne Craig-Whytock, author of *The Seventh Devil* and *The Devil You Know*

"The Blue Water Mysteries delivers once again! *Lost Like Me* follows *The Dead Lie* with another multi-layered mystery, featuring memorable, complex characters and surprising plot twists. You won't be able to put it down!"—Travis Tougaw, author of *Foxholes*

"In the second book in her Blue Water Mystery Series, author Ivanka Fear has crafted a tightly-plotted page turner. A young woman mysteriously disappears from her home in the middle of the night, and despite all efforts, three weeks later she is still missing. This is the intriguing premise of *Lost like me*, a twisty, clever mystery that kept me guessing right to the end. A great read."—J. Woollcott, award-winning author of the DS Ryan McBride Belfast Murder Series, *A Nice Place to Die* and *Blood Relations*

"A gripping mystery thriller that keeps you turning the pages. *Lost Like Me* is full of dark secrets, missing persons, and crazy twists. Ivanka Fear keeps us guessing to the very last page!"—Joseph Souza, bestselling author

"*Lost Like Me* has everything a novel you can't put down should have––plus more. A solid mystery, great characters, and surprise twists and turns spattered throughout, readers will be anxiously waiting for more."—Lynn Chandler Willis, award-winning and bestselling author of *What the Monkey Saw—A Death Doula Mystery*

"What starts off as a simple missing person investigation develops into something far more involved and sinister. As Cheryl MacGregor delves more deeply into the case, it threatens to put both her life and marriage in jeopardy. Another well-crafted tale in the Blue Water Mystery series from a very accomplished author."—David Weller, author of *Secret of Heathcote Manor*

Chapter One

Cheryl MacGregor

Sunday early morning July 5

A shrill ring pierces the darkness. *That* can be nothing good.

We're both startled from our sleep, but Jim's the one to answer since the phone lies on the nightstand next to his side of the bed. I switch on the lamp and watch his expression change from groggy to alarmed.

"What? What is it? What's going on?" I whisper, fearing we've been discovered. Signaling me to be quiet, Jim turns away, covers one ear, and ignores my mouthing and gestures.

"No, I haven't seen her since Friday afternoon at work. I have no idea." Worry laces his words as he adds, "The police? What did they say?"

"Police?" I scream the word, unable to control my terror despite the fact I might wake our eleven-year-old son and six-year-old daughter, who lie safely tucked in their rooms across the hall.

"I see. I'm sure there must be a logical explanation. I'm sorry I can't tell you anything useful." It kills me, not knowing what he's talking about. "Well, keep me posted, and let me know what I can do to help."

Jim turns to me and explains the call was about Julia, his receptionist at MacGregor Realty. Danny, her boyfriend, is out of his mind with worry. She's missing. As in gone, disappeared, vanished. "Her car's in the driveway, and it looks like she's home, but there's no sign of her, and no one knows where she is."

A wave of relief runs through me. Although I should be upset by this news, I had imagined so much worse. The possibility of Stefan showing up to exact vengeance for his son's death has nearly paralyzed me since the crash upon my return home from Croatia this past fall. Although the police determined that the truck smashing through the glass doors into the *Gazette*'s lobby was a fluke accident, I'm still not convinced. I narrowly escaped death when the vehicle stopped within a hair's breadth of me, no one in the driver's seat. The official report stated the unlicensed teen driver rolled out of the truck and fled the scene when he lost control. Once I realize the phone call isn't a threat to us, the nosy reporter in me takes over, and I envision the byline. Local Woman Goes Missing—by Cheryl MacGregor.

Things like this don't often happen in our mining community in the middle of absolutely nowhere, so it'll be the story of the decade. Well, Lake Kipling's story of the decade, anyway. And it's the story *I'm* going to write.

Most of the time, I report on council meetings, which is about as exciting as watching snow melt. And there's plenty of it to watch up here. I hate it, but I endure it. At least we're safe. There's the occasional break-in or drugs found in someone's possession, but that's as sensational as it gets.

"Oh, my God! What do you think happened to Julia?" I'm already preparing to take notes in my head.

A lost girl. Just like me. I know what Jim's thinking, but not saying. He's wondering whether she took off, left her old life behind to start fresh. Maybe she doesn't *want* to be found. But Jim, of course, didn't tell Danny that.

Julia Brenner has been Jim's receptionist for the past six years. Danny Anderson joined the small sales team last summer. He and Julia became friends, then started officially dating after the Christmas party. Some firms frown upon that sort of thing, but Jim doesn't mind if it doesn't interfere with their work. Jim's a romantic at heart.

I certainly wonder if Julia simply ran off. But then again, maybe something terrible happened to her. It's scary. When you think of the miles of forest and lakes surrounding Lake Kipling, there's a chance she might never be found. That was why I chose to move up north when I became Cheryl MacGregor. I knew no one would come looking for me here. It's nothing like the city of Hamilton, where I was born and raised. The city where I met Jim, my savior. The love of my life.

It's the perfect place to get lost.

It's also the perfect place to get rid of someone. Maybe Danny killed her, and he's covering up by reporting her missing. He doesn't seem like the type, but you never know what people are capable of. Not really.

In any case, I'm excited about this. Julia is missing and needs to be found. Dead or alive. Of course, I want her to be safe and sound, back home where she belongs, or living the life she wants to live elsewhere.

Jim says she'll likely turn up tomorrow. People usually do in cases like this.

But if she's still missing, I need to find out what happened to her. There's a whopper of a story here, and I'm going to be the one to write it. Being a reporter, you have to always be on your toes. Because you just never know. That big story could be right around the corner. It all starts with one phone call in the middle of the night.

Chapter Two

Danny Anderson

Two hours earlier

At 2:15 a.m., Danny Anderson picks up the emergency key under the flowerpot next to the front door and enters his girlfriend's house, his hand shaking as he turns the key. Danny's worried about Julia. He's been trying to call for the last hour but can't get through.

Why isn't she answering?

Upon entering the house, Danny notices a light emanating from down the hall. A sense of relief washes over him. Walking toward her room, Danny assumes he'll find Julia in bed, exhausted from her late night out with the girls.

But that's not what greets him when he walks through her doorway.

The lamp on the nightstand sheds light on a half-empty mug of cocoa and a half-eaten Twinkie. Fuzzy slip-on slippers lie tossed on the floor in front of the table. The clock radio, on the other nightstand, is tuned to the local station, the volume on low. On the bed, the pillows sit propped up and the covers thrown down, with a closed mystery paperback novel on top of the sheets. The chair next to the bed holds a patterned sundress and a white sweater folded over the back, along with a canvas purse. It looks as though she's gotten up to use the bathroom and will be back any minute.

The bathroom door, though, stands partly open, with the lights off. Danny flips the switch, wondering if she's in the near dark, sick to her stomach after a night out drinking. A used bath towel hangs over the edge of the tub. The counter holds a curling iron and hairbrush, along with assorted cosmetics. But Julia's not there. She's not in the spare bedroom, either.

"Julia! Where are you?" he shouts, wandering through the kitchen and living area, although it's obvious she's not there. "Julia!" Considering she may have decided to throw in a load of laundry when she got home, Danny descends the wooden steps to the unfinished basement and strides across the cement floor. Something brushes against his legs, startling him. The house isn't empty.

Julia's cat, Cleo, is home. Alone. Danny wonders what the hell happened to Julia. Her car sits parked in the driveway, but she's obviously not in the house.

Maybe she stepped out for some reason.

Danny exits through the front door and jogs up and down the road, looking for some sign of Julia. She knows a few of her neighbors, but it's too late to be visiting anyone. Besides, there are no lights on at any of the houses.

I should have called the cops when she told me someone was following her the past few weeks.

Julia had repeatedly said she felt someone watching her. She didn't provide any evidence to prove her suspicions. But now, her abruptly abandoned house, along with the possibility of a stalker, confirms her fears were justified.

Danny goes over the scenario in his mind several times before picking up the phone and dialing 911 to report Julia Brenner missing. He prays they'll believe him when he insists something has happened to her, although he's not sure the provincial police in Lake Kipling will respond immediately to a report of a 24-year-old woman missing after a Saturday night out on the town with her friends. But he hopes the bizarre circumstances surrounding her disappearance will make the cops take him seriously.

"It looks like she's been snatched right out of bed," he exclaims, his voice quavering. The story he tells the dispatcher convinces her to send a couple of officers to 66 Clapton Ave. in the nearby village of West Kipling just after three o'clock in the morning.

* * *

Officer Aaron Parker

A disheveled young guy with dirty blond hair, in his mid to late twenties, greets the uniformed officers.

"You've gotta find her. Before it's too late. Please…" The anguish on his face seems genuine, but there's a nervousness just below the surface.

"We're here to help," Officer Logan Murphy assures him, indicating Danny should take a seat on the couch. "We need to ask a few questions about your girlfriend and when she was last seen."

"No. You *need* to look for her right away," Danny insists, remaining rooted at the front entrance. "She was just here. The cocoa wasn't completely cold. We can't waste time."

The two officers exchange a look, trying to determine exactly what's going on. "What do you mean, she was just here?" Officer Murphy asks. "Were you with her?" He's likely thinking this could be a domestic situation that got out of control. Has he hurt her? Did she run away from him?

"No, but she was here," Danny persists. "Her car's in the driveway. And she should be in her room. But she's not."

Aaron Parker's gaze follows Danny's eyes to the hallway. A soft light casts a glow. For a moment, he's afraid of what they might find.

"When was the last time you saw her?" Logan Murphy moves past Danny into the living area.

"Friday night."

"Not tonight?" Aaron Parker clarifies. "Can we have a look around?"

"No." But when he raises his eyebrows, Danny adds, "I mean, no, I didn't see her tonight, and yes, you should look in her room. But we need to hurry and find her before she gets any farther away."

Officer Murphy follows his colleague down the hall to the open bedroom, and they take in the scene. "Have you checked the whole house? Could she be in the basement?"

When Danny confirms that he's been through the house several times, Officer Parker asks, "And were the doors locked? What about the windows?"

"Yes, everything was locked up tight, with the curtains and blinds closed. Are you going to go look for her?" Danny appears increasingly agitated with each passing minute; sweat is forming on his brow.

"What about her cell phone?"

"No. She couldn't find her phone Friday night. I thought maybe she'd forgotten it at work. So I called her home number, but I couldn't get her. It rang busy the first couple of times, then no answer."

"Can you think of any place in the village she might be?" Aaron Parker leads the way back to the front door. "Anyone she might be with?"

"No, there's nowhere for her to go. Her friends and family live in Lake Kipling." Danny's eyes flicker back and forth between the two officers, as though hoping they'll come up with a reasonable explanation for Julia's absence.

"Is it possible she went out for a walk? Does she have a dog?" Logan Murphy asks. Logan, a more seasoned officer, in his late thirties, tries to calm Danny. "In most cases, when adults go missing, they turn out to be not missing at all. Usually, they show up on their own after a while. Sometimes, people just need a break from their routine or their family. Is it possible something was bothering her, and she went out to clear her head?"

"No, no dog. Just Cleo, her cat. And she wouldn't go out by herself this late at night. Look at this place. No one in their right mind would go for a walk in the middle of the night," Danny points out, as though it should be obvious.

Julia's small bungalow sits on the left-hand side of a dead-end road. Brush and trees border two sides of the property, leading to the woods that surround the village, with its population of 429, according to the sign. On the other side of the house, a fence runs along the side yard, separating it from an empty lot. The closest neighbor lives about 100 feet away, adjoining the vacant property. Across the road, a wooded area leads to a small lake. Danny is familiar with that area. He explains the two of them have walked along the path through the woods on several occasions. "But never at night."

After thoroughly checking the interior, careful not to touch anything, the officers turn on the outdoor lights and shine their flashlights around the property. Julia's locked red 2004 Sunfire sits on the driveway alongside her tiny white-sided bungalow. There's no sign of activity outside.

"Do you have a recent picture of Julia?" Officer Murphy asks.

As Danny pulls out a wallet-sized photo of a pretty, brown-eyed brunette, Officer Murphy fires off some routine questions for him. "Does she have any physical or mental impairments? Any medical issues? Has she been depressed lately? Does she take any medications or recreational drugs? Any problems with alcohol?"

Danny answers with a quick no to each of the questions. "Except for her inhaler sometimes. She has asthma."

Officer Murphy instructs Danny to phone Julia's family and friends. "Maybe someone came and picked her up. We'll do a slow tour around the area, see if there's anyone out on the streets. Then we'll check the outskirts of town, along the highway."

* * *

Danny

The first person Danny calls is Julia's best friend, Sheila Grey, whom she's known all her life.

"Hey. Do you have any idea what time it is?" Sheila mumbles.

"Sorry to wake you. It's Danny. I'm worried about Julia."

"Julia? What's wrong with her? Is she sick?" Sheila's voice rises in alarm. "She only had a couple of drinks." Sheila and Julia had been out with a couple of other friends for dinner, drinks, and entertainment by a local band.

"No...well, I don't know." It's possible Julia suddenly got ill and called for an ambulance. "I'm at her place. Her car is here, but I can't find her."

There's a moment's silence on the other end before Sheila says, "That's weird. Where could she be?"

"I'm hoping you might have some idea. When did she leave the bar?"

"We all left sometime before twelve-thirty. The band finished at midnight, and we hung around a bit, then said our goodbyes and headed out. The three of us left together in Nell's car, and Julia drove off in hers." Sheila, Nell, and Rachel live right in town, not out in the boondocks. Lake Kipling, with its population of about 7000, is the major community in this area of Northern Ontario. But Julia had decided to buy a house in West Kipling last year. She had saved enough to move out of her parents' place, and prices were considerably lower here than in the main town.

"Did she say anything about going anywhere else? Can you think of some reason she would have left the house without her car?"

Sheila tells him that, as far as she knows, Julia was going straight home to bed. She had mentioned having to get up for an early church service and lunch at her parents' house the next day.

After explaining how he drove to West Kipling when he got worried because Julia didn't call when she got home, as she said she would, Danny tells Sheila what he found when he got to her house. "The police are here, looking for her around town. Can you check with Nell and Rachel and call me back?"

There's a note of alarm in Sheila's voice when he mentions the police. "So she's really, truly missing? Oh, my gosh!"

"I'm going to call her parents. I know they'll freak out and blame *me* when I give them the news."

Following up on Sheila's suggestion that Julia might be sick, Danny checks in with Lake Kipling General Hospital. No one has been admitted during the last few hours.

After hanging up, Danny makes the dreaded call to Julia's parents. Her dad answers. "Hello? Who is this?" His voice conveys annoyance at being awakened in the middle of the night.

"It's Danny. I'm worried about Julia. She wouldn't happen to be there, would she?"

"Why would she be here? Isn't she at her place?" Mark Brenner's voice rises, his panic immediate. "What's going on?"

Danny explains the situation. Mark says he'll be right over and hangs up without a goodbye.

By the time Officers Parker and Murphy return from searching the village, Mark is waiting for them, standing on the street next to Danny who has been given the third degree by his girlfriend's father. "Any sign of her?" His voice trembles as he explains that he left his wife at home to call family members. Mark says it's best to keep her at arm's length from the situation until he knows exactly what's going on. No point in having her hysterically pacing around Julia's house.

The officers report the village is quiet, not a soul out. Sheila calls back to say neither Nell nor Rachel know why Julia wouldn't be home. Julia's mom phones to say she's contacted all the family members. No one has heard from Julia. No one has any idea where she could be. Danny can think of only one other person who might have any knowledge of Julia's whereabouts. He calls their boss, Jim MacGregor.

"Jim, I'm sorry to bother you. It's Danny. Julia's missing. Do you know where she might be?" He explains once again that Julia has disappeared from her home after a night out with friends. "It's as though she vanished into thin air."

Chapter Three

Detective Scott Evans

Sunday morning

"The forensic team is here," Office Murphy announces.

Officer Logan Murphy stands at the other end of the small hallway leading to the bedrooms and bathroom. He's a bit older than me, with receding brown hair, and a pleasant enough clean-shaven face. When I arrived on the scene in the early hours of the morning, he's the one who briefed me on the facts.

"Good. Hopefully, they'll be able to tell us if anyone else was in the house with her." I'm not seeing any evidence of that, though. The upset boyfriend and father have been questioned and sent home to wait by their phones in case Julia tries to contact them.

I leave Julia's bedroom and walk toward the front entrance. Aaron Parker, a younger officer, steps aside to allow me access to the door.

Everything is neat and tidy in this small bungalow where Julia Brenner lives alone with her cat, who I'm told was hauled away in a cat carrier by Julia's father. The scene in the bedroom indicates she was settled down, reading, before going missing. Nothing indicates she didn't plan to return to bed.

The bathroom confirms she had been preparing to go out at some point. That fits in with what the boyfriend told the police about her evening with friends.

I open the front door as two male and one female crime scene officers slip underneath the yellow police tape and approach the house with their equipment. After the usual exchange of words, they get down to business. Their focus, of course, is on the bedroom. They'll be looking for fingerprints, hair or fiber samples, and body fluids. Given that Danny said Julia thought she had been being followed for the past few weeks and that she suddenly vanished, there's reason to suspect someone has taken Julia against her will.

Officers Parker and Murphy remain in the hallway while the team does their sweep of the bedroom and bathroom. Another team of officers scours the surrounding treed area with high-powered flashlights, searching for any sign of Julia. Maybe she's wandered off for some reason.

Maybe someone dragged her into the woods.

For the second time this morning, I comb through the house. In the kitchen, everything looks spotless. The kettle Julia used to boil water for hot chocolate sits on the stove. Everything else is put away. On the floor, the cat's dishes sit half full of dry food and water. Traces of wet food remain in one dish, and a quick look inside the recycling box reveals an empty cat food tin. The small living room is furnished with a sofa, a television on a stand, a coffee table, a floor lamp, and a few decor items. In the spare bedroom, cardboard boxes and storage tubs occupy the small space, as is the case in the studded but unfinished basement.

When I return to the living room and peer out the front window, a black Toyota Rav4 pulls up behind a row of police cruisers. An attractive young woman with medium-length, curly black hair exits the vehicle, ducks under the police tape, and marches toward the house as though she owns the place.

What the hell does she think she's doing? Who the hell is she, anyway?

I intercept her before she reaches the door. "Stop right there! This is a crime scene."

She stops briefly, then boldly meets my eyes. "I realize that. I'm with the *Lake Kipling Gazette*. Cheryl MacGregor. I'm covering this story. I'd like to speak with the detective in charge."

The name rings a bell.

How the hell did the press get wind of this already?

"I'm Detective Scott Evans. We have no comment on the situation at the present time. We'll be in contact with the media once we have more information. You can leave your card if you like." I expect her to hand it over, turn around, and skedaddle, but she stands her ground.

"Well, I might be able to shed some light on the *situation*," she says, indicating she somehow knows more than I do. "If you're interested, that is." Her brown eyes bore into mine, and she raises her eyebrows as though she's challenging me to send her away.

I don't rise to the challenge. Instead, I ask what she knows. Any information I can get in this case is more than welcome.

"Julia is my husband's receptionist at MacGregor Realty. She's worked for him for six years. Early this morning, we got a call from her boyfriend, Danny Anderson. He said she's missing." Cheryl pauses for effect. "He has no idea what's happened to her, and neither do her family or friends."

I'm already aware of this. But as she's personally involved with the missing woman, I could use her interference to my advantage.

"What else did he tell you?"

Cheryl elaborates by repeating what Danny told the officers when they responded to his 911 call.

"How well do you know Julia and Danny?" Maybe she has some insight into their relationship that might help.

"I wouldn't call Julia a close friend, but she's more than an acquaintance. I see her when I stop into Jim's office to visit and at staff parties. It's a small sales team, just Jim, Ellen, Rob, and Danny, who joined the firm last year. Julia answers the phone and greets customers, does some of the paperwork. I don't know Danny that well, apart from what Jim's told me."

"Would you be willing to come down to the station to give a statement?"

Her eyes leave mine, and she becomes aloof, putting her arms protectively around herself.

What is she hiding?

"I'm not sure what else I can tell you." Her gaze falls to the ground. Then she tilts her head back up and asks what *I* think happened to Julia.

I haven't got the foggiest idea. No plausible explanation at this point. Of course, I keep that to myself. "We're actively investigating all possibilities."

* * *

Danny arrives at the police station to give his formal statement. It's mid-morning, almost ten hours since Julia was last seen. As he sits in the small, gray-walled room, I wonder what he's thinking. Does he realize he's a suspect?

"Thank you for coming to the station, Danny. I know you've already gone over this with the officers who responded to your 911 call and with me, but we need to file an official report and get your statement. I'll be leading the investigation into Julia's disappearance." I sit down across from him at the table, noting his sallow complexion framing the bags under his eyes.

"I understand. Whatever it takes to find Julia." He repeats what he's already said and what he probably told Julia's family and friends, as though it's a rehearsed speech.

When Danny stops talking, I start questioning. "You said Julia's home phone was busy when you first tried to call. Who do you think Julia might have been talking to?"

"I don't know. I've talked to her friends and family and our boss, so it couldn't have been one of them, or they would have said so. At least, they didn't admit they had talked to her. Wouldn't you be able to find out by checking phone records or something?" He sits up straight as though that idea just occurred to him.

"We'll be doing that. Has Julia mentioned anyone she's been in contact with recently other than her regular circle of friends? Maybe someone new? Or someone she used to know who's come back into her life?"

Danny says he can't think of anyone. "Except..." he leans forward across the table. "Like I said, she thought someone was stalking her."

I ask about his relationship with Julia. Danny says they met a year ago at work, became friends, then started dating after Christmas.

"It got to be more serious a couple of months ago. Sometimes she stays overnight at my house, and sometimes I stay at her place."

"Any plans to move in together or get married?" I want details about this relationship, whether there was any tension.

Danny says they talked about him moving in with Julia, but no one knew that. "Julia's parents are religious and old-fashioned, so she didn't tell them. She didn't want anyone to know we were sleeping together," Danny admits, looking a bit sheepish.

"What can you tell me about her relationship with her parents?"

"Strained." He hesitates, stares down at his hands. "She loves her family, but made it clear she likes her independence. That's why she moved out of her parents' house last fall. They didn't want her to leave. She told me she had saved up some money and had been planning to move out for quite a while."

"And how do Julia's parents feel about your relationship with her?"

"They like me okay, I guess. We get along decently, but I haven't gotten to know them that well yet. I've been to a few family dinners, and they were polite. Julia and I don't spend all that much time there, to be honest." Danny shrugs.

"I see. What about the rest of her family? Does she maintain close contact with them?"

"They all live in the area. She visits her grandparents sometimes. And she has an aunt and uncle she stays in contact with. Her cousins still live at home. I guess it's what you'd call a normal family relationship. I wouldn't really know about that."

"You're not close with your family?"

"I don't have a family. I was raised in foster homes."

"Are you from the area?" By area, I mean the vast expanse of Northeastern Ontario, next to the Quebec border. I myself was born and raised in the area.

"No, I just moved up here from the city. Toronto. I wanted to get away from all that, you know?"

"Well, Lake Kipling's about as far away from that as you can get." I know all about Toronto. I lived there for several years while attending school, but

I couldn't wait to get back home.

I thank Danny for coming into the station and tell him I'll be in touch as soon as I have any information to share.

As I escort him to the outer office and the row of chairs that make up the waiting room, a familiar face turns in our direction. Cheryl approaches, puts her arms around Danny, and pats his back.

"Have you come to make a statement about the case?" I ask once Danny has exited the building.

"Not exactly. But I did want to talk to you again."

I escort her to the office that's made available for my use when I work out of the Lake Kipling division. We head down the hall into the small private space, and I close the door.

"Have a seat. So, to what do I owe the pleasure of this visit?"

"I'd like to offer my services."

"Really? And what services would those be? What exactly are you offering, Mrs. MacGregor?" I can't help myself. The corners of my mouth twitch upwards.

"I want you to give me exclusive information on this story for the *Gazette*. In return, I'll do whatever I can to help you find Julia," Cheryl states matter-of-factly, like she's playing some version of *Let's Make a Deal*.

I offer a curt reply, hoping to discourage her before she goes any further. "I'm sorry, this is a police investigation, not an amateur game of hide and seek." With that, I rise, ready to escort her out.

"I'm going to investigate, regardless. It's part of what I'm trained to do, as an investigative reporter," she insists. "And it's personal as well. I want to find out what happened to my husband's receptionist."

"I can't stop you from pursuing your story. But interfering with a police investigation is against the law, a fact I'm sure you're well aware of." The last thing I need is some busybody nosing around where she has no business being.

"I won't interfere," she says, standing up as well. Lifting her head and looking me directly in the eyes, she adds, "But, I *am* going to find out what happened to her."

CHAPTER THREE

This woman has a lot of nerve.
I like that.

Chapter Four

Cheryl

Well, he certainly doesn't have the best social skills. I offer to help find Julia, and he snickers and practically kicks me out the door. I'll have to take matters into my own hands. Since Detective Evans called him in for questioning already, he's obviously thinking the same thing I am—Danny Anderson is connected to Julia's disappearance. It's always the spouse or better half when it comes to murder. Hopefully, this *isn't* murder.

The best place to start looking for Julia is the place where she went missing. Driving along the Trans-Canada Highway, a two-lane road between Lake Kipling and West Kipling, the raw face of nature strikes me, as always. Trees border the highway cut through rock, with a few homes and businesses dotting the landscape. Not exactly wilderness, but if you look beyond the roadway, there's not much out there but forest and lakes. One certainly wouldn't want to wander off the main thoroughfare.

Fifteen minutes down the highway, at the West Kipling sign, two roads lead to the rest of the residential area. The first turnoff to the left takes a couple of winding turns, and I end up at Julia's house for the second time today.

Police tape surrounds the property. The cruisers haven't all left; they're probably still searching the area. About a dozen or so homes line the street. I park across from the next-door neighbor's house and set out on my door-to-door interviews hoping since it's Sunday, most people will be home or on their way from church. At the first door, an elderly woman answers my knock.

"Good afternoon. I'm Cheryl MacGregor from the *Lake Kipling Gazette*. I'm doing a story about your next-door neighbor, Julia Brenner."

I'm well aware my investigative nature can be a handicap. My trip to my parents' homeland last fall got me into trouble when I pried into their past. I stick my nose in where it doesn't belong, in both my job and my personal life. It's a wonder I haven't had it bitten off by now, or at least broken. But I get answers.

The little old lady doesn't seem to be put off by my forthright manner and my intrusion on her Sunday. In fact, she seems happy to have company and invites me in.

"Why, hello, dear. I'm Mavis Kaufman. Why don't you have a seat on the sofa while I put the kettle on."

"Thank you. That's so kind of you, Mrs. Kaufman." The next thing I know, I'm in her living room having a cup of tea and homemade scones.

"Call me Mavis. I met your husband when he brought the kids to stay with Julia last fall while he went to the funeral. What a lovely family you have. I'm so sorry about your parents, dear."

Tears well in my eyes at the reminder that I won't be seeing my mom and dad again. "Thank you."

Her cat jumps onto my lap to console me. I stroke her silky gray fur, and the purring calms me. Mavis pats my back.

I wipe the drops from my cheeks, trying to focus on Julia. I've got a job to do. "I'm wondering whether you noticed anyone around the neighborhood or heard anything strange last night. Julia was out with friends and got home sometime after midnight, but then went missing shortly after. The police are investigating her disappearance."

"Oh, dear, yes, it's an awful thing, that is. One of the police officers talked to me early this morning. He wondered if I'd seen anything. I told him I worried she was dead when I saw all those police vehicles on the road. Such a pretty young girl. I couldn't imagine anyone would want to hurt her."

"Yes, she's a lovely girl. Jim and I are very concerned about her. This is more than just a news story for me. I want to find her and make sure she's okay." I'm hoping my altruism will make Mrs. Kaufman more talkative. "Did you see anyone around last night or early this morning *before* the police came?"

"Why, yes, I did. I was up using the washroom when I heard an engine. As I looked out the window, a vehicle drove by and stopped in the driveway behind hers. It was her boyfriend's car. I didn't think anything of it at the time. I went back to bed."

"And you heard nothing else?"

"The police, of course."

"*Besides* the police."

The doorbell rings, and Mrs. Kaufman excuses herself to answer the door. When she returns, she is accompanied by Detective Evans.

"Mrs. MacGregor, what are *you* doing here?" His tone tells me he's annoyed for some reason.

"It's Cheryl. And I'm conducting an investigation into Julia's disappearance, remember?" He obviously has a short memory.

"As I told you *before*, this is a police investigation. I'm a police detective. Here's my badge." He pulls out his credentials. "Now that I've shown you mine, show me yours."

I stand and show my press card, which indicates I work for the *Gazette*. He's unimpressed. Detective Evans shakes his head and says we'll discuss this later.

"I've already told this nice young lady everything I know," Mrs. Kaufman informs the detective when he asks about last night.

"Well then, I guess I'm not needed here." He shoots me a dirty look as though I've stepped on his toes. "So, have you made any progress in your investigation, Mrs. MacGregor?"

Chapter Five

Scott

Absolutely unbelievable! *She acts like she's in charge.*

"Well, it seems like the only people who were at Julia's house last night were Danny and the police." Cheryl backs away, sensing my irritation at her interference.

After speaking with Mrs. Kaufman myself, I thank her and head for the door, Cheryl following. We go out without speaking onto the paved road where our vehicles wait. I expect her to get into her Rav and drive home to her husband.

"I'm going to ask the rest of the neighbors what they saw." She hesitates at the side of the road, daring me to stop her, those gorgeous eyes staring me down.

"The hell you are. This is *my* investigation. Go home."

She raises her eyebrows. "Go home?"

"Fine. Don't go home. But I'll be the one doing the questioning here." I stride toward the house next to Mrs. Kaufman's. Cheryl accompanies me without a word.

She's going to do whatever the hell she wants. I might as well keep an eye on her while she's doing it.

A young couple with a small child lives in the two-story yellow-sided house. They allow us in no further than the entrance hall. I toss Cheryl a stern look to remind her who's in charge. Showing my ID, introducing the two of us and explaining why we're here, I ask if they noticed anything unusual in the neighborhood last night. Mr. and Mrs. Caron, who stayed up late, saw Julia's Sunfire drive past at about 12:45, just before they went upstairs to bed. Their bedrooms face the back, so they had no idea there were police on the street until their little girl woke them at eight in the morning.

They steer us toward the exit when Cheryl speaks up. "So you didn't hear anything else?" Cheryl addresses the wife, even though I've already ascertained the answer.

"No, we were asleep," Mr. Caron answers, and his wife nods. "We'd had a busy day shopping in town and working in the yard, so we were tired."

"It's too bad you weren't up during the night to witness anything, but I know what it's like having a child. You must have been exhausted." Cheryl directs this to Mrs. Caron. "I'm sure you slept right through."

"Actually, I did see something, but it's probably nothing." Mrs. Caron finally speaks for herself. "I was in the bathroom and glanced out the window, probably around twelve thirty, before Julia got home. I thought I saw a little pinpoint of light flickering over to the left. It could have been coming from Julia's yard."

She tells Cheryl she's not sure what she saw, and she may have been imagining it.

I thank them for their help and we leave. Cheryl voices her opinion that someone could have been skulking around Julia's backyard waiting for her when she got home.

The house across the road is currently empty. It's up for sale by an agency other than MacGregor. We walk past as Cheryl continues prattling on about the light in Julia's back yard.

"It's our first real clue. Now we just have to find out who was waiting for her and where they took her. Was it someone she knew? I'll bet one of the people on this street saw something. All we need is a description of any vehicles or people hanging out around Julia's house last night, and we'll have a suspect. Why don't we each take one side of the street and interview the rest of the people on the street? It'll be quicker that way."

I can't allow her to do interviews without me. It's not professional, to say the least. Although she did get tea and scones at Mrs. Kaufman's while I got the cold shoulder, and she finagled information out of Mrs. Caron when I hit a wall. Maybe people here are more comfortable talking to a local female reporter than they are answering questions from the police. It probably seems less official.

Hell, maybe I can get a coffee at the corner store while she takes over my job.

"That's not going to happen. You won't be questioning anyone."

She raises her eyebrows again. "Oh? Really?"

I narrow my eyes. "And I hope I don't need to tell you that any information you may have about this investigation is confidential until it's officially released to the press." I want to make sure she's not blabbing all over town. "And that means you can't share what you know with anyone, not even your husband."

It's been over twelve hours since Julia went missing. She hasn't been in touch with her friends, family, or workplace. The search of the village and nearby forest has uncovered no evidence of her whereabouts. It looks like she really *is* missing, possibly abducted.

Chapter Six

Cheryl

July 6

The next morning, I drop the kids off for summer day camp at Lake
Kipling, which our small town was named after. A drop in the
bucket compared to Lake Ontario, the Great Lake on the shore
of which the great city of Hamilton appears as a dot on the map. But here,
we're surrounded by lakes. More than you could ever count. The town of
Lake Kipling barely registers as a grain of sand in a sea of lakes and trees,
green forests reflected on blue water.

Back home, I enjoy a second cup of tea while going over my notes gleaned
from yesterday's interviews, despite the threat of being slapped with an
obstruction of justice suit. No one saw or heard anything to indicate that
someone other than Julia's boyfriend and the police were at her house in
the early hours of the morning. One of the people on the street confirmed
what the Carons said about Julia coming home at 12:45 a.m. Someone else
noticed a police car coming down the road just after 3 a.m. Apart from that,
it doesn't seem the neighbors will be of any help in solving the mystery of
Julia's disappearance. I type up a short description of Julia and a few basic
facts about the circumstances of her disappearance. After doing a load of
laundry, making the beds, and cleaning up the kitchen, I check in at the
newspaper office to give my boss the article and a photo of Julia from one

of our real estate ads for Wednesday's weekly paper.

To top off a busy morning, I'll treat myself to a nice meal. Lunch at the restaurant near the real estate office, then I'll drop in to visit Jim. If Danny is at the office and I can grill him, so much the better. As I head out in my Rav4, I go over what I know about this case. It's kind of a locked room mystery. Only the victim isn't trapped *in* the locked room; she's missing from it. Why did she leave so suddenly? Where did she go? How did she leave? Was she alone? Did she expect to return right away? What stopped her from coming back?

The diner close to Jim's office offers good luncheon specials. It's a two-minute drive from the newspaper office. As I turn left off Prospect Ave. I look in my rearview mirror and notice a car tailing me. It pulls in beside mine at Kirk's Diner. As he parks the vehicle, rock music blaring, I recognize the driver.

"Why are you following me?" I exit my car and stride toward Detective Evans, who's swinging his long jean-clad legs around, getting out of his own vehicle, a silver Camaro. If I didn't know who he is, I'd think he's just some guy trying to look cool to impress the girls. *I'm* not impressed.

"I'm not. Don't flatter yourself. I was just stopping to get some lunch. But now that you mention it, maybe I should be following you to make sure you're not doing anything stupid," he says, wagging his finger at me.

Well, isn't that nice?

"If Julia *has* been taken by someone, it's not safe for you to be going around by yourself asking questions," he adds.

"I'm glad to hear you're concerned about my well-being, but, trust me, I can handle myself." I narrow my eyes, trying to look tough.

"I'm sure you can. But stay out of it. Leave it to the professionals. So, can I buy you lunch?"

Well, I wasn't expecting *that*. I accept his offer, thinking that perhaps he might be friendlier and more open about sharing information outside the police station and away from the crime scene. After we order burgers and fries, he asks how long I've lived in Lake Kipling.

I tell him we moved here almost twelve years ago. It's no big secret. When he asks where I'm from, I tell my usual vague lie. "I'm from a lot of places. We had to move around because of my dad's job. He was a manager for a retail chain out west, and he got transferred every couple of years. My boyfriend and I decided to head out east, and this is as far as we got." I've rehearsed this so many times, I've got it memorized. But there's a lot more to my story.

"Why'd you stop here?"

"Honestly, I liked the idea of a cozy little community like Lake Kipling." This isn't honest at all; I love the city, loved living in Hamilton, and would have probably stayed there if it weren't for... But a little white lie doesn't hurt anyone.

"What about you? Did you grow up here?"

"No, actually I'm from Kapuskasing." A couple of hours north. "I was born and raised there, but I attended school in Toronto. After spending a few years in the city, I was ready to move back north, so when a job opportunity came up at the Lake Kipling police department, I took it. A couple of years ago, when I was training to become a detective, I began working out of Northeastern headquarters."

"You seem young to be a detective." And a good-looking one. Brown hair with a slight wave, brown eyes, and just a hint of facial hair to make him look tough and sexy. Tall and lean, but he obviously works out. Not that I should be noticing. I'm happily married.

"I'm thirty-four. It's my second year of being a detective." He smiles and says he won't ask my age, but his detective skills tell him I'm quite a bit younger.

"Thirty." Turning thirty-one this year, but I keep that to myself.

"Really? I would've guessed a lot younger."

"Thanks, I guess. I've been with the *Gazette* for the last three years. Earned my Arts degree in English, took some journalism courses, mainly through correspondence." I offer him some information about myself that's true. "They were only too happy to have someone on staff who actually had a good grasp of the written language." I laugh, to show I'm not an academic snob. He laughs along, and it puts me at ease knowing he has a sense of humor.

"So, off the record, what do you really think happened to Julia?" While he's in a good mood, maybe he'll let something slip.

"Are you trying to pry information out of me?" He leans forward with a wolfish grin and whispers, "It's going to take a lot more than a lunch date."

Is he hitting on me? He knows I'm married.

"I'm just trying to help." Feeling the heat on my face, I move my gaze away from his intense eyes. "I have a story to write, but I'd like to see her found unharmed."

"Well, I'm not sure there's much story to tell. There's no sign of a struggle at her place, and no sign of her." It sounds like he doesn't think she's a missing person at all.

"So you think she just left?" That's what's most plausible. What I don't know is why. "Did she take money out of her bank account or take anything with her?" When I left my old life behind, I took a few personal belongings, family photos, and cashed out my bank account. I also brought my purse and wallet. I left the rest behind, wanting to get away as quickly as possible.

"We'll be checking into the bank account. Like Danny said, it didn't look like anything was missing from her house. Her purse, wallet, and keys are still in her bedroom. If she did leave, she certainly left a mystery behind for her family and friends. Does she seem like someone who would do that?"

He's turning the tables and grilling *me* for information. I guess that's to be expected. He's the detective, after all. "No, not at all. She came to work for Jim after high school, and she's stayed with the firm. Her family's from here. Danny is her first serious boyfriend, from what Jim tells me, and they were getting on well. She has friends here that she grew up with. So, no, I can't think of any reason why she would just up and leave. I can't imagine where she would go. Jim finds it hard to believe she would leave voluntarily, but he thinks it's a possibility." I don't tell him that I think she may have left suddenly because something unexpected happened. Something awful, something horrific, something unspeakable. Something she just couldn't deal with. Like what happened to me.

It's all speculation on my part, but if anyone can get into her mind, it's me. I've been a missing girl for almost twelve years. I know why someone might want to disappear off the face of the earth. Running is the only way to escape your demons. I wonder what demons pursued Julia.

"So you think someone may have taken her?" he asks, and my eyes meet his.

"Well, I don't think she was abducted by aliens, but yes, someone could have taken her." Either she left on her own because she was running *from* something, or someone took her away with them. But without a struggle. Those seem to be the only two logical possibilities, given the state in which she left her bedroom.

"Assuming it wasn't aliens…" Detective Evans smirks, "Who do you think would have taken her? And how?"

"Obviously someone she knew."

He nods. "Considering the state of her house, that's exactly what I'm thinking."

When we finish our meal, the waitress brings one bill. I insist on paying my half. We head out to our cars, and he waves goodbye as I drive toward Jim's office.

Jim sits at his desk, going over paperwork. "Hey," he says when he glances up to spy me in the doorway. He stands as I approach and leans down to kiss me. My husband's toned body, black wavy hair, a lock or two falling across his forehead, brown eyes, a five o'clock shadow showing off his strong jaw, would attract any woman. It's his kind, gentle nature that's most endearing, though. That's what I fell in love with in 10th grade. Although his looks may have been a big factor in it. "What's up?"

"Do I need a reason to drop in on my handsome husband?"

I thank God for Jim every day. I don't deserve him. He saved me from myself and my own impulsive actions. Not once did he complain about leaving behind his life, his home, his friends. He never blamed me for uprooting him and moving 300 miles from the city he loved. Jim took on his new identity as my husband, and together, the three of us were reborn. We were nineteen when we vanished into thin air. And I was pregnant. Everyone assumed we just ran off together. Only our parents knew where we were and who we had become. No one knew why we had left.

"I didn't know you were coming. I would have saved the bagged lunch for tomorrow if I'd known. We could have gone out." Jim lowers himself into his chair, indicating the empty bag.

"It's okay. I've already eaten. I figured you'd be too busy closing that sale." I don't mention my lunch date. "Besides, I'm working on Julia's disappearance. I had a meeting with the detective on the case. Thought I'd drop by to say hello and also to see if Danny might be in."

"Any new developments in the investigation?"

"No, Detective Evans doesn't seem to have any information yet. I think he's hoping I might be able to help find Julia." I'm pretty sure he's just using me, but it might keep me in the loop.

"I'm constantly looking at the door, expecting her to come through it," Jim says, looking in that direction now. "I can't believe she's gone."

"I know. The circumstances of her disappearance are so weird, with her leaving everything as though she expected to come right back. And her car's still there. It's like someone just picked her up out of bed and walked off with her."

"Maybe someone she knew came and picked her up?"

That was exactly how I disappeared. Jim took me away with him.

"Maybe. But, it's pretty quiet out there, so a car coming down the road would be obvious." I already confided in Jim everything I knew about the case, even though Detective Evans told me to keep it to myself.

"Danny should be back anytime, if you want to talk to him. He's out showing a property to an older couple looking for a retirement spot. I told him to take some time off, but he wants to keep busy."

I nod. Keeping busy is important when you're under stress. I settle myself into one of the comfortable leather chairs in front of Jim's desk and tell him I don't want to keep him from work any longer. Picking up a real estate magazine, I start to flip through it. Jim has done well enough these past many years to provide us with a comfortable home of our own, and my part-time earnings from the newspaper helped pay the bills. But it was only this past winter we were able to pay cash for our large brick and siding split-level house and move out of the modest three-bedroom sided bungalow. Thanks to the life insurance.

I glance up from my magazine every once in a while to watch Jim work and think how lucky I am to have him and our kids, a lovely home, and a decent job. I'm still mourning the loss of my parents, but I try to focus on the positive. Not everyone has what I have.

Fifteen minutes later, Danny enters the main office. I get up to greet him. "How are you holding up?" I know it's a silly question. I never know what to say to people. Especially when they're grieving. And having someone you love disappear out of your life is a lot like having them die on you. Only worse. I'm well aware of that.

"Okay, I guess. I keep thinking she'll call and explain what happened." Danny looks haggard, especially for a young man in his mid-twenties. He's tall and lanky, with dirty blond hair and stubble on his face. Usually, he's clean-shaven. Nice looking, but obviously under a lot of strain right now. Circles under his eyes and stooped shoulders show his fatigue. I wonder whether it's because he thinks Julia left him, or because he's terrified she was abducted. Or is he worried someone will find out what he did to her?

"I'm sure Detective Evans will do everything he can to find her." I watch his reaction for clues. Is he hopeful she'll be found alive and well? Is he afraid she'll be found dead? Afraid the evidence will point to him? "Have you thought of anything else that might help his case?"

"No, I told the police and the detective everything that happened that night. I don't know where she could be. All her stuff was still in her closet, including her suitcase and overnight bag."

"What do you think she was wearing?" This could be a clue. If she dressed to go out, maybe she was expecting someone to pick her up. Although, that doesn't explain why she left her purse behind.

"Her pajamas and robe weren't on the bed or the chair where they usually are. Not in the closet, either. But her slippers were still there." He's quiet for a minute, as though thinking something through. "So she must have been barefoot. Why would she go outside in her pajamas and robe? And why didn't she put her slippers on?"

I don't have any answers. I try to think of a reason why I would put my robe over my pajamas, not put on my slippers, then head out of the house without my purse, without my keys. I can't think of one. Yet the fact is, Julia *did* leave the house.

"When did you last see Julia?"

"Friday after work. We had takeout pizza for supper and watched TV at my place. She couldn't find her cell phone, said she couldn't remember where she might have left it, so she called from her home phone to let me know she made it home safely sometime around 1:30. She had plans to go to the Northern Bar and Grill with her friends Saturday night, and wanted to have the day at home to do a few chores and get ready to go out. The last time I talked to her was about five o'clock Saturday, just before she was ready to leave."

"And she seemed okay?"

"She was fine. That's why I just don't get it. It's not like we had a fight or anything. She wouldn't just walk out on me. Something terrible must have happened." Danny's lower lip quivers, and he grabs hold of the edge of his desk.

"What do you think could have happened?

"I don't know. Maybe she went out to the backyard because she heard something. Maybe she thought she saw something. What if she went out the back door and it locked behind her by accident? What if she fell and she's hurt somewhere out there in the woods?" Danny reaches for the phone and calls the police station as this realization hits him.

Not long after his call, Detective Evans bursts through the door. He tilts his head in my direction. His frown indicates he's not pleased to see me, but he must remember it's my husband's office because his expression softens. "I got a message saying you wanted to see me," he says, turning to Danny. "Have you remembered something important?"

"She has to be in the woods." Danny explains his theory. "That's the only thing that makes sense, dressed the way she was, and with her car still there. She must have slipped out of bed and stepped out the door for something. Maybe there was a wild animal out there. What if it was a person?" Danny paces back and forth, running his fingers through his hair, as he speculates what might have happened to Julia.

Detective Evans assures him that the police are still looking in the woods and elsewhere as well. "We already have posters up around town here and in West Kipling. The radio station is putting a call out for anyone who's seen her to come forward. There's a missing persons police bulletin out for the province and for Quebec as well. But if you're sure she was wearing her pajamas, we should do a more thorough search of the immediate area. Maybe we've missed something. I'll get the K-9 unit out there tomorrow morning."

"She could have wandered away by now if she got lost. You need to have them look farther into the forest."

Detective Evans confirms that they'll be doing just that. Then he beckons me to join him outside. "I don't want him worrying any more than he already is, but I'm wondering if Danny's right and she's lost in the forest, maybe got disoriented. There's a lot of area to cover. It's been over thirty-six hours, and no one's heard from her. I could really use your help."

I'm astonished, but thrilled, that Detective Evans is actually soliciting my services as an investigative reporter. "What can I do?"

"Try to keep Danny calm. And make sure he doesn't run off somewhere."

Chapter Seven

Scott

July 7

Early the next morning, the Northeastern Region canine unit, consisting of six officers and their service dogs, arrives at Lake Kipling. I brief them on the case, and they're accompanied to West Kipling by four officers from the local division to extend the search deeper into the forest.

I give Officer Murphy, one of the accompanying officers, the house key Danny turned in, and tell him to hand over the sundress and sweater from the chair by Julia's bed to the dogs' handlers so they can pick up her scent. I instruct him and his partner to do a second search of the immediate forest surrounding Julia's house and have the two other officers conduct another door-to-door search in the village. Given Danny's insight into what Julia was wearing when she went missing, we need to act on the assumption that she couldn't have strayed far from home, especially if she was barefoot. Regardless of that, the K-9 unit will be going out to the highway to search the forests on either side of the road, just in case.

As we hadn't made headway in locating Julia the last couple of days, I secured a warrant yesterday afternoon to check her bank and phone records to see whether she had planned to leave voluntarily. According to her bank manager, there have been no unusual withdrawals from her account.

What I find interesting is that the phone company has no record of any conversations from Julia's residence the night of her disappearance, except for an outgoing call at 5:12 p.m., the 911 call at 2:47 a.m., and, of course, the calls Danny later made to friends and family. There's no evidence that Julia spoke on the phone with anyone the night she disappeared.

Danny has lied about the phone calls. When he's brought to the interrogation room for another round of questioning, I inform him the woods are currently being searched by officers and their dogs. "I'd like to go over your statement once more. I have a few questions about what you said regarding Julia's disappearance."

"I already told you everything. What else do you want to know?" Danny fidgets with his fingers.

"Tell me again why you went to Julia's house at 2 a.m."

"Julia was supposed to call me when she got home from her night out with friends. She didn't call, and it was getting really late, so I tried to call her. The line was busy, then it just rang and rang. I was worried, so I drove to her place to make sure she was okay."

"When exactly did you call? How many times?"

"I tried to call a little after one o'clock, then again just before one thirty. The line was busy. I didn't know who she was talking to, but I thought maybe it was Sheila. So I waited, then tried again. It rang with no answer. I kept trying till a quarter to two. Then I decided to head out and check on her."

"If you thought she was talking on the phone with her friend, why would that be a cause for alarm? Why were you so concerned that you drove all the way there in the middle of the night?"

"She was supposed to call me. It's not like her to say she's going to call and then not call." Danny drums his fingers on my desk. "And she's been kind of on edge lately."

"In what way?"

"Like I said before, Julia told me she thought someone had been following her the last few weeks, watching her. I never noticed anything when I was with her, and she didn't tell me who she thought it was. I'm not sure if she knew. But she kept her doors locked when she was home alone. So when she didn't call and I couldn't get her on the phone, I started to panic. How many times do I need to repeat this?"

"Sometimes you remember details when you go over things. Is it possible she was on the phone with someone she just met? Or an old friend, maybe?"

"There isn't anyone. Not that I know of. But she did say she felt someone was watching her," Danny reiterates, his face getting increasingly red and splotchy.

I can't put my finger on it, but Danny is hiding something. I turn the conversation away from the phone call and ask again about his relationship with Julia's parents. "You said you and Julia didn't spend much time at her parents' place. You gave the impression that she's not close with her family."

"Well, no, I didn't say that. It just seems their relationship is a bit strained."

"What makes you think that?"

"She visits them, but I get the feeling it's more out of a sense of duty than actually wanting to spend time with them."

"Do you have your own key for Julia's house? Would her parents have one?"

"No, I don't have one. She told me she put a key under the flowerpot in case she locked herself out. But if she went out the back door and didn't realize she'd locked herself out...and then something happened..." Danny's eyes go wide. "The key was still there, so nobody took it and broke in. And I'm pretty sure no one else had a key. Her parents didn't visit that often."

"Who did? Any other family or friends?"

"Her friend, Sheila."

I conclude the interview by asking Danny to call if he remembers anything else that might be helpful.

The judge has issued a warrant allowing me to go through Julia's personal belongings. She agrees the strange circumstances of Julia's disappearance, and the length of time passed without anyone hearing from her are reason enough to suspect she may not have left of her own volition.

It's possible someone has taken and harmed her, or worse. Nine times out of ten, it's the spouse or boyfriend. I'm not sure about Danny. He seems genuinely upset, but I've seen this before. The perp disassociates from the act and presents as the victim. It could be he's done away with her and can't face it. Or, he could just be good at fooling everyone. So many people are.

As Danny exits the one-story red brick police building, I call Julia's best friend and ask her to come down to the station.

Sheila Grey, dressed in jeans and a peach-colored tight-fitting V-neck top, is a good-looking blond girl of the same age as Julia. She sits on one of the waiting room chairs, legs crossed at the ankles and blue eyes darting around the room.

"Miss Grey, thank you for coming down to the station so promptly." I assume she must be on her lunch hour. I motion for her to follow me to my office and begin by asking how long she's known Julia.

"I've known her all my life. We played together at the park when we were little and went to school together. She's my best friend. Are you going to find her?" She looks to me for assurance, chewing on her long pink fingernails.

I affirm that we're doing everything we can, then ask about Julia's other friends. She tells me there are four of them who have been close throughout their school years and continue to maintain contact. "We get together a couple of times a month, all of us. Everyone's busy with their own lives, but we still go out for dinner or a movie, maybe out to the bar. Sometimes, it's just two or three of us at each other's place, hanging out."

"So, you and Julia hang out at each other's place?"

"Sure. She comes to my place; sometimes I visit her in West Kipling. It's kind of cool that she has her own place." Sheila uncrosses her ankles and then crosses them the other way. "I'm still home with my parents. In between boyfriends right now."

I ask if she has a key to Julia's house. She doesn't. When I ask whether Danny has a key, she says she doesn't know. "What can you tell me about Julia and Danny's relationship?" If anyone can enlighten me, it's Julia's best friend.

"They've been dating for about six months. I think it's pretty serious. Julia hasn't really had a steady boyfriend before. We've been out together a few times on double dates. But I don't know him that well."

When I ask what Julia's family thinks of Danny, she tells me as far as she knows, they think he's okay.

"Can you think of any reason why Julia would take off unexpectedly?" I ask.

She twirls her hair and taps her foot. "No, not really. Why? Do you think she ran away on purpose?"

"We have to consider all possibilities. Was Julia worried about anything lately?"

"No, I don't think so."

"What about her family? How did she get along with them?"

"Okay, I guess. She moved out because she thought her parents would keep treating her like a kid as long as she lived at home. I'd move out, too, but I'm not very good at saving money. It would be nice to have some privacy." Sheila seems to envy Julia's freedom. It makes me all the more curious about the family dynamics in Julia's childhood home.

"Does Julia get along well with her parents?"

"Sure."

"Would they have a key to her house?"

"I don't know. They helped her move out and into her new place. But I don't know if she gave them a key."

I'm not making much progress with my interview of Julia's best friend, who I suspect is holding something back. After giving her my card and telling her to call if she thinks of anything that might help us find Julia, I escort her back to the main office.

I find myself wondering whether my new detective buddy, Cheryl MacGregor, might be more successful in getting information out of Sheila than I am. She might be more receptive to confiding in another young woman, one who's personally concerned about her friend's well-being.

I pick up the phone book and look up MacGregor. No listing. But I do find MacGregor Realty.

"MacGregor Realty. Jim MacGregor speaking." It seems the boss is answering the phone now that his receptionist is missing. I identify myself and ask how I can reach Cheryl.

He hesitates before giving me her number.

She picks up on the second ring and answers with a hello that sounds guarded, almost suspicious. "Hello, who is this?"

"It's Scott Evans. I was wondering whether we could meet to talk about Julia."

A huge sigh escapes her. "Of course. I can come down to the station."

"Actually, can we meet somewhere more private?" When she doesn't respond, I add, "How about The Pond? It's a nice day, and I wouldn't mind getting out of the station. I could use some fresh air and a change of scenery." Somewhere more casual, less official. Just two new friends discussing her husband's missing receptionist.

The Pond is a nature area on the edge of town with walking trails and park benches surrounding a marshy pond, a gazebo on a grassy hill overlooking the water. She agrees to meet me there.

"Have you eaten yet?" I ask, thinking it's a nice day for a picnic.

Too bad she's married. I haven't been inclined to go on a second date with anyone in ages. This job wreaks havoc on my personal life.

Chapter Eight

Cheryl

H e's right. It *is* a nice day to be out. The sun beams down, and the temperature is about 75 degrees, with a few wisps of clouds in the sky. Heading out on the highway toward the outskirts of town, I wonder what Detective Evans wants to discuss with me. And why meet at The Pond? I had the impression he wanted me to keep my nose out of his business. Now, all of a sudden, he wants to meet for lunch. What's he up to?

I arrive first and park in the small gravel lot facing the pond. People stroll along the edge of the water, enjoying the weather and nature. Canada geese and ducks float on the surface and lounge on the surrounding grass. I walk along the shore, not straying far from my Toyota. Five minutes later, he roars up in his silver Camaro, music blasting. After handing me a bag of food, he removes two drinks from his cup holder.

"Hope burgers and fries are okay again," he says, eyebrows raised, as I take the bag from him.

"Sure, sounds good." I head up the hill toward the gazebo he points toward. "You said you wanted to talk to me about Julia. Do you have some new information?"

"Not really, more questions than answers."

Once we're seated inside the gazebo, drinks between us on the bench, I hand him a burger and fries. He explains there are some discrepancies in

Danny's account of what happened the night Julia went missing.

"What kind of discrepancies?"

"Well, for one thing, he *claims* he called Julia several times between one and two o'clock. The line was busy at first, then kept ringing."

"But you think he's lying? He'd have to know you would check the phone records." I don't see Danny being so naive as to think the police wouldn't find out Julia wasn't on the phone.

"Possibly. Or maybe the phone was off the hook for a while. But Danny used her phone to call 911, so we know it was in working order at that point."

"That's strange. Were the phone lines down for a while, maybe?"

"No, not anywhere else in the area. The other thing that's bothering me is Danny gave me the impression that Julia wasn't close to her parents. It makes me wonder if they had a falling out, maybe because of him."

I don't know the details of Julia's relationship with her parents, but Jim never said anything to make me think there was a problem. "I wasn't aware of any falling out."

"I didn't get much information about the parents from her best friend, Sheila Grey. I was wondering whether you'd talk to her. He leans in toward me. "You seem to have a way of getting people to open up. And since you're going to butt in anyway, I thought maybe you could help me out. Unofficially."

"Unofficially? What does that mean?"

"That means you hand over any information you find about Julia to me. No one else. This is just between the two of us."

"Is that some sort of rule in the detective handbook?" I'm not really sure what the protocol is. I've never been involved in a murder investigation before. Not that it's necessarily murder.

"You'll find I'm not a 'by the book' kind of guy." He flashes that unnerving smile of his. "Those are *my* rules. If you want to help find Julia, you need to remember I'm in charge here." His eyes pierce mine as he tries to get his point across.

"Of course. You're in charge." Whatever it takes to make him trust me to be a part of this investigation, I'll do it. Even if it means lying to him about my compliance and cooperation. This could be the one for me—the story that will make my career. My big break.

I already have a story that would make the headlines, and in the city newspapers, for that matter, but of course, I can't tell it to anyone. Because it's *my* story. And it's the story that would break *me*. So I've had to keep it quiet all these years.

But this could be it. Not only is it big news, but it involves me personally. Since Julia is my husband's receptionist, I have the inside scoop. I want in on this at any cost. So I can write a great article. And, of course, help find Julia.

But I'm not about to tell him that. "Have you spoken to Julia's parents yourself?"

"I did. They're both understandably distraught. Neither of them seemed to have anything negative to say about Danny, but I didn't exactly get a warm, fuzzy vibe from them when I asked about him. Officer Parker spoke to her dad the night she went missing. He said he appeared to be suspicious of Danny. I suppose that's a normal reaction, though, for a father, being suspicious of his daughter's boyfriend. I don't suppose you'd have any opportunity to chat with Julia's mom? Get her honest opinion of Danny? And I want to remind you, this is a police investigation. Whatever you find out, you tell me. No spreading information about the case in the media or gabbing around town, not even to your husband."

I'm flattered to not only be included in Detective Evans' investigation, but to be sought out for my ability to interview people. It's what I do best, and I'm glad he finally recognizes that. The only problem is, as good as I am at keeping secrets, I hate to keep secrets from my husband. Especially when they include another man. "I can do that, no problem," I agree despite my reservations. "It sounds like you think Danny might have something to do with Julia's disappearance."

"I don't know at this point. I do know the circumstances of her disappearance don't make sense. People don't normally vanish out of their homes suddenly."

I'm sure there are plenty of cases of people leaving their homes without notice. I left mine behind. But I understand what he means. It's the strange circumstances—how she left everything behind without warning—that make this a baffling case. I ask whether he has checked with her bank. When he tells me there were no unusual withdrawals or deposits, it makes me wonder how she was able to get away. It takes money to start a new life. When I left, I withdrew enough to get by for the first several weeks. So did Jim. And we took Jim's car. We had the means to leave and to live until we found jobs. I wonder how Julia thought she would manage without a vehicle, without her wallet, and with no money.

"If she left voluntarily, she had to have help," I tell Scott, going from my own experience. I find myself thinking of him as Scott now that we're partners in crime.

"That seems logical. With no sign of a struggle and nothing missing, she must have willingly left with someone. And there's one obvious person, as far as I'm concerned."

"Danny?"

"Danny."

I'm sure we're both hoping he's working with her, helping her to run away from her parents and start a new life. The alternative is too frightening to think about. If he's not helping her escape, what has he done with her?

Chapter Nine

Scott

By the end of the day, the K-9 unit has covered a large area of the forest surrounding West Kipling. They arrive back at Lake Kipling to present their findings. The dogs picked up Julia's scent in one area of the forest.

"In the woods in front of her house. A path leads to a small lake," Officer Grant Beausoleil reports. "But there was no sign of the woman or evidence of a struggle."

"Any idea how long ago she had been there?" I ask.

I'm told it could have been anytime within the last week, depending on a variety of factors, such as weather conditions. They couldn't narrow down the time frame any better than that, but it was clear she had been in the woods by the lake not long ago.

I mull over this new information and think about how to proceed.

Picking up the phone, I ask Danny to meet me in front of Julia's house. Taking her spare house key with me, I let the officer at the front desk know I'll be out in West Kipling following a lead.

Just after six o'clock, I pull up in front of Julia's house. The street is quiet, as usual. Mrs. Kaufman sits on her front porch. When Danny's black Ram drives up behind me, I get out of my dark, unmarked Ford to greet him.

"Thanks for coming out so promptly, Danny."

"Do you have any new information?"

"Just following up on an idea. I'm wondering if you could show me where Julia might go for a walk. Did she go down any particular street...? Or anywhere else...?"

Danny points out there aren't that many streets in town, so she would have walked on all of them at any given time. "There's not much to see. But she does like to go down to the lake. When the weather's nice, she takes a blanket and a book with her."

"Do you know when she would have last been there?"

"Last week, we were down to the water for a picnic, but otherwise, I don't know. Could have been anytime." Danny shrugs.

"Would you mind taking a walk there with me now? Maybe show me the path you took when you were with her?"

"Sure."

The two of us cross the street and enter the wooded area. The sun filters through pine and birch trees as we follow the dirt path. We reach the water's edge in about four minutes.

"Do you run into many people out here?" A rough trail indicates people have been trudging through.

"I've seen people walking along the lake sometimes. This is the edge of town, so I guess it's a good spot for people who like nature." Danny scans the area, as though expecting someone. "Mostly people who live here, I suppose."

"Do you know anyone here?"

Danny explains he doesn't really know anyone, but Julia sometimes talks about her neighbors, and he'd see them around when they went for a walk. "Just to wave and say hello, that's about it," he responds with another shrug. "Out here, everyone waves to each other, whether they know them personally or not."

"Did you ever notice anything strange here or around town? Anyone who didn't seem to belong?"

"There's a lot of strange people around, but no one seems to be dangerous."

Danny shows me where he and Julia shared a picnic supper last Tuesday. The grass is a bit flattened, but otherwise, there's no other sign of anyone

44

having been here.

We walk back toward the house, and I thank Danny once again for his cooperation. As Danny pulls away, I head for the front door. Donning plastic gloves, I insert the spare key and step inside. It's time to search through Julia's personal items. I have her parents' permission as well as my warrant.

Once in the bedroom, I call the number I've memorized. There are two reasons why I want to see her. One is that I know she's going to involve herself anyway, and I'd rather have her work for me than against me, so I may as well take her up on the offer to use 'her services' in an unofficial capacity. The other reason is that I'm interested in seeing her on a personal level. Although I know she's unavailable for anything more than friendship, I enjoy her company. Something about that attitude of hers gets to me. That and the way she looks. But she's clearly out of bounds. I know that.

"Hello?"

"Hi, it's Scott Evans. Can you meet me at Julia's house?"

"Now?"

"Yes, if you can."

"I don't know. It's kind of late. I was just finishing up the supper dishes. Is it important?"

"I think so, but if you're too busy with dishes, it can wait till tomorrow."

There's a slight hesitation on the other end of the line, then she says, "I'll be right there."

I use the next twenty minutes to take another walk through the house and around the outside. I wonder what it is I'm missing.

I'm also looking forward to seeing her again.

Chapter Ten

Cheryl

What does he want? I haven't had a chance to talk to Julia's mom or Sheila yet. There's nothing for me to report. I spent a couple of hours at the office after meeting with Scott, then came home to make dinner. I hope he's not expecting me to have new information already.

"That was Detective Evans. He wants to discuss the case." Although I hate to give up my evening with my family, I'm interested in knowing if Scott has news about Julia. "He asked to meet at Julia's house. I'm not sure why."

"I'll finish cleaning up the kitchen and get the kids to bed," Jim generously offers. I love this man. He's always thinking of others. Me, in particular.

When I arrive in West Kipling, Scott meets me at Julia's front door. He must have heard me drive up. It makes me think if Julia was awake reading in bed, she would have had a warning. Julia would most likely have heard a vehicle pulling up outside her house.

"Thanks for dragging yourself away from the sink." His mouth twitches in acknowledgment that I've given up my dishes for him. "I was just meeting with Danny, checking out the woods along the lake, and I thought it wouldn't hurt to have a closer look inside the house while I was here. Danny says he doesn't think anything is missing, but it occurred to me that it might be a good idea to have another set of eyes and a woman's opinion. You're a woman, an attractive young one, like Julia, and you know her. I thought maybe you could get into her head better than I could."

I'll chalk that up as another compliment. Or two. Although I don't know what my looks have to do with my opinion, and I'm sure there must be women on the police force who could assist him. "So now it's okay for me to be in her house?"

"The tape's down. Forensics is done. But I'm not." He hands me a pair of plastic gloves and tells me we'll start in the bedroom. "I want you to have a look at her closet and drawers. Check to see if it looks as though she's taken anything, if there's any sign she may have packed lightly."

When I enter the room, I'm shocked. I had been told the circumstances surrounding her disappearance but seeing it for myself is beyond disturbing. Scott, hearing me gasp, says, "Everything's been left the way it was when officers answered the 911 call. The place has been swept for fingerprints and other evidence. Still, I don't want anything disturbed for the time being. Have a look around and tell me if anything strikes you as odd."

What strikes me as downright eerie is the fact that Julia isn't in bed, when by all appearances, she should be. Besides the turned-down bed and paperback, nightstands holding her snack and clock radio, a six-drawer dresser completes the furnishings. A jewelry chest sits on top, a necklace and earrings beside it, along with a silver tray holding some hand lotions and perfumes, a couple of stuffed animals, and some framed photos. One of Julia's family, another of Julia and Sheila as kids, and a recent photo of Julia with Danny. The open closet door reveals neatly arranged clothing. There's nothing to indicate someone took Julia by force. There's nothing to indicate she didn't plan on coming back to bed.

"What are you thinking?" Scott studies me as I scan the room.

"I don't think anyone was here with her."

"That's what I thought. Does this look a bit staged to you, though?" His question catches me off guard. I ask what he means and he suggests that perhaps someone set it up to look like she had been in bed.

"Why would someone do that?"

"What if she did this herself? What if she's faking a kidnapping to worry her parents? People have done that sort of thing before. She wouldn't be the first."

"I think that's kind of far-fetched. It's a silly way to get back at one's parents. She's an adult, not a sulky teenager. If she wanted to get away, she wouldn't have had to create some elaborate hoax. I wonder, though. Did she have any history of sleepwalking?"

"I hadn't thought of that," Scott admits, eyes roaming around the room as if he expected to find a clue he missed before. "But if that's what happened, why hasn't she come back?"

He tells me to have a closer look, being careful not to disturb anything more than necessary. The closet holds her clothing, a suitcase, and an overnight bag. A small hamper holds a few dirty clothes, including a bra and some underwear. In the drawers, I find more clothing—underwear, socks, sweaters, jeans, t-shirts. It doesn't look as though she's taken anything as far as I can tell, but then I can't say for certain. It's the nightstand holding the cup of hot chocolate that interests me the most. That's where I would keep my most personal belongings. I open the drawer underneath the shelf that holds a row of books.

A flashlight, some headache pills, antacid, a notepad and pen, a checkbook, a couple of bookmarks, an address book, some envelopes containing cards and letters, a small photo album, and a journal.

"I wonder why she didn't use one of her bookmarks to keep her spot?" I lift the book and notice a crease created by tossing it aside. "And why didn't she finish the chapter? It looks to me like she was suddenly interrupted from her reading. Personally, I don't like to stop in the middle of a chapter."

"Is there anything else that seems strange?"

"Well, yes. If I were a single woman with a steady boyfriend, I'd have birth control pills or condoms in my nightstand drawer." I feel the red creep up my cheeks. "But maybe things hadn't gone that far."

"Danny admitted they were having sex." Scott appears not to share in the slightest the embarrassment I'm feeling. "Maybe he brought his own condoms."

"I think you should have a good look at her journal and letters. Maybe there's something there to indicate whether she took off intentionally," I suggest, changing the topic. "If there was something bothering her, there's a chance she recorded her feelings in writing. Women do that sometimes." I do, but I camouflage my reality with fiction. I don't want anyone reading my mind.

I ask if I can look in Julia's purse. He nods. The usual items—keys, wallet, Kleenex, headache pills, mints, hairbrush, lip balm, hand lotion, pen and notepad, dental floss…and something unusual.

"What's this? Is it an inhaler?" I pull out the canister and hold it up. "Wouldn't she take this with her if she decided to leave?"

Scott sidles up next to me and takes a look. Something about him makes me nervous, being this close. I remind myself that I'm alone in a secluded area of the village in a bedroom with a police detective, not just some man I met a couple of days ago. It's perfectly safe.

"I wonder whether she uses it regularly," Scott remarks. "Or if she has a spare one."

We leave Julia's belongings where we found them, except for the journal, letters, cards, photo album, address book, and checkbook. Scott places those in a plastic evidence bag and takes them with him.

In the bathroom, Julia's curling iron sits on the counter along with her cosmetics. Like Danny told the police—she would have gotten ready for her Saturday evening out and was supposed to be going to church the next day. I think it's possible she was going to wear the same sundress she had worn the night before, the one with the sweater hanging on the chair next to her bed. This doesn't look like the scene of a crime. It doesn't look like the home of a woman who was planning to run away, either. So, what happened to her?

A quick look through the kitchen and living room doesn't send up any red flags. In the basement laundry room, the washer is empty, and the dryer contains towels ready for folding. There's an exercise bike in one corner of the unfinished basement, storage boxes piled in one section, and a litter box under the stairs. Julia clearly doesn't spend much time down here.

Scott tells me about his discussion with Danny during their walk down to the lake.

My mouth flies open. "You don't think she's in the lake, do you?"

"The K-9 unit found evidence that she's been there sometime during the last week, but they didn't take the dogs out on the lake. Danny said they sometimes went there together; sometimes she went on her own. So, it's not unusual that the dogs picked up her scent. Given the fact that there's no evidence of a struggle, I think she went off on her own or with someone she knew." He's trying to reassure me she's still alive and well somewhere.

I agree that it appears Julia left voluntarily. There's nothing to contradict that. "But why didn't she take her purse, at least?"

Scott shrugs. The big question is, why would she intentionally make it appear as though she vanished into thin air? And, if she had help, who did she voluntarily leave with?

"It's going to be dark soon." I know Jim will start to worry, even if I'm with a police detective. Neither of us forgets Stefan is a constant threat. "If we're done for now, I'd like to get home."

"Of course. Thank you for coming out. I appreciate it. I'll see you out." He appears to be all business, his manner and words professional.

As he walks me to my car, he asks if he can see me tomorrow. I stop in my tracks.

"To explore the evidence I've just bagged." There's something in his eyes and his mischievous grin that tells me he's interested in exploring more than just the evidence. Or it could be my overactive writer's imagination. I don't know. There's something about him...

"Yes, I'll give you a call." I open my door and slide into the driver's seat. As I pull away, I glance into my rearview mirror to see him watching. I have the feeling this case is going to put me in the path of danger. In more ways than one.

Chapter Eleven

Scott

July 8

The completed forensic report is faxed through to my attention. I'm hoping it will give me some direction. In the absence of evidence to the contrary, I'm going to conclude that Julia Brenner left of her own accord.

The report indicates there were six unique sets of fingerprints collected from inside the house. One set is Julia's. Her prints were on the mug, the curling iron, the hairbrush, and on most of the other surfaces that were dusted. The other set of prints found throughout the house belongs to Danny, two others to Julia's parents, and one set to her best friend, Sheila Grey. I was told these people had all been in Julia's house on several occasions and had agreed to being fingerprinted and providing hair samples. So, who belongs to the set of unidentified prints?

Another friend? Or someone else?

The hair samples collected from the bathroom belong to Julia and Danny. The bed sheets have been recently changed and indicate she was alone the night she went missing.

I take out the evidence bag containing the items from Julia's nightstand. The checkbook stubs show no sign of unusual payments, which confirms what the bank manager said. In the photo album, I find pictures of Julia at various ages with her family. Her address book contains the usual phone numbers—family members, friends, employer. She turned 24 recently; several cards wish her a happy birthday.

I sit back and open the journal. According to Cheryl, this is how women sometimes express their thoughts and feelings. The writing is legible, but it's not exciting reading. I find myself hoping Cheryl will call soon. I want to know whether she's learned anything useful from Sheila or Julia's mother. I also want Cheryl's take on the journal entries to be sure there's nothing incriminating in them.

Who am I kidding? I want to see Cheryl. Period.

Chapter Twelve

Cheryl

I kiss Jim goodbye after breakfast, and he sets off for the office, while I get Brent and Jamie ready for camp, then make a couple of calls before leaving the house. Judy Brenner agrees to see me this morning, and Sheila Grey says she can meet during her lunch hour at a fast-food place close to work. I'm eager to hear what each of them has to say.

As I pull up outside Julia's older two-story red brick family home on Pinecrest Ave., I consider how traumatized her parents must be. It's a parent's worst nightmare, having your child disappear and not knowing what happened. I don't know what I would do if Brent or Jamie ever went missing.

After parking my car in the wide driveway beside the dark blue sedan, I stroll next to a lush lawn and well-tended flower beds. Mrs. Brenner answers the door on the second ring.

"I'm Cheryl MacGregor. I spoke to you on the phone earlier."

Julia's mother, an attractive brunette in her forties, wearing a yellow print dress, escorts me to the beige floral French provincial sofa with a cat curled up in one corner. The formal furnishings match the original woodwork of the home.

"Cleo is staying with us until Julia comes back. Can I get you something to drink?" Judy Brenner asks politely, playing the proper hostess, her shaky voice failing to hide the stress caused by the situation. "Coffee or tea, or a soft drink?"

"Tea would be lovely, thank you." It occurs to me that Julia wouldn't leave her cat alone. So, she didn't leave of her own volition. But then again, she probably knew her mom and dad would look after her. I left Lulu with my parents when I ran off. It was for the best, not knowing where Jim and I would end up.

As Judy prepares tea in the kitchen, I take the opportunity to snoop. Framed photos on the fireplace mantel portray a happy family. A vase of freshly cut flowers sits on the entrance table. Across the hall is the formal dining room with its cherry dining set. A portrait of The Last Supper hangs on the wall facing the hallway.

Judy returns with a tray of flowered teacups, a teapot, cream, and sugar. "I hope Earl Grey is okay."

"Yes, that's perfect."

After Judy pours the tea with trembling hands, I remark what a lovely home she has. Judy thanks me and says they raised their daughter here. Her bottom lip quivers. "Now it's just the two of us, of course. Julia decided she wanted to be on her own last summer, although she was more than welcome to stay home. I always assumed she would live here until she got married. If she hadn't moved out, this wouldn't have happened." Judy breaks down.

I do my best to console her. "The police are actively looking for Julia. I'm sure Detective Evans will do everything he can. In most of these cases, the missing person turns up unharmed."

Judy wipes her tears and blows her nose. I wait for her to compose herself, then continue our conversation. "Jim and I are both very fond of Julia and want to see her back home safe and sound. My boss at the *Gazette* has given me the go-ahead to write about her disappearance. I'm hoping someone may come forward with useful information when they read the articles I'm writing."

I stop talking for a minute to let her process what I just said before starting my interview. "Do you mind if I ask you some questions about Julia?"

Judy blows her nose and says she is happy to answer any questions to get her daughter back. "What do you want to know?"

"Is there any possibility Julia may have left on her own and not told anyone she was leaving?"

Judy declares that Julia wouldn't do that. "She's a good girl. A good daughter. She wouldn't do that to us. When she wanted to move out, she talked to us about it. Although we didn't agree with her leaving, we had no choice but to accept it."

"So you were on good terms, then, after she left home?"

"Yes, of course. She doesn't visit quite as much as we'd like, but she's been busy with work, and with that—" Judy stops suddenly. "Well, with her friends."

"And her boyfriend, Danny?"

"Yes, I suppose so."

Judy doesn't seem to want to elaborate on Danny and Julia's relationship. "Do you know Danny well?"

"Julia brought him home for dinner a few times. She told us they worked together and became friends and were dating. But we could see there was obviously more to it."

"And what did you and your husband think of Danny? Did you approve of the relationship?"

"We'd like Julia to find a nice Christian boy to marry. We don't want things to end up like they did…" She stops again and fidgets with her hands.

"Like they did?"

"We want Julia to be happy. We worry she might be taken advantage of, like some girls are. We wouldn't want her to get hurt. She's our baby."

"I'm sure Julia can take care of herself. She seems to have a good head on her shoulders. And Danny seems like a nice guy. Do you have any reason to think he might hurt Julia?"

"No, but I thought he seemed a bit possessive. He kept touching her and finishing her sentences for her. She stopped coming to church every Sunday once she started seeing him. And now she's gone. Maybe if we had made it clearer that we didn't think he was suitable for her…but we were worried that would have made things worse between us."

"Danny is worried about her, too. Is there an old boyfriend or someone new in her life who might know where she is? Anyone she might have gone off with?"

Judy insists that Julia hasn't really had any other boyfriends. "She went on a few dates, mostly boys from church, but never brought anyone home before Danny."

I thank Judy for the tea and tell her to call anytime she wants to talk. As I walk to my car, I think that if I were in Julia's position, I would probably have moved out, too. I can feel the oppression in the very air of this house. I find myself wondering whether Julia moved out of a controlling household into a controlling relationship. Maybe Julia had a reason to want to escape her life. Much like I did.

I stop at home to do chores and make notes about my visit with Mrs. Brenner. Before I leave for my lunch meeting with Sheila, I call Detective Evans and tell him I think it's possible Julia may have wanted to escape her overly protective parents.

"Maybe she just needed a break. Although there is something that bothers me," I say.

"What's that?"

"Julia's mother said they thought Danny seemed a bit possessive."

Chapter Thirteen

Scott

Everything points to Danny. Time to put the pressure on. I call MacGregor Realty.

"Hi, Jim. It's Scott Evans. Is Danny in?"

"Yes, he's here. Is there anything new in the investigation?"

"I'm afraid I can't share anything at this point. Can you let Danny know I'd like him to come down to the station as soon as possible?"

It seems that Cheryl isn't giving out information about the case to her husband. She's able to keep secrets from him. I wondered whether she would be able to do that.

I'm in the middle of reading Julia's journal when Officer Murphy informs me Danny Anderson is waiting.

"You're not telling the truth about Julia's disappearance." I confront him with this accusation as I enter the interrogation room and slide into the chair opposite him.

"What? What are you talking about?" His legs bounce on the polished epoxy flooring. "I've told you everything I know."

"There were no calls to Julia's number the night she went missing. You said you tried to call between one and two o'clock, and the line was busy at first. The phone company has no record of calls that night other than the outgoing call after 5 p.m. and your 911 call before 3 a.m."

"I don't understand. I called her number, probably about ten times that night."

"Maybe the phone was off the hook for a while."

"Maybe."

"But you didn't notice that when you called 911?"

"No. I don't know. I guess I was too worried to notice if it was off the hook," he says after some hesitation.

I'm wondering whether he's going to change his story. But he has nothing more to say.

"There's something else I'd like to ask you. In Julia's journal, she says she wishes you could move in together."

"She said she couldn't when I asked her. Said her parents wouldn't approve."

"She wrote that she wishes the two of you could move away."

Danny shifts in his chair and stares ahead at the wall. "You think I had something to do with her going missing, don't you?"

I ask him straight out if he had anything to do with Julia's disappearance.

He denies it. "I have no idea what happened to Julia. You should be looking for her instead of asking me the same questions over and over again. If *you* can't find her, I will." His face red and fists balled up, Danny pushes back his chair and rises.

I advise him not to leave town.

He's hiding something.

Chapter Fourteen

Cheryl

Sheila and I meet at a fast-food restaurant close to the women's clothing store where she works. She recognizes me from the description I gave her, and waves as I enter. When I join her in the booth, she offers to order for me. Being calorie-wise, I opt for a chicken burger instead of a hamburger this time.

After explaining once again my connection to Julia, I ask if she knows any reason why Julia would want to disappear.

Sheila hesitates, then says no.

"I was over at Julia's parents' house this morning talking to her mom. She seems nice, very concerned about Julia."

"Mmhmm. I bet they're really worried about her." She pops a few fries into her mouth.

"I was hoping you could tell me more about Julia's relationship with her parents."

"She loves her parents. They're kind of strict, though. Very traditional. Julia doesn't like to disappoint them, but she wants her freedom. That's why she moved away."

I nod, hoping I'll come across as empathetic. "What about Danny? Julia's mom said she thought he was kind of possessive about Julia."

"Danny? That doesn't sound like him. Julia told me he's a great guy. He doesn't seem to mind her going out with her friends or working late hours when she's needed."

When I ask whether there were any past boyfriends or new friends in Julia's life, Sheila blurts out, "Just the guy who…"

"What guy?'

"I don't know his name. Just some guy she went out with years ago. But she hasn't been seeing him, as far as I know." Sheila stops eating for a minute, her brows furrowed.

"What did Julia's parents think of that guy?"

"He was the devil, in their books."

"A bad influence?"

"Julia was only seventeen. He was a few years older. I never met him. Julia was pretty secretive about their relationship, but she told *me* about him. She thought she was in love, and they were going to get married. But then, the next thing I knew, they broke up. I think her parents had something to do with that."

Still, Sheila doesn't think Julia would run off without telling her parents she was leaving. "That's not like her."

"What do you think happened, then?" Surely, Julia would have confided in her best friend if she ran away.

"I don't know. But I hope they find her soon."

I'm not any closer to figuring out why Julia disappeared, but I *have* found some interesting information about her parents, as well as her relationships with guys.

After lunch, I call Scott to see if he has time to see me this afternoon. He says he always has time for me. Well, that's quite a change from a few days ago. I'm making progress. He's starting to take me seriously.

When I meet him at his office, he says he's been going over Julia's journal.

"Have a seat." He indicates the chair on the other side of his desk. Handing the journal over, he points out the entries where Julia wrote about getting away with Danny.

I ask if there's anything else to indicate she planned to leave home.

"Yes, actually. The letters in her drawer are from some girl named Rebecca. She must have confided something to her. Here, read this one." He hands over a piece of writing paper decorated with flowers, and points to the last paragraph.

I know how hard it must be, with what happened. But maybe it's time you put the past completely behind you and concentrate on the future. Let me know what you decide. I'm here for you.

Friends forever,

Rebecca

"It sounds like Julia wanted to get away from here." I glance up at Scott, who is now standing and looking over my shoulder.

"That's what I think, too. I wonder who Rebecca is."

"There's one way to find out."

I make a call and get the answer. "Mrs. Brenner says Rebecca Collins used to live next door. She and Julia were good friends until Rebecca moved away in eighth grade."

"Where did she move?"

"Her dad got a new job in Ottawa."

"Let's check the bus station and see if Julia bought a ticket to visit Rebecca." Scott holds the door open for me.

Finally, we've got some evidence to indicate where Julia might be.

Chapter Fifteen

Scott

We head west in separate vehicles on the Trans-Canada highway to the Northern Travel bus/train station. Five minutes later, we arrive at the small terminal located in a strip mall on the edge of town.

I show the middle-aged man at the counter my badge and ask if he recalls a young woman purchasing a ticket for Ottawa in the last few days. Cheryl pulls out a picture of a pretty, wavy-haired brunette with brown eyes to spur his memory.

"There was a ticket sold to Ottawa," he says after looking at the photo. "Could have been that woman. I'm not sure. I don't remember everyone who buys a ticket." He doesn't seem to be inclined to offer more information.

"Could you check your records?" I ask, hoping to prod his memory.

The man looks up the bus ticket sales for the last week. "Yes, there were two tickets sold to Ottawa this past week. One Friday morning. Another Monday."

"Could you take a closer look at the photo?"

Cheryl hands the photo back to the man.

He shakes his head and says, "I don't know. Looks a bit familiar, but I can't say for sure. I just sell tickets. I don't memorize their faces."

After thanking the man for his time, Cheryl and I walk back to our vehicles, ready to head back to the station. "There's a good chance Julia got on that bus Monday morning. I'm going to call Rebecca Collins to find out if she's there."

I dial the number I've recorded in my notebook. There's no answer, so I leave a message.

"If she got on that bus, someone had to give her a ride to the terminal in Lake Kipling," Cheryl states. Of course, she's right. "Maybe Danny?"

"That seems most likely. Unless she got a neighbor from West Kipling to take her. Or she arranged for someone pick her up."

"In her pajamas and robe, though? That doesn't make sense."

I pick up Julia's journal again and ask Cheryl to have a read through it. "See if there's anything important I may have missed." Having the opinion of a woman close to Julia's age might bring some insight into Julia's frame of mind and maybe Cheryl will find something more to indicate Julia left of her own accord.

Cheryl flips the pages of the lined notebook and comments that Julia writes in it most days, but not every day. Some of the entries are only a few lines long, whereas others are several pages. She notes that Julia kept a record of her appointments and recorded her weight every so often.

Then Cheryl settles back and starts reading aloud from the beginning. The first entry is dated May 15, the Friday of the May long weekend. It's a short entry, written in the morning.

I can't wait till work is done. I'm all packed. I really need to get away.

The next entry is May 19.

It was an amazing weekend. It's the first time I've been to Montreal, and the first time I've ever stayed in a hotel like that! I'm not sure how Danny afforded it. A long drive, but worth it. Great scenery along the way.

Julia describes her visit to Mont Tremblant and Old Town Montreal. They had left work early Friday to drive to Mont Tremblant, where they stayed at the Fairmont Hotel. It's a long journal entry, which continues the next day.

I could see myself living in a city like Montreal. So much action compared to what I've been used to. I couldn't leave my family to move that far away, though. And Danny likes living in Lake Kipling, says he's had enough of the city. Oh well, I can always dream.

The rest of the entries Cheryl reads are about work and everyday stuff, like what Julia's been reading and watching on TV. She writes about going out with her friends and with Danny. She talks about her feelings for Danny. One of the entries catches Cheryl's attention.

"Here's something." Cheryl practically shouts in my ear as she lifts her head.

I think I'm really in love this time. I know I thought that once before, years ago. I was such a fool. Mom and Dad were right about him. Still, I wish it hadn't turned out the way it did. I'll never get over losing my…Well, there's no point in dwelling on the past.

I assume she's talking about losing her virginity and comment that I don't see what that has to do with her being missing now.

"It's this guy she's talking about. According to Sheila, Julia never had a boyfriend before except this one guy her parents hated. *This* is the guy. Do you think she might have started to see him again?" Cheryl asks. "I wonder if that's what Rebecca meant about leaving the past behind."

"I didn't see any more mention of anyone other than Danny."

Cheryl reads on. On June 5th, Julia wrote something else that catches her attention. "I think I found something,"

I saw him today. He didn't notice me. I was shopping for

64

new sandals. It's time to throw out the old ones. I found a nice pair of white Birks slip-ons at a good price.

Chapter Sixteen

Cheryl

July 9

I need to find out more about the old boyfriend. The next day at noon, I meet up with Sheila at the same fast-food restaurant. I'm tired of burgers, but fries are always good. I pair them with a healthy salad this time, copying Sheila's order.

"I wanted to ask you about Julia's ex-boyfriend. You said you didn't know his name."

"That's right. I didn't." Sheila tilts her head and narrows her eyes. "Why are you asking about him? He's been gone for, like, seven years."

"What about her parents? Would they know?"

"No, Julia said she didn't tell them about him. It was a secret relationship. Julia was afraid her parents wouldn't let her out at all if they found out about him. She said he didn't go to church, and he was kind of wild."

"But you told me her parents thought he was the devil. Now you're saying they didn't know about him." I'm sure I've caught her in a lie, but she doesn't bat an eye.

"They didn't at first, but they found out she was seeing *someone*. Then they broke up, and Julia didn't see him anymore. That's all I know."

"Do you know how old he was? Where was he from? What did he do for a living? Anything at all?" There's no way Julia's best friend doesn't know this guy.

"She just said he was older. From here, I guess. I don't know what he did for a job or whether he went to college or anything. She just said she knew her parents wouldn't approve of him. Somehow, they found out, and that was the end of it. Her mom said he was just after one thing."

I ask Sheila if she knows whether Julia has had any contact with this guy since they broke up seven years ago. It's a small town. You'd think they'd have a hard time avoiding each other.

"She never mentioned him again after the breakup."

I wonder whether she really broke up with him. Or did she keep seeing him behind her parents' backs? Is she with him now? I know what it's like to be attracted to the wrong guy. The guy I fell for years ago was bad news. By the time I found out who he really was, it was too late. The relationship didn't end well for either of us.

"So you have no idea who he is, and neither do her parents?"

Sheila confirms she doesn't know anything else. I give her my card and tell her to contact me if she thinks of anything that might be helpful in locating Julia. Before we get up to leave, it occurs to me that she might know Rebecca.

Sheila twirls a lock of her hair. "She and Julia were friends. Rebecca went to a private school, so she wasn't part of our crowd. But she was Julia's next-door neighbor, so the two of them hung out together outside of school. How do you know about her?"

"Her mom mentioned her. Do you happen to know when Julia and Rebecca last saw each other?"

"Rebecca moved away at the end of Grade 8."

That's exactly what Julia's mom told me. The letter we found in Julia's drawer is dated June 16th of this year. Apparently, they have remained friends for the past ten years. Julia may have confided in Rebecca.

"She did visit her once in a while. Last summer was the last time, as far as I know," Sheila adds.

After lunch, I drive directly to the police station, hoping Scott is there. I'm in luck.

"I think Rebecca is the key to Julia's disappearance," I say, rushing into his office, excited that I may have solved the mystery. It's possible she told Rebecca things she wouldn't tell Sheila because Rebecca lives hours away and is less apt to spread her secrets around Lake Kipling.

Scott looks up from the paperwork on his desk. "Sorry to burst your bubble, but Rebecca returned my call this morning. She says she hasn't seen Julia since last summer and has no idea where she might be. They stay in contact through mail and phone calls, but Julia never mentioned leaving."

"Do you think she might be hiding something? Protecting Julia?" I can't believe there isn't more to this. I'm sure Rebecca must know what's going on in Julia's life. Friends tell each other everything. Then I remember how I kept what happened with my boyfriend, Darko, from my best friend, Haley, who I had known all my life. Only Jim knows the darkest of my secrets.

"That thought crossed my mind. That's why I put in a call to the Ottawa detachment. I'm having them check Rebecca's parents' house and Rebecca's apartment in case Julia did go to Ottawa and wants it kept secret."

I've got a definite feeling that Rebecca is connected to what's going on with Julia. I think there's something in Julia's past that has caused her to leave town suddenly. Maybe it has to do with the old boyfriend. What is Julia running from? I know all about running. I ran from my past, and I hope to God it never catches up with me.

Scott says he'll let me know if he hears anything from Ottawa. In the meantime, he tells me to keep my ears open when I'm around Danny. Maybe he'll let something slip. Scott is convinced that Danny is involved in Julia's disappearance.

* * *

July 10

"Is Danny in?" I ask Jim as I join him for lunch at the office. It's Friday and he's ordered Chinese food for the two of us.

"No, not today. He called this morning and said he was taking the day off. I'm surprised he's been to work this week at all. I guess reality is finally sinking in," Jim remarks, getting up to bring his lips to mine.

My arms wrap around his neck as I return his kiss. "That's probably a good idea. He needs some time to himself. I'm sure he must be going crazy wondering where she is and why she left." I'm hoping Julia will miraculously show up this weekend.

Jim asks whether Detective Evans has concluded that Julia took off on her own. "I still don't understand why she left her house so suddenly, leaving her stuff in her room like that, and not packing a suitcase. And not to tell anyone she was leaving? Why would she do that? What does the detective think happened?"

"I don't know. Let's just hope she's found safe, whatever her reasons for leaving." I scoop rice onto my plate.

I'm not supposed to talk about the case.

While Jim and I enjoy our lunch, the phone rings. It's Detective Evans looking for me. Jim raises his eyebrows as he hands the phone over.

"Julia's not with Rebecca," Scott reports. "At least, that's what Rebecca and her parents told the Ottawa police, and there's been no sign of her in the area. So, we're back to square one. But I did get an anonymous phone tip claiming someone fitting her description was seen earlier in the week on a trail in Emery Provincial Park north of town. I'm going to have an unofficial look around the area this afternoon. Care to join me?"

I watch as Jim bites into a chicken ball and feel a pang of guilt for keeping things from him. When I hang up the phone, I tell Jim I'm meeting with Detective Evans after lunch.

"You're seeing an awful lot of him." Jim sets down his fork. "Have there been more developments in the case?"

"Not really. But we're looking into a few things."

After lunch, I give Jim a peck on the cheek and head for the door. He pulls me back into a passionate kiss. "I love you," he reminds me. "But I hope this investigation comes to an end soon and you have more time for me instead of hanging out with your new detective friend."

"Why? Are you jealous?" I tease.

"I saw the way he looked at you. And I don't like it one little bit." He pulls me closer. "Just remind him you're very much taken," Jim adds, as his lips trail down my neck.

"We're just working together; there's nothing more to it." I don't mind a bit of jealousy. I'm flattered Jim thinks another man might find me attractive, but I assure him he has nothing to worry about. "You know how much I love you."

"I trust you completely," he says. "Him, not so much. Besides, I want Detective Evans out of our lives before he uncovers something that should remain buried in the past. Before he becomes a threat to our family."

Jim's right, of course. The last thing we need is some hotshot detective finding out what I've done. I need to watch my step.

Chapter Seventeen

Danny

Danny Anderson slams the door to his pickup and drives down the Trans-Canada highway toward West Kipling. It's been one week since he last saw Julia. He misses her. He needs to know she's all right. The police seem to be concentrating their efforts on questioning him. He wonders whether they're going to arrest him and stop actively looking for Julia.

Detective Evans' continued focus on the phone calls gets Danny thinking. There has to be an explanation for the line ringing busy when he tried to make the calls to Julia's home phone. He has an idea.

Taking the first turn into West Kipling, Danny continues through to Cook Ave., passing about a dozen homes, both one and two-story houses, some with peeling siding, some in significant disrepair, and others boarded up and abandoned. For not the first time, Danny questions Julia's choice to move out of Lake Kipling. West Kipling doesn't have much to offer other than cheap housing.

Danny doesn't see anyone as he drives through the village. The post office and variety store/gas station sit on the corner of the second exit off the highway. They're a five-minute walk from Julia's house. Apart from that, there's nothing but houses and the surrounding forest and lakes. Of course, the gold mine across the highway occupies a large part of the wilderness. It would have employed thousands a decade ago, but it's abandoned now.

Against Danny's advice, Julia sometimes walks down the lane leading to Millcroft Mine.

Leaving his car on the road, Danny jogs to the back of the small bungalow. He doesn't have a key, but he doesn't need one. On the deck, Danny locates the phone box holding the wires that connect Julia's phone to the phone company. Scanning the secluded back yard, he kneels and removes a screwdriver from his pocket.

When he finishes doing what he came for, Danny sits on one of the metal bistro chairs and closes his eyes, thinking about Julia. A noise from inside snaps him to attention. At the kitchen window, a shadow moves behind the curtains. Someone is inside the house. Relief courses through him.

She's back. Finally.

Chapter Eighteen

Scott

This feels like a wild goose chase. If she were running away, it makes sense she went to Ottawa. It doesn't make sense that she's wandering around a provincial park. But I need to follow up on all tips. I'll have a look and see if there's anything worth pursuing in the area. So many of these anonymous calls end up being a hoax or some overzealous amateur sleuth. In any case, it gives me another opportunity to spend more time with Cheryl. I've come to enjoy her company. In a platonic way, of course.

We take my Camaro to Emery Park, which is about a two-hour drive from the station. During the trip up north through the wilderness, Cheryl and I discuss the possibility of Julia being there. Neither of us think it's likely.

"How did she get there?" Cheryl speculates. "Someone had to pick her up and take her there. Why would she be hiding out in a park? The person who took her had to have camping gear and supplies if she was going to stay for any length of time."

"If Danny took her, he couldn't have done it the night he reported her missing. It's a four-hour round trip. If he was at her house at three a.m., that's less than three hours from the time she was with her friends. The timeline doesn't work," I add, thinking aloud.

"Unless she was somewhere else that night and taken to the park the next day," Cheryl suggests, and out of the corner of my eye, I see her head turn, watching me.

"That's possible," I concede, keeping my eyes on the winding road. "But I don't buy it. It's more likely she went to Ottawa. Maybe she went to Montreal from there. It's a big city to get lost in. She wrote in her journal about how much she liked Montreal. If I wanted to get away and start a new life, I'd do it there, not in the middle of a forest."

"No, you're right. But the forest could be a temporary hiding spot till things settle down. After a few weeks, when the search for Julia isn't so intense, maybe she'll head for the city."

There's a lull in the conversation, so I steer it away from Julia. I want to find out more about Cheryl. I ask how long she and Jim have been married. She told me she moved to Lake Kipling with her boyfriend about twelve years ago. Is Jim the boyfriend she was talking about?

"It'll be 12 years in December." That answers my question. Same guy. The boyfriend became the husband. "How about you? Married?"

"No, still single. I value my independence." I turn slightly toward her for a split second, flashing her a smile.

She asks whether there's been anyone special in my life.

"I've had girlfriends, but didn't want to settle down. Maybe someday." Maybe with someone like you, I think, but don't dare say it out loud. She'll think I'm hitting on her. "This job isn't the most conducive for family life," I say instead. Which is true.

She's suddenly quiet. The only sound is the radio playing Bon Jovi's "Shot Through the Heart". She seems lost in her own thoughts. Sad, in a way I haven't witnessed till now.

"Have you two thought about having kids?" I continue the conversation about family, wanting to know more about her marriage.

"We have a son. He's eleven. And a daughter, six."

Shit! She's got kids? Why didn't she mention them before? I try to hide my disappointment. A husband is one thing, but being a mother is another.

"Really? You were just a kid yourself when you had your son, then."

"Nineteen," she says. "I was just nineteen. Some girls end up having to raise a kid on their own, but Jim took care of me. He set aside his own plans when I told him I was pregnant. He's always been there for me."

Great. Just great. Jim, the martyr. Jim, the hero.

We approach the provincial park, which is about twenty-five square miles of forest, lakes, rivers, and streams. There are hiking trails throughout and it's a popular summer spot for fishing, canoeing, swimming, and picnics. I've been many times and know the trails well.

At the main gate, I show Julia's photo. The girl in the booth shakes her head, says there are tons of people who come through here. I park in the main lot, go into the park's office and try again, getting the same response. After grabbing a map of the park, we head out on the main trail.

As Cheryl leads the way, I notice the way her jeans fit. Trying to get my mind back on business, I survey my surroundings. According to the phone tip, a woman matching Julia's description was spotted on the 1.5 km long Bog Boardwalk trail. I watch for signs indicating the various trails that break off from the main one. A backpack slung over my shoulders holds bug repellant, a supply of water, granola bars, and trail mix. I pass the bug spray over to Cheryl, who's swatting at mosquitoes and deer flies, then douse myself with it. We're not here to sightsee, but I notice a variety of plants amongst the pine, birch, and spruce trees. The Bog trail veers off to the right and follows along a large pond, the boardwalk meandering through wetlands. We cover the trail in about an hour, taking our time to look for clues among the vegetation.

"I spent quite a few summers here as a kid." I tell Cheryl about my childhood as we stride along the boardwalk, hoping to find out more about her in the process. "Canoeing, fishing, swimming, hiking. My parents took me and my brothers camping when we were young. In the evenings, we'd roast hotdogs or marshmallows and sing songs or tell ghost stories. How about you? Did you go camping when you were a kid?"

"No, it was just Dad and me. No family camping trips."

"Where out west did you live? I've been to Alberta. It's amazing—the mountains and glacier-fed lakes." I can't imagine why anyone would want to move away from all that nature.

"We moved around, but not to the mountains. Never settled for long in any one place to get to know the area or make friends."

"That's too bad."

She doesn't respond, and I get the feeling she doesn't want to talk about her childhood. I'm about to say I'd like to take her camping sometime, but then I get an image of her husband and kids tagging along, and I'm not keen on kids. "What about Jim? Does he like to go camping?"

"No, Jim and I have never camped. The four of us take day trips and go hiking or swimming, go on picnics."

"You should try camping sometime." We circle back to the main trail. "There's nothing to indicate that Julia's been here. That's what I figured."

"What's that?" Cheryl runs ahead and stops to point at something caught between the boards up ahead. When I reach the spot she's referring to, I see it's just another piece of garbage. Although the park is fairly clean, there are always people who can't be bothered to carry their waste back to the car or campground or seek out a waste receptacle.

"It's a Twinkie wrapper," she says, peering through the crack.

"That doesn't necessarily mean she was here." I'm not nearly as excited as she is. "Other people eat Twinkies." Still, it *is* a clue. It supports what the caller said. I pick it up, using the plastic gloves in my pocket. "I doubt we'll be able to get prints off it."

"If she was here, where is she now? At one of the campsites, maybe?" Cheryl's eyes sparkle.

There are about one hundred serviced campsites in the park. The best thing to do, I say, is split up and meet back at the office in a couple of hours. I hand her a bottle of water and a granola bar and tell her I'll see her at about seven o'clock.

There's no chance that anyone will have seen her, but I make my way around the campground, announcing myself at each tent entrance, knocking on trailer doors, asking people I meet. No one has seen her, or if they did, they don't remember. I'm not in the least bit surprised.

I know Julia hasn't been here.

When I meet up with Cheryl, she says she had no luck, either.

"That's what I thought." I nod. "I know there's a lot of ground here we haven't covered, but I think we should call it a day."

In the car, we munch on trail mix as we head back to Lake Kipling. I'm thinking how nice it's been spending the day together and what kind of excuse I can come up with to see her again.

"So what do you think we should do now?" Cheryl asks as we drive past a continuous sea of trees. If someone were to get lost out here, it's not likely they'd ever be found.

"What?" I turn my head to catch her expression. For a moment, I think she's talking about us. "What do you mean? What should we do now?"

"To find Julia, what do you think I mean? Will you send a search team to Emery Park?"

"No. We don't have concrete evidence to prove she's there. I can't waste police resources on a whim." I've already wasted the K-9 unit's time and spent most of my week looking for a woman who has probably run away to start a new life.

"So you're just going to assume she's run off and stop looking?"

"No, but I can't justify spending all my time on this one case."

After a moment's silence, she responds. "Well, I'm going to keep looking for her, with or without your help."

I'm glad to hear that because it gives me hope that I'll be seeing Cheryl again. Even though it would be best if I didn't.

Chapter Nineteen

Danny

When Danny circles around the front of Julia's house, he doesn't see anyone. The front door is locked, with no vehicle in the driveway or on the street other than Julia's and his own. Yet, he's sure he heard a noise inside the house and saw a shadow at the window. He rings the doorbell and pounds on the door.

Maybe it was just my imagination. Wishful thinking. I'm seeing and hearing things.

Danny peers in basement windows and listens for any sign of someone inside. All's quiet. Julia isn't here, after all. He's been hoping beyond all hope that she has somehow miraculously turned up.

Danny isn't sure whether he should report this to the police or not. It won't look good that he's been hanging around Julia's house, snooping. Detective Evans is already suspicious of him. He needs to direct attention away from himself.

When he arrives home, he fixes himself a ham and tomato sandwich, topped with a slice of processed cheese and a side of potato chips. The phone rings. The call is coming from Julia's house. Danny picks up, anxious to hear her voice. The movement of a chair sliding across a floor, followed by a click is the only sound. The line goes dead.

Chapter Twenty

Cheryl

Saturday, July 11

I 'm not ready to give up. I tell Jim it seems Detective Evans is ready to walk away from the case. Or at least not actively pursue it.

"Well, that's good news. Maybe I'll see more of you then." Jim rolls out of bed and pulls on his pants. "It'll be a week tonight. And since he's found no evidence to the contrary, I think we have to assume Julia is fine. She must have had her reasons for wanting to get away suddenly. I know the circumstances are strange, but you should know better than anyone that sometimes you just need to leave."

"You're right." Still, I can't help but want to know what happened to her. I won't let it go until I find out. I'm like a dog with a bone.

We start our day like most Saturdays. Brent and Jamie are already up watching cartoons in the family room. I put on a pair of comfortable shorts and a t-shirt and head to the kitchen to start breakfast. Jim checks on the kids, then comes up behind me and puts his arms around my waist as I crack eggs into a bowl.

"They'll be busy for a while. We could go back to bed." I feel his smile as he moves his lips down my neck.

We've just spent the last hour in bed, not sleeping, and already he wants a replay. I suggest maybe we could wait till tonight. We've both been too busy all week to tend to everyday chores. "I've got a long list of things for you to do." Turning to face him, I put my arms around his neck. "If you do a good job of working all day, I'll make sure you get rewarded tonight." With a kiss, I seal the promise.

He sighs and asks what he can do to help with breakfast. By ten o'clock, we're all in front of the television, eating pancakes, bacon, eggs, hash browns, and toast.

Leaving the kids to their cartoons, Jim and I enjoy a second cup of coffee on the back deck overlooking the lawn and flower gardens.

Our new home is located on Birch St., in the center of town. There aren't many newer brick houses this size in Lake Kipling, so when this one came up for sale before Christmas, Jim and I snapped it up, thanks to my inheritance. The school is almost across the street, and it dead ends after that, so it's a perfect spot for raising kids. No through traffic. A double garage and paved driveway accommodate our vehicles, and a good-sized porch allows us to relax as the kids ride their bikes out front. The backyard deck, surrounded by a variety of roses, is perfect for barbecues and eating outside; the decent-sized yard holds a wooden playground that Jim built and flower beds for me to putter around in.

After breakfast, Jim gives the kitchen a good clean, runs the vacuum over the carpets and sweeps the floors while I work on the four bathrooms. When the cartoons are over, Jim gets out the lawnmower and trimmer and takes Brent and Jamie outside to play. Cookie, the multi-colored Yorkie Poo pup we bought the kids for Christmas, joins them. We had to give up our beloved Ivy for adoption when Jim developed a severe allergy to cats last year.

While Jim takes care of the lawn, I straighten up and dust. We're just a typical, happy little family living in a small town. I'm so grateful my life has turned out this way. My high school sweetheart, the boy I fell in love with at first sight, has grown into the most wonderful family man. And every time he looks at me or touches me, it still sends a tingle through me.

I don't deserve Jim.

The temperature is in the low seventies, with the sun beaming down on the deck, warming my shoulders as we relax over a late lunch of pasta and salad before I head out for groceries.

"Can you fix that leaky tap in the bathroom while I'm out? And throw in a load of towels into the washing machine? Oh, and don't forget to put new batteries in the smoke detector," I instruct my husband before heading out to his new vehicle.

The grocery store I usually frequent is a ten-minute walk from our place or a one-minute drive. Since I'm planning on stocking up for the week, I take the Jeep.

Danny's apartment is not on my way to the grocery store, but that's where I end up. He lives in a small apartment complex on Governor's Road, the main drag in Lake Kipling. His car isn't in the back parking lot. I suppose he could be driving around, looking for Julia. That's what I would do if I were in his shoes. I knock on the door of his second-floor apartment in case he's there, but of course, he isn't, so I check in with the superintendent. Introducing myself as Danny's employer's wife, I ask when he last saw Danny.

"Not since yesterday around noon." The man eyes me from head to toe. He's probably in his mid-thirties, a bit rough around the edges with his scraggly blond hair and beard.

I wonder whether Scott informed Danny about the anonymous phone tip. Does he know that Julia was supposedly sighted in Emery Park? Is that where he is now, looking for her himself?

When I return home from my shopping trip, Jim helps me put away the groceries and prepares the steaks I've bought for the barbecue. We'll have a nice family dinner outside, pop a kid-friendly movie into the player, send the kids to bed afterwards, then enjoy a glass of wine while we watch a romantic comedy. After that, we'll spend some quality time in bed, as promised. While I prepare the salad, my mind wanders. What does Detective Evans do on a Saturday night?

Chapter Twenty-One

Scott

Another Saturday night and I'm home alone. I could go to the bar for a couple of beers with the guys from work, except most of them are spending the night with their wives or girlfriends. I could go on my own and sit at the bar, munching on nachos and nursing a beer in front of one of the sports screens. Or, I could go to the pickup bar downtown and see what happens. The problem is, that wouldn't get my mind off *her*. I'd still be thinking of her if I were with someone else.

The best thing for me to do is work; I've brought home some files to flip through. Then, I'll put in a video, some action film with lots of shooting. Maybe Bond. There's a man who doesn't let himself get sidetracked by a woman. Uses her to his advantage. Gets the job done, no matter how tempting the distraction.

I've got no leads in Julia's case right now, so I open my file on the suspicious transactions case. The facts and figures from Northern Lights Raceway, south of Lake Kipling, aren't adding up.

Then there's the file containing complaints from residents. Low-flying planes above homes in the area are waking people at night. A check with the small airport north of town shows they haven't registered flight plans. And noise complaints about motorcycles roaring down the highway are coupled with people feeling unsafe in their communities. Black leather jackets prominently display the logo of a well-known biker gang, prompting parents to keep their children under constant surveillance and their teenagers home by 10 pm. Although the organization has a reputation for causing trouble, officers have no concrete evidence to charge these local members with criminal activity.

However, there's also been an increase in drug possession charges in the last few months in the northeastern area. No doubt that's connected to the biker gang.

Going over the files gives me a headache. Time for a beer, takeout pizza, and TV. Yep, this single life is living the dream.

I wonder what Cheryl's doing with her Saturday night.

Chapter Twenty-Two

Cheryl

July 12

We sleep in again Sunday morning. I'm the first to wake, with my back to Jim, his arm around me, snoring in my ear. Over the past several days, he's been even more affectionate than usual. Is he jealous of the time I spent with Scott this past week?

Last night, I suggested a Sunday drive. When I open the blinds, dust motes float in the morning rays. I check on Brent and Jamie, who have a plastic town playmat with toy vehicles spread out in the family room, then head for the shower. By the time I'm dressed in shorts and a T-shirt, Jim is making coffee. He greets me with a kiss and says we'll grab breakfast on the road. I pack the cooler with ham and cheese sandwiches, mini muffins, and fruit drinks, then stuff towels and our swimsuits, along with insect repellant, into our beach bag.

Fifteen minutes later, we pull out of the driveway. Our destination is Emery Park. Jim stops at the drive-thru for more coffee and breakfast sandwiches. It's going to be a long trip, my second in two days. I don't tell Jim that.

I packed a couple of picture books and a portable CD player for Jamie, and Brent brought his electronic game. It's a boring drive for kids. We turn off the highway onto Emery Road and head north. Trees, trees, and more trees. Open road and trees.

"Are we there yet?" Jamie asks ten minutes into the trip. "I hope they have swings." I tell her it's going to be a while. Jim tosses me a quick look with raised eyebrows. I'm sure he's wondering why we're traveling so far for a swim and playground equipment.

"Why are we going to the forest, anyway? Sounds bor...ring." Brent sing-songs his two cents.

"There are nice walking trails there. Lots of lakes. I'm sure you'll see plenty of birds and other animals. We'll be adventurers out in the wilderness." I hope Brent is going to be agreeable about this. If he starts complaining, Jamie will follow suit, and it'll seem more like an eight-hour drive.

"You like being an adventurer, don't you, Brent?" Jim tries to get Brent on board with this family outing. "Like Tom Sawyer?" Jim had read *Tom Sawyer* to the kids a few months ago. Brent thought Tom was pretty cool at the time.

"Will there be a cave?" Brent asks.

"And gold treasure?" Jamie bounces up and down in the back seat, as much as her seat belt will allow.

"This land was built on gold, so you never know." Jim turns an ordinary trip into storybook magic. "You'll have to keep your eyes open. Maybe you'll find some yourself. Or you might find other treasures, like nice, shiny pieces of rock."

Jim can get the kids excited about anything. Even rocks. I've got an ulterior motive for going back to Emery Park, and I'm thankful to Jim for making this an adventure rather than a fruitless search for a missing girl. I'm looking forward to spending time as a family, not as the amateur sleuth I've been pretending to be.

At the main gate, Jim pays the fee and continues to the parking area near the beach and playground. He removes our gear from the Jeep and we head to the change rooms. A sandy beach fronts an area of blue water bordered by green forest. Many families gather on the sand and in the water, enjoying the sun's warmth. I smile at the thought that I belong to the 'happy families group'. My life could have gone so differently. After splashing about in the water for an hour, we change back into shorts and t-shirts and watch the kids on the playground. Jim hauls the cooler out, and we enjoy our picnic lunch at a shaded table. I'm worried Jamie will be too tired for a walk, but she seems eager to get going on our adventure.

I've indicated I'd like to hike the Recreational trail, showing Jim the map that says it's easy and family-friendly. I've also chosen it because it's not far from the Bog trail that Scott and I already checked out. If Julia was on the Bog trail, she might just as easily have been on the Recreational trail. Maybe I'll find some sign that she's been there. Like another Twinkie wrapper.

This trail is a dirt path through the forest. Brent runs ahead, with Jamie tagging close behind. They're looking for gold while I look for Julia. Jim takes my hand and shouts for Brent to stay on the path and slow down, or he might miss the treasure. Eyes riveted to the ground, I search for clues.

The vastness of Emery Park and the surrounding area grips me and instills a sense of fear. If Julia were here on her own, she'd be terrified at night. I certainly would be. Does that mean someone is with her? No one at the campsite admitted to having seen her. Is a wrapper and an anonymous call enough to go on? Or has someone intentionally tried to get Detective Evans sidetracked? Is Julia nowhere near here? Has she gone to Ottawa or Montreal? Does Danny know where she is?

Brent shouts, "Ta-da!" He runs around in circles shouting as he waves something in the air. He's really excited about what he's found. I run to catch up.

It's gold.

Chapter Twenty-Three

Scott

Monday, July 13

She's talking a mile a minute. I tell her to slow down. It's Monday morning at Northeastern headquarters, and I'm in my main office, writing reports and once again perusing the files on suspicious transactions at Northern Lights Raceway, when I get her call.

Cheryl called Lake Kipling station and was told I'm back at Northeastern. I hadn't expected to hear from her again. She's obviously dug up something.

"I found a bracelet," Cheryl says, speaking slowly and clearly now. "I think it might be Julia's. It was on a trail at Emery Park. Jim and I went there yesterday. I'm planning on taking it to the office later this morning and asking Danny if it's hers."

"What makes you think it's Julia's? It could belong to anyone."

"What if Julia dropped it on purpose? Like a clue? What if she wants to be found?"

"If Julia wanted to be found, she'd go back home. There are plenty of people around Emery Park she could approach for help."

"What if she can't ask for help? Maybe someone's threatening her? Or maybe she's being kept there forcibly against her will? Maybe Julia's lost her memory?"

"Cheryl." There's a note of exasperation in my voice. "You're grasping at straws. I know you want to find her, but I really don't think Julia's at Emery Park."

The silence at the other end of the line makes me wonder if Cheryl's mad at me for not making finding Julia a priority. But I've got a drug problem and a biker gang in the region that needs my attention, as does the raceway financial issue.

"Well, I'm going to talk to Danny, anyway."

I don't try to discourage her. Every clue needs to be followed. If Julia's in trouble, it's my job to help her. And besides, every lead that turns up leads me to spend more time in Cheryl's company. I can deal with that.

"Okay. Let me know what you find out, one way or the other."

"I will."

I try to concentrate on what I was doing but find myself tapping my pen on the file folder, hoping she'll call back and tell me it's Julia's bracelet. Because I'd like to prove Julia is alive and well. I'd also like to see Cheryl again, though I know I need to put her out of my mind for good. She's married, with kids. Maybe if I'd met her before Jim did... There's no point in fantasizing about what could have been. Back to work.

A couple of hours later, I'm having lunch at my desk when she calls. I expect her to tell me it's not Julia's bracelet.

I can't understand what she's saying. "Calm down, Cheryl. Tell me what happened."

"It's Danny."

"What's Danny?"

"He didn't come to work today. Jim called him, but there was no answer, so I stopped by his place this morning. The superintendent hasn't seen him for a few days," she says all in one breath. "He's gone."

Chapter Twenty-Four

Cheryl

If this is Julia's bracelet, it means she was in Emery Park. Maybe she's hiding out, maybe she's being held there and got away for a while, maybe she's afraid, maybe she's playing a game, maybe she's dead, maybe... My mind goes through all the possible scenarios, thinking this is crazy.

I can't ask Danny since I have no idea where he is. My next best option is to ask Julia's best friend. Not bothering to call first, I drive to the women's store where she works.

It's almost noon when I arrive at Chic Boutique. Sheila is helping a woman try on cocktail dresses. Somebody must be getting married. I think back to my own simple civil ceremony at the town hall. Just the two of us, the officiant, and two witnesses we didn't know. Not very romantic. I wasn't showing yet, just over two months pregnant. We had waited until we obtained our new IDs and were married as Jim MacGregor and Cheryl Novak.

While I'm waiting, I browse through racks of dresses, pants, and tops. The sales racks have some nice pieces that tempt me, but there's nothing I need, and I'm not ready to think about cool-weather clothing. As I flip through the new fall fashions, I wish Sheila's customer would hurry up.

The woman chooses a lilac sleeveless dress, and Sheila brings it to the counter. After she rings her through, I catch Sheila's eye.

"Hi," She greets me in a friendly manner, assuming I'm there as a customer. "What can I do for you?"

Taking the bracelet out of my purse, I ask if it's Julia's. It's a simple gold twisted chain with a clasp.

Sheila shakes her head.

"Can you tell me what Julia wore the last time you saw her? Her clothing, shoes, jewelry?"

"Sure. She wore her printed blue and white sleeveless sundress and white sweater, white sandals, and her moonstone necklace and earrings. And her canvas white purse."

I recall seeing those items in Julia's room the day Scott allowed me in.

"Will you be going to lunch soon? Maybe we could talk?"

Twenty minutes later, we're at our usual fast-food restaurant. "Danny's gone. He didn't show up for work, and he's not at home. I think he may have joined Julia."

Sheila's eyes widen. "Do you know where they are?"

Setting aside my promise not to share information about the case, I inform her Ottawa and Montreal are being considered as locations Julia may be.

Sheila nods, "That makes sense."

"Has Julia ever been to Emery Park?"

"I don't know. She likes nature. Most of the time, she stays close to home. One of the things she likes about her new house is the woods and the lake. She spends a lot of time there, hiking, picnicking, reading. I don't know about Emery Park."

"Have you been there? What about Danny?"

"I went camping a couple of times with my family when I was a kid. I don't know who Danny would go with. He moved to the area last year and doesn't have family here. And I don't think he has friends apart from his neighbors and people at work."

As much as I want Julia to be at Emery Park, I'm doubting she's there. It's a red herring. I've been thrown off track and need to get back on course. "Do you think it's possible she went out to the lake the night she went missing?"

"I don't know why she would," Sheila answers, slowly, then adds, "unless she was with someone."

I can't think of a reason why Julia would go into the woods at night; it would be too scary, too dangerous. But I also can't imagine why she would leave her house dressed as though she were coming back to bed. So, I suppose all possibilities are on the table.

"The doors were locked, and she didn't take the keys from her purse. The spare key under the flowerpot was still there. How could she have locked herself out? If she planned to go out, why didn't she take her keys? Or use the spare key to get back in?"

"Maybe she did take her keys."

I must look stumped because Sheila elaborates. "Maybe she took the extra set of keys she keeps in the drawer in the entrance hall. Did anyone notice if they were missing?"

"There were extra keys?"

"Yes, a car key and a house key. Julia keeps them on a key ring in the drawer. When she steps out, she grabs her second set of keys. And if she locks herself out of the car, she has a second key stashed away. The flowerpot key was for emergencies. She hardly ever used it."

That piece of information is a game-changer for me. If Julia's second set of keys is missing, that means she intentionally left the house and planned to return. If the keys are still in the drawer, that means... Well, I'm not sure what that means.

Chapter Twenty-Five

Scott

It's the third time she's called today. She tells me it's not Julia's bracelet. Of course, I'm not surprised. "I think it's clear the two of them ran off together. Maybe they're getting married. For all we know, they could be back next week, after a honeymoon. Her parents will be so relieved they won't protest the marriage. Maybe that was the plan all along—to make her family worry."

"You mean you're not coming back to Lake Kipling?" When I don't answer right away, she adds breathlessly, "To find them?'

She wants to see me. I wasn't sure if she felt that spark between us, but clearly, she did. I'm not sure if I can handle seeing her again. She and Jim have kids. I don't want any part in breaking up a family. I need to keep my distance and leave our relationship as a mild flirtation. I won't be seeing Cheryl MacGregor again.

After a moment's hesitation, I say, "No, I'm not coming back. The Lake Kipling police can handle it from here, if further investigation is warranted. It's obviously a romantic story—a case of two young people running off together. Julia wanted to get away from her parents so she could make her own choices. Danny's got a history of moving from home to home. It's not a crime to take off and start a new life."

There's silence on the other end of the line. I hope I've made it clear that the police will still be on the lookout for Julia even if I'm not actively out searching myself and that I'm not interested in seeing her personally.

"Okay."

Okay? What the hell does that mean? She says goodbye and hangs up the phone, leaving me to decipher the meaning of 'okay'.

I focus my attention back on the files in front of me. In the last several months, provincial police have made several drug busts in the small communities of Northeastern Ontario, but they haven't been able to ascertain the source of these drugs. No one's talking. The quantities seized have been for personal use, and the arrests have resulted in nothing more than possession charges. I'm thinking the biker gang is involved. But whatever connection exists between the drugs and the biker gang isn't apparent to law enforcement officers working the case. I need to find that link.

Shit! I can't concentrate with Cheryl still on my mind. I tap my pen against the top of the open folder and wonder if 'okay' is the last thing she'll ever say to me. When the phone rings again, I'm almost relieved.

"Cheryl MacGregor is here at the station asking if she can borrow the spare flowerpot key Danny handed in for Julia's house to pick up some paperwork her husband needs for a real estate deal that's closing this week," Officer Murphy reports. "Of course, I told her no, but she won't leave. I thought maybe you could talk to her." He clears his throat and passes the phone over to Cheryl.

"Um, I didn't realize I'd need your permission to pick up some papers. Sorry," she apologizes. But I don't think she's sorry at all. "I don't want to cause any trouble. I'll just slip in and out quickly."

"Why don't you tell me the real reason you want the keys to Julia's house? What are you up to?" The accusation in my voice is clear and meant to scare her off.

"Nothing. I've got some papers I need. That's all."

I know damn well there are no real estate papers. She wants to snoop in Julia's house, looking for clues that aren't there. Cheryl MacGregor is looking for a story, and runaway sweethearts aren't newsworthy enough. I could simply tell her no, but I suspect she'll find a way around that. I close my file, putting off the motorcycle gang and drug problem until tomorrow.

"Go home, Cheryl. Make supper for your husband and kids or whatever it is you normally do. We'll make sure we return any real estate papers in Julia's house to your husband's office. Stay away from her place. I don't want to see you arrested for a break-and-enter." I hang up, not allowing her the opportunity to argue.

I inform Staff Sergeant Cardiff that I'm returning to Lake Kipling to tie up some loose ends in the missing persons case. Mainly keeping Cheryl's nose out of what doesn't concern her. After grabbing a few things from my apartment, I'm on Highway 101 heading back south. Back to the mysterious disappearance of Julia Brenner and the boyfriend who reported her missing a week before he himself disappeared.

And back to the woman I should be running from.

Chapter Twenty-Six

Cheryl

G o home and make supper? Or get arrested? I don't think so. If Detective Evans can't be bothered to find Julia, I'll do it myself. Officer Murphy is obviously not going to hand over the key to Julia's house, so I'll need to think of some other way to get in.

I try Julia's mom. "Hello. Mrs. Brenner? It's Cheryl MacGregor. I wondered whether you would have a key to Julia's house."

"No, I don't. I thought the police had a key. Did they lose it?"

"No, no, it's not that. I was hoping I'd be able to pick up some real estate papers that Julia took home with her. The deal is closing soon, and Jim needs them." I hate to lie to the poor woman, but Scott has given me no choice. "Can you think of anyone else who might have a key?"

No luck. Mrs. Brenner pumps me for information about Julia, and I inform her that Danny is missing as well and that Detective Evans believes they ran off together. Judy is already aware of this; Detective Evans called her, but she doesn't believe Julia would do that to her. "She would have called to say she's okay, at the very least."

I agree the circumstances of Julia's disappearance are strange and tell Judy I'm still trying to find out where her daughter is. Although I don't want to give Julia's mom false hope, I want her to know that Julia hasn't been forgotten.

It's time for me to come clean with Jim. I've been keeping secrets from him, and I don't like it. If Detective Evans is putting this investigation on the back burner, then it can't hurt for me to tell my husband all the details.

When I enter his office, Jim stands and greets me with a kiss. I tell him I have a confession to make. "I've been keeping something from you." As I pull away, I note his worried look.

Sliding into a comfortable leather chair, I tell him everything. Everything about the case, but nothing about the fact that I find Detective Evans attractive. Nothing about the fact that I sense Scott might be attracted to me. Because it doesn't matter. As much as I like spending time with Scott, I would never allow it to become anything more than a work relationship, maybe a friendship.

"I can't believe you didn't say anything about being in Emery Park with him," Jim responds when I tell him about the excursion with Scott.

"I knew that if I told you anything at all, I'd end up telling you everything. And Detective Evans said I wasn't supposed to share confidential information with anyone, including you. But now that he's not actively pursuing the case, I don't see why it matters anymore."

"I know you've been working closely with Detective Evans." Jim leans over his desk to take my hand, his touch casting all thoughts of Scott Evans out of my mind. "And I can't say I'm sorry to see that relationship is over. I was a bit jealous, to tell the truth."

I stretch across and stroke his stubbled cheek, assuring my husband there is nothing to be jealous about. Not on my end, anyway. "You know you're the only man for me. I've loved you since the first time I met you. And I will always love you. No one else."

Jim doesn't respond for a moment, and I wonder if he's thinking about Brent's biological father. But that's ancient history. Jim and I were on a break then, attending different universities. Stupid me had suggested we should take some time apart to focus on our studies and make new friends. I made bad friend choices and focused my time on the wrong guy. One time. That's all it took to get pregnant. But Jim didn't hesitate to take me back when I needed a strong shoulder to cry on. He's my rock. Solid. And sexy as ever. If the office door weren't partially open…

Jim breaks the silence as he leans back in his chair. "What about your article? How are you going to write about what happened to Julia if you don't know for certain?"

"There won't be much to report, that's for sure. But what I'm really concerned about isn't my job, it's Julia. I just want to be sure she's okay."

"So do I. What do you plan on doing now?"

Breaking into Julia's house.

"I was hoping to have another look inside Julia's place, but Detective Evans won't allow me to have the key." Maybe Jim will have some suggestions about how to break and enter without attracting attention.

"That's probably just as well. I don't want you getting into trouble."

"I don't see how having a look around her house could get me into trouble." He's not going to help me. But I won't lie to Jim. I'm going to Julia's house, and I want him to know that. How I get in—well, we'll discuss that later. "I'm going to have a look around West Kipling again."

Jim sighs and tells me to be careful, whatever I decide to do. As I'm about to leave, he stands and adds, "We had a key to her house last summer for the Open House. It's not likely still here but let me have a look before you go."

Ellen, an older woman, in her fifties, well-dressed and attractive, is at her desk in the main office. Standing in the doorway, Jim asks, "Do you remember the Open House at Julia's? You did the showing. Did Julia get the key back when she bought the house?"

"I would assume so," Ellen replies, glancing over at us. "But if we neglected to give it to her, it could be with the file."

Unlocking the cabinet, Jim flips through the files. "Here it is. 66 Clapton Ave. But I don't see any... Hold on." He digs amongst the folders. "It slipped out of the file. Here it is."

Jim takes the tiny brown envelope and places it in the palm of my open hand. "At least you won't be breaking and entering in the conventional sense." He shakes his head saying he's not keen about this but knows he can't talk me out of it. Jim knows me better than I know myself.

The investigation into Julia's disappearance is still open. With or without the great Detective Scott Evans.

Chapter Twenty-Seven

Scott

No Cheryl at the station. No answer when I call her. I have a bad feeling about this. Grabbing the key to Julia's house from her file, I inform Officer Murphy that I'm heading to West Kipling, where I hope I won't encounter the nosy Mrs. MacGregor committing an illegal act. Although I don't voice this last part aloud, Officer Murphy raises his eyebrows and nods as though he's read my mind.

It's mid-afternoon when I pull up behind Cheryl's Toyota. The streets are quiet as usual, with Mrs. Kaufman sitting on her front porch, reading. She waves as I drive by. I get the feeling not much gets past Mrs. Kaufman's eagle-sharp vision, even at seventy-plus years.

The crime scene tape is long gone. The front door is locked. Fishing the key out of my pocket, I slip it into the keyhole and turn the knob. Not wanting to startle Cheryl, I announce myself as I open the door. No answer. Nothing seems to be disturbed in the main area of the house. Assuming she's in the bedroom or basement and didn't hear me, I walk down the hallway, peering into the rooms. A check of the basement tells me the house is empty. Yet, her car is parked out front.

Where the hell is she?

I head outside, check her vehicle, and gaze down the road, wondering how I could have missed her. Running around the side of the house, I search the backyard. It's a good-sized lot, backing onto the woods. Between the deck and the woods, an overgrown lawn stretches for about 100 feet. Seeing no sign of Cheryl or anyone, I circle around the other side of the house and stand on the street, turning my head in all directions. It's like the story Danny told about Julia. She should be there, but she's not. Deja vu.

On the off chance that someone did abduct Julia, it's possible other people could go missing. First Julia. Then Danny. Two people connected to this house are unaccounted for. Now Cheryl. Was Danny here looking for Julia when he went missing? Some irrational part of my brain is buying into the alien abduction scenario.

Increasingly worried about Cheryl, I jog down the street to continue my search. Mrs. Kaufman rises from her porch swing and waves her arms. "Are you looking for Cheryl?"

The panic that assaulted me moments ago dissipates as I realize she knows where Cheryl is. "Yes," I say, breathless, "Have you seen her?"

"She's in the woods," she says, as though that's a normal place for her to be. "We had a nice chat, and then she said she was going to take a walk around the lake. She's such a nice girl. I hope everything's okay." Extra wrinkles form on her brow.

When I ask why she thinks things might not be okay, she responds by saying it's my behavior that concerns her. "You seem worried about her."

"I expected her to be in the house and was alarmed when she wasn't there. I'll head over to the lake. Thanks."

Mrs. Kaufman offers some grandmotherly advice. "She's married, you know. A wonderful husband and two lovely children." When I nod, she continues, "I hope you remember that."

"Our relationship is purely professional. We're working together to find out what happened to Julia."

Something in her eyes tells me she doubts that. The fact that my feelings for Cheryl are blatantly obvious to a woman who barely knows me makes me wonder who else has noticed. I thank her again and head across the street to the wooded area leading to the lake.

A few minutes later, I arrive at the spot where Danny told me they had their picnic almost two weeks ago. A variety of grass and vegetation grows between the shore and the woods. There's no evidence anyone was here. And no sign of Cheryl. I follow the worn-down dirt path that meanders through the trees and comes out on the shore at various spots. Dirt and stones line the shallow edge of the lake, but from what I can see, it gets deep quickly. I scan the perimeter of the blue water. It wouldn't take long to drag the bottom of the lake, or pond as I'd refer to it. A sudden sound snaps me out of my morbid thoughts, and I whirl around to see Cheryl approach.

My heart flutters, seeing her unharmed.

"Do you think she could be in the lake?" Her question takes me by surprise. It's exactly what I was thinking—Julia and Danny had an argument, and things got out of control. Domestic violence accounts for a large percentage of the murders in this country.

"What do you think?"

Cheryl gazes across the lake. "I think we should consider it. I checked the house again. They weren't there."

Who wasn't there?

She answers my question before I voice it out loud. "The extra keys in the entrance table. They're gone."

"Extra keys?'

She explains that Sheila told her Julia kept an extra set of keys in a drawer by the front door. "So she must have gone for a walk, expecting to come back shortly," Cheryl continues. "Her sandals are gone, too. The new white ones she wore out to dinner that night. They're not at the front door mat or in her front closet."

"You think she slipped on her robe and sandals, grabbed her keys, and went for a walk alone in the woods well after midnight? Why would she do that?"

"Maybe she heard a noise or saw someone and went to check it out. Maybe someone she knew pulled up in front of the house, and she went out to talk to them. I don't know. I've been trying to think of a reason why she would leave the house suddenly. From her front window, all I saw was the woods, and I wondered whether she simply walked out the front door and kept walking straight ahead—into the woods and into the lake. I know it sounds silly."

"I don't think it's silly. We don't know her frame of mind at the time. She may have gone to the lake. But..." Although it's not impossible, it's highly improbable. "I don't think she'd go alone. Someone was with her."

"Unless..." she continues, ignoring my suggestion. "What if my sleep-walking theory is correct? Is it possible she walked into the lake without waking up? By the time she woke up, it was too late. She was drinking that night. What if she got drowsy, set aside her book, fell asleep, then got up and walked into the woods while still sleeping? Has anyone ever died while sleepwalking?"

"I've read of cases where that's happened." I recall an incident from the local area. But I don't believe that's what happened to Julia. Especially since Danny is now missing. "I think it's more likely Danny came to Julia's door that night, and she went off with him. Maybe he wanted to talk about something, like moving in together, and they got into a heated argument, with him losing control. I don't know whether he planned to hurt her or whether it was an accident, but it's possible Danny killed Julia. Maybe he disposed of her in the lake. The search didn't show any evidence that anyone was dragged through the woods, but she may have gone willingly, or he forced her at gunpoint and knocked her out. He could have pulled her into the lake or carried her in if she was unconscious."

Cheryl nods. Is she actually agreeing with me? "I hate to think that. But you never know. We're all capable of murder."

The expression on her face scares me—the vacant stare. It's only there for a second or two, but, in that moment, I fully believe she's capable of murder. "Are we?"

The moment passes, and she shakes her head. "No. I don't know. I suppose it all depends on the circumstances. What do you think about Danny?"

In this particular scenario, with Danny going missing the week after Julia disappeared, I consider whether he got scared and took off before he could be arrested. He was lying about something. The phone calls he claimed he made, but didn't, back me up. "I think either Julia and Danny concocted this whole escape plan together, or Danny killed Julia and went on the run because he was afraid he'd be caught. I'm not sure which, but there's been no evidence of foul play so far, so until we find concrete evidence to prove otherwise, we have to assume they're together."

"I hope you're right." Cheryl appears unconvinced as she stares at the blue water. She looks like a lost little girl. I'm tempted to take her in my arms, comfort her, to say everything's going to turn out just fine. Then I recall what Mrs. Kaufman told me to remember: She's married, with kids.

End of story.

"We should go back," I say, thinking there's nothing more to find here.

Cheryl turns and leads the way back on the path through the woods. Watching her curvy shorts-clad figure, I give myself a mental slap. I jog to catch up as she disappears into the trees. I'm right behind her when she suddenly stops and turns to face me. In my attempt to stop myself from knocking her over, I grab her around the waist, and we stumble around in an awkward dance. Without thinking of the consequences, I bring my mouth to hers and kiss her. Not a 'we're friends', chaste kiss. A hungry, passionate, 'I need you kiss.' I've thought about doing this since the moment I first saw her exit her car and march up to the front door of Julia's house eight days ago. And I have no excuse for my behavior other than the panic that coursed through me earlier when I thought she might have been abducted.

She doesn't pull away. Once I eventually release her, she brings a hand to her mouth, then slaps me, turns around, and runs. I'm left standing there like an idiot, feeling both ashamed of what I've done and confused by her reaction.

When I return to the house, Cheryl's car is still parked on the street, and the door is unlocked. I enter and call her name.

"I'm in the bedroom. Come here."

I stand frozen at the end of the hallway, unsure of whether to join her in the bedroom. It's going to put us in a very uncomfortable situation. I realize I may be about to cross an ethical line. One that will cost me my job and Cheryl her marriage.

"Are you coming?"

CHAPTER TWENTY-SEVEN

I take the first step and cross the line.

Chapter Twenty-Eight

Cheryl

I *can't believe he did that. I can't believe I let him. How am I going to face him again? What's more important, how am I going to face Jim? Isn't there some sort of ethics code manual warning detectives not to kiss their work colleagues?*

But right now, I need to focus on what happened to Julia. When Scott insisted Danny and Julia ran off together, I wondered why she didn't take anything with her. It just doesn't make sense. I still believe she left the house with the intention of coming back. It's her purse sitting on the chair beside the bed that makes me certain I'm right. It contains her inhaler, as well as her wallet and keys. Why wouldn't she have grabbed it if she meant to be gone for days?

I want to have a closer look in her room to see whether there's a prescription receipt for more than one inhaler. If she knew she was going to be gone for any length of time, she would have brought her medicine, even if Danny took care of the money they needed to make their escape.

I rummage through her purse, hoping to locate a receipt, and find the inhaler that *was* there is now missing. Scott calls my name and I tell him to get in here. But he just stands in the doorway, his eyes glued to me.

"Scott?"

"Cheryl?" He doesn't enter. "What's going on here?"

"It's her inhaler. It's gone."

CHAPTER TWENTY-EIGHT

"What?"

"Her inhaler isn't in her purse anymore. Did you take it into evidence?"

"No." He sets foot in the room and asks if anything else is missing. "What about clothes? Suitcases still here?"

I take a quick inventory of Julia's closet; her suitcase and overnight bag are still here, exactly where they were before. Something looks different, though. "I think there are more empty hangers now." I check her dresser drawers. Again, it seems some underwear and socks are missing. I'm also sure there were more T-shirts and jeans before.

Scott takes photos of the closet, the open drawers, and the rest of the room. "We can compare these to the photos taken the night she went missing." He's all business again, as though nothing happened between us. It's as if I imagined it. "If you're right, it could mean either Julia or Danny came back to get what she needed."

"So she's alive?"

"It looks that way. Like I've been saying all along, they probably ran off."

"Why go to all the trouble of reporting her missing first, then meeting up with her later? Why didn't they just leave together? And why come back for her stuff?"

Scott says we may never know. "By the way, how did you get in? I've got the spare key."

"Jim had a key in the file from the Open House for the property."

He doesn't say anything about the fact that I shouldn't have used the key to enter someone else's house, especially this house. I'm aware I could be arrested for illegal entry, not to mention tampering with a possible crime scene. But then, Detective Evans doesn't seem to adhere to proper police protocol.

"You should give that to her family."

He's giving up on finding Julia. Maybe he's right. There's nothing more to be done. "Hopefully, she'll contact her parents and let them know she's safe," I say, still skeptical.

"I hope so. We should go." Scott clears out of the bedroom, and I follow at a safe distance. I don't want to chance colliding with him again.

"You'll be going back to Northeastern headquarters, then?"

"That's the plan. I do have other cases that need my attention."

When we're at the front door, Scott turns around and heads back to the bedroom. "Just a minute."

I lift my hands, palms up, and shrug when he returns.

"Just checking to make sure the phone's working. I want to have another look outside."

My curiosity gets the better of me, and I follow him out the back door. It's the phone box on the back deck that has his attention. Scott removes plastic gloves from his pocket and touches the cover on the box. It opens easily. I point out something wedged between the boards. It's the head of a small screw nail.

"It looks like someone may have tampered with the wires," Scott concludes after examining the inside of the box. "But everything seems to be connected properly now."

"What do you think that means?"

"It could mean Danny messed with the wires after I told him the phone company had no record of incoming or outgoing calls that night."

"Why would he do that?"

"If it looked like someone tampered with the phone line, it would give credibility to his claim that he tried to call and the line wasn't worrying properly."

"Or maybe someone actually disconnected the phone line, and Danny *couldn't* get through," I suggest, giving Danny the benefit of the doubt. "Remember the light Mrs. Caron saw out here just before Julia got home?"

We're kneeling on the deck next to each other, thinking the same thing. If someone messed with the phone box, then Julia may not have left voluntarily. Either Danny or someone else wanted her phone line disconnected for a reason.

"So, I guess I'll be spending more time working out of Lake Kipling, after all." He rises and extends his hand to help me to my feet.

I was afraid he was going to say that. As much as I want to find out what happened to Julia, I don't want to risk my marriage to do it. And Scott Evans is a definite risk.

Chapter Twenty-Nine

Scott

S he's acting as though nothing happened. Regardless of what's going on between the two of us, I need to pull myself together and concentrate on the case. The possibility of the phone wires being tampered with isn't enough to send the crime unit back here. The fact that someone's been here and taken some of Julia's things doesn't necessarily indicate there's been a crime. There's no evidence of a break-in. Julia's spare keys must have been used to enter the house. I'm interested in knowing whether Danny has packed his own belongings as well. If so, it would be reasonable to conclude he's shacked up with Julia somewhere.

"I'd like to check out Danny's apartment." I'm trying my darndest to keep things professional between us. "But it'll be difficult to get a warrant when I can't prove a crime has been committed."

"I can probably get in his apartment."

Although I'd appreciate that, there is no way I'm going to condone illegal entry into a possible suspect's residence. I disregard her comment and tell her I have work to do at the station. After securing the house, we return to Lake Kipling in our separate vehicles.

Officer Parker is at the front desk when I return. When he asks if there are any new developments, I tell him it looks like she ran off with her boyfriend, but until we hear from them, I'm keeping an open mind.

Alone in my office, I close the door and open the Brenner file. One set of prints found in Julia's bedroom and bathroom belongs to neither family members nor known friends. Two pieces that don't fit into this puzzle. An unknown person has been in Julia's bedroom. Someone has likely messed with Julia's phone line.

It's not looking quite as though Julia left her home voluntarily.

As I'm considering my next step in the investigation, which seems to be far from over, Cheryl calls. I greet her in a professional manner, trying to push that kiss out of my mind.

"Hey," she says, as though we're old friends. "Jim's working late at the office. Do you want to come over for pizza?"

After what just happened between us? Another date with Cheryl, initiated by her this time. She's inviting me over when her husband's away. I should suggest we meet elsewhere, somewhere public, but instead, I tell her I'll be right over. Like a moth to a flame. Like an idiot to a married woman.

When I arrive at the address she's given, I park on the dead-end road behind her Toyota. A kid bikes up and down the double drive. Cheryl calls from the front porch, "Jamie! It's time for pizza!"

"Yay!" The kid leaves the bike on the front lawn and runs to the porch as I amble up the driveway.

I'm glad I opted not to bring a bottle of wine and a bouquet of flowers. Obviously, I'm not here for a romantic dinner, husband or no husband. Upon entering Cheryl's house, the first thing that hits me is the aroma of pizza. The second thing that hits me is a yapping furry ball doing his darndest to send me flying off the hardwood flooring.

And I quickly realize this is a family home—Cheryl's family, Cheryl's home. As I follow her past the formal living/dining room on the right, straight ahead into the family room and kitchen area, I dodge an assortment of toys. Although the place isn't untidy, it looks lived in. Like Cheryl, it's attractive, but feels comfortable. This is a place where you could put your feet up and not get reprimanded.

"The pizza was delivered a few minutes ago," Cheryl says. "I'm keeping it warm in the oven." She has the kitchen table set for four. "If you want to wash up, there's another bathroom upstairs. Brent's using the powder room."

Upstairs, I catch a glimpse of what I assume is Cheryl and Jim's bedroom as I pass an open door. The bed's made, with a flower-patterned duvet, and an ensuite is visible to the right. Across from their room is Jamie's, with ponies adorning her comforter, and toys strewn about the carpeted floor. Beside her room is the main bathroom. Brent's room, next to it, is decorated in a car motif. Across from that, I find what's obviously an unused guest room.

Following a self-guided tour of the upstairs and washing my hands, I join Cheryl and the kids at the kitchen table. It's a scene of domestic bliss, but I'm a fish out of water. Why she invited me over, I don't know. Maybe to drive home the fact that she's happily married? I don't belong here. Cheryl does her best, though, to make me feel like I do.

"Brent, Jamie, this is Mommy's friend, Detective Evans."

Jamie glares at me. Brent politely says hello, and I respond in kind. I'm not good with kids.

"We've got plain pepperoni on one and three meats and mushrooms on the other. I hope that's okay. Just help yourself," she says, pointing to the boxes on top of the stove. After I've placed one of each on my plate, Brent does the same. Cheryl serves Jamie a piece of pepperoni pizza and takes two for herself, peeling off pieces of meat and cheese for the excited pup. "Here you go, Cookie."

Not sure how to start the conversation in the current circumstances, I ask Brent about school.

"Bor...ring." He rolls his brown eyes.

Cheryl nudges him.

"It's okay, I guess." His brow wrinkles under wavy black hair. "Are you really a detective? Do you have a gun? Did you ever shoot anybody? Did you catch any bad guys? I saw you drive up through the window. Where's your police car?"

Nosy kid. Like mother, like son.

"Detectives don't always drive a police car. This is my own personal vehicle."

"Your Camaro is way cooler than a police car, anyway," he shrugs.

The kid and I have hit it off. All it took was cars. If there wasn't a husband on his way home soon, I'd be confident the evening would end with his mom and me getting comfy on the couch. But with Jim coming home, I want to make sure I keep my distance from his wife. I don't trust myself after what happened in the woods this afternoon.

We all have seconds of pizza, after which Cheryl suggests the kids go play in the back yard, while she cleans up the kitchen. I watch through the patio doors as Jamie swings on the wooden playground in the left corner of the yard and Brent shoots hoops on the pavement behind the garage. "You won't arrest me, will you?" Cheryl walks up behind me. "I don't know if it's against the law."

I'm stumped. Why would I arrest her? An extramarital kiss isn't against the law. "Of course, I won't arrest you." Besides, the kiss was initiated by me. And that's as far as it's going to go. Nothing illegal happening here.

"I took all the proper precautions," she continues in a low voice as I turn to face her. "I don't think anyone will know, unless you tell them. Except for Jim. I'm going to have to tell him, but he's used to me doing things like this. He didn't pack his suitcase. I don't think anything is missing from his closet."

"What?" I'm totally lost here. "You'll need to be clearer, Cheryl. I don't know what you're talking about." If she and Jim have an open marriage, I don't want to be involved. If he's leaving her, for whatever reason, that's a different story.

"I went into Danny's apartment. I know I probably shouldn't have, but I wanted to see whether he'd packed up his stuff."

"You...what?"

"I didn't break in. The super let me in. I met him before, and he knows I'm Danny's boss's wife and that I'm worried about him." She says this as though she's just checked in on a sick friend.

"I don't believe this!" As my voice gets louder, she tells me to shush. "You tampered with potential evidence. If it turns out Danny did something to Julia..."

"I didn't tamper with anything. I wore gloves, removed my shoes, and I touched as little as possible. I don't think anyone will know I was there."

I take a minute to calm down. "Okay. What's done is done."

"I just wanted to help. I thought you wanted to know the state of his apartment."

"Yes, I do," I concede, "but not this way. Tell me what you found, and then we'll pretend none of this ever happened." I'm talking about more than the illegal entry, and I hope she understands that.

Danny's apartment apparently looks like he was planning on coming right back. Like Julia's place, there is evidence to suggest he hadn't expected to leave for long.

We sit down at the kitchen table and Cheryl describes his place for me. The remnants of sandwich fixings sit on the counter. A loaf of bread, the ends of a tomato, half a bag of chips, an empty plate, and a knife smudged with margarine lie beside an open box of granola bars and an unopened bottle of beer. A TV tray is set up in the living room in front of the couch with the remote sitting on it. In the bedroom, Danny's dirty clothes are on the floor, as though he changed quickly and didn't have time to put them in the hamper. Everything else looks tidy. There's a suitcase in his closet, and clothes on hangers, clothing in drawers. The door and windows are locked.

"What do you think happened?" I'm hoping she has some suggestions.

"I don't know. Maybe he found out something about where Julia is, and he dropped everything to go look for her."

"And maybe he found her?"

"Maybe."

I let that register in my brain. "What if she didn't want him to find her?"

"You think Danny could pose a threat to her?"

"You're the one who told me her parents thought he seemed possessive. What if they had a fight, and she got away from him that night and kept running?"

We sit in silence for a while, then I ask if there is anything else I should know. There isn't. That sounds like my cue to leave. Thanking her for the pizza supper, I say goodbye to Brent and Jamie and see myself out. I'm not sure what's next. Either in regard to the missing persons or my relationship with Cheryl.

Chapter Thirty

July 14

The next morning, Danny Anderson's Visa card is swiped in the small city of Northern Bay, about two and a half hours south of Lake Kipling. $246 worth of various baby products is carted out at Walmart.

The middle-aged cashier comments, "Isn't it nice of you doing all the shopping for your wife. I hope she's feeling better soon."

That same evening, a note is slipped into a mailbox. Typed in standard font, the note reads: **I saw what you did.**

Chapter Thirty-One

Cheryl

"She's pregnant?" Scott has just called to tell me the news. It makes perfect sense. Julia's parents are old-fashioned. They wouldn't approve of a baby out of wedlock. "Do you think they took off to get married?"

"Possibly. In any case, it looks like Danny was in Northern Bay yesterday. I think we can assume they're still somewhere in the north."

I know what it's like to be pregnant and on the run with your boyfriend. I didn't want to be found. But then, I had more serious reasons for wanting to disappear than a fear of disappointing my parents. I ran because I was terrified.

There are two things that cross my mind when I hear the pregnancy news. First, I wonder if her best friend knows. Second, I wonder why she didn't write about it in her journal. I need to know where Julia's old journal is—the one that comes before the May 17 long weekend. Did she mention the pregnancy before that time?

"I'm going to go see Sheila. Can we meet at Julia's place later?" I ask. "I want to search for her old journal."

Scott agrees to be there at two o'clock.

Sheila meets me at the fast-food restaurant, and we settle into a booth with our orders. If I keep eating all this fast food, I'm not going to fit into my shorts much longer. Taking my time to bring up the topic of pregnancy,

I ask Sheila about her life. There's a better chance she'll share her secrets if she thinks of me as a friend, not a reporter.

"How's work going?" I initiate a casual conversation before grilling her about Julia once again.

"The usual." Obviously not something she's passionate about.

"And your friends? Been out anywhere fun lately?"

"Nope, not really."

The friendly approach doesn't seem to be working. I examine her carefully, taking in the pretty made-up face, blond hair, and fashion clothing on her shapely body.

"Are you seeing anyone? You told me you and Julia sometimes double dated."

"No one special." I think I'm really striking out, but then she adds, with a bit of a giggle. "But there is someone I'm interested in. I doubt he knows I'm alive, though. He's a bit older than me. Probably not interested, but he was kind of flirty when he talked to me. Really cute guy."

"Oh, well, you never know. Have you tried asking him out?" Finally, a topic she wants to talk about. Guys.

"No, it was just business. He asked some questions about Julia."

"He did?" Now I'm really interested. Someone has been asking questions about Julia. Someone other than me and Scott. Obviously not Danny, either. "What kind of questions?" I lean forward, expecting to hear something that will help us find her.

"About her being missing. He's a cop."

The heat flows from my neck to my face, and I hope I'm not too visibly red. Has he been flirting with other women? Not just me? Is that the kind of guy he is? Not wanting to show a personal interest in Scott, I direct the conversation away from him and focus on Julia.

"Speaking of cute guys, I just found out something about Danny," I whisper, indicating I'm letting her in on a secret. "He was seen in Northern Bay buying baby stuff. Julia's pregnant."

Sheila's mouth flies open. "She's pregnant again?"

What does she mean by 'pregnant again'? When Sheila sees my reaction, she clamps her hand over her mouth and says, "I wasn't supposed to tell anyone."

"Tell what?" I've finally hit on something.

She clams up. We eat the rest of our lunch in silence. Just as Sheila's about to get up and leave, I put my hand on her arm and tell her she can trust me. "I'm on Julia's side. I won't tell her secrets. I just want to make sure she's okay. I got pregnant when I was eighteen and ran away from home. I know how scary it is to be young and pregnant and on the run. Believe me, I've been there myself."

Sheila appears to relax a bit and sits back down. "I promised her I wouldn't tell anyone."

"I understand." I need to convince her to confide in me. "But the thing is, I'm worried about her. Detective Evans told me something that makes me wonder if someone else is the father."

"Who? Julia never talked about anyone else, just Danny."

Scott isn't going to be happy I'm sharing information he told me in confidence. "Some fingerprints found in her bedroom don't belong to family and friends. What if she was seeing someone else? Maybe she ran away from her parents and Danny because she was afraid to face them. But if Danny's found her and he's possessive, like Julia's mom claims…" I trail off, letting her imagine what he might do.

"Ohh…!"

"I don't know how Danny feels about raising another man's baby…" If I can get her to think the worst of Danny, maybe she'll let me in on the secrets Julia shared with her. I have no idea how Danny feels about being a father to someone else's kid. Jim, thank goodness, has always treated Brent as his own flesh and blood. Not every woman is as lucky as I am.

"She'll want to keep the baby," Sheila states in no uncertain terms. "She never got over it seven years ago when she had to give up the baby."

"She gave it up for adoption?" Something I never considered doing.

"No, she had an abortion," Sheila whispers. "She didn't want to. Her parents told her it was the only thing to do."

I'm not one to judge. Every situation is different. My own birth mother considered abortion before handing me over to my parents. And I have no idea what Julia must have gone through. "What about the baby's father?"

"I don't know. She never told anyone who he was."

Chapter Thirty-Two

Scott

There she is, on the front porch steps, when I pull up in front of Julia's house. Cheryl comes running up to me as though she's ready to jump into my arms. She's excited to see me, and my hopes are aroused until she blurts out, "Julia was pregnant before! It's not the first time! We need to find her old journals."

Wow! How did she manage to find that out? Obviously, I've underestimated Cheryl's ability to pry things out of people.

"Sheila told me. I know it's Julia's personal business, and I promised Sheila she could trust me to keep it secret, but if Julia's in danger, you need to know. Jim says I'm always sticking my nose in other people's business, but I'm just trying to help."

Once again, I use the spare key to open Julia's front door. Cheryl wants to go through the boxes and tubs in the spare room and the basement. She's sure there must be more journals packed away somewhere.

We begin in the spare room. As we're opening boxes and tubs, checking through the contents, neither of us speaks. It always seems obtrusive to me, going through people's personal belongings, but it's part of the job. At least in this case, there hasn't been a murder on the premises.

The first few boxes contain photo albums, mementos from her childhood, some old schoolwork, old cards and letters, report cards, and her diploma. There's nothing of value, except to Julia. Then Cheryl lets out a squeal when

119

she opens a box with paperback novels and finds some old journals mixed in with them.

There's an assortment of various types of notebooks with decorative covers. Although nothing identifies them as diaries, it's evident that's what they are as soon as we open to the first page. The most recent journal is near the top. It begins on December 4, 2008, seven months ago. Cheryl digs out all the journals and piles them on the floor, about a dozen of them. One stands out from the others. It's a thick, lilac-colored diary with a padlock, the tiny key still attached to the clasp.

Cheryl opens it and reads aloud the handwritten words on the inside cover.

To my best friend, Julia:

Although we won't be together as we begin this new stage of our lives, I wish you all the best in the future. Here's a little something for you to record your Grade Nine adventures.

Love forever,

Rebecca

"Rebecca gave this to Julia as a parting gift when they finished Grade 8 and she moved to Ottawa," Cheryl says, carefully flipping through the pages. "Then Julia must have continued writing. There's probably ten years' worth of her life recorded here." She gestures to the stack of journals.

"I've got a lot of reading to do." I scoop up most of the journals off the floor, leaving the rest for Cheryl, and take them out to the living area.

She suggests she help. "Why don't you start at the end, and I'll begin with Grade 9, and we can meet somewhere in the middle. "We may as well get started now, if you're up for it."

That sounds like a plan; there's a lot to get through, and it's not clear what we're looking for. "I'm up for it if you are. Reading women's diary entries is one of my favorite pastimes."

She gives me a quizzical look and sits on one end of the sofa, giving me lots of room. I decide it's prudent to take the opposite side, as far from her as possible. We begin the tedious process of skimming through Julia's life as she saw it. I'm glad she's assigned herself the high school years. I don't imagine there's much there to explain Julia's disappearance. Likely just a teenage girl's angst. Since I've got this year's journal, I start at the end, on May 16, and work my way forward. I suspect that if there *is* anything to find, it will be in the entries from the last few months.

The next ten minutes are spent in this way, the two of us immersed in Julia's life, when I read something that catches my attention. A possible lead. "Listen to this. There's something here about the Millcroft mine."

Lake Kipling literally sits on gold. Situated within the Canadian Shield, a large area of Precambrian rock, the town's mine shafts are located along the Main Break. We learned all about it in school. Tourists can read about it on the many plaques along the mining heritage tour.

I'm not sure how much Cheryl knows about it, so I fill her in. "Millcroft Mine was the last of the local mines to shut down. The buildings surrounding the lagoons and quarries are still standing, but the corporation that owns the mine declared bankruptcy. The whole area is blocked off at the main road leading into the complex, and the gates to the mine are locked. But, according to this journal entry, Julia has managed to trespass on the property." I read aloud Julia's journal entry, dated May 5, 2009.

I went to Millcroft Mine today. It was a nice spring day to explore. I know I shouldn't go there, but I'm curious to know what's happening. Danny said I should mind my own business. Maybe he's right.

"What if she went to the mine the night she disappeared?" Cheryl asks.

I shake my head. "She wouldn't go there when it's pitch black. It's too dangerous even during the daytime, much less alone in the middle of the night. Why on earth would she do that? Unless Danny went with her. But I can't imagine what they'd be doing there."

"It doesn't make any sense," Cheryl agrees, crinkling up her cute, slightly upturned nose. "But then, neither does anything else in this case."

Chapter Thirty-Three

Cheryl

Scott's vehicle heads down Clapton Ave., and we end up at the intersection of Governor's Road, which is also the highway through town. As we travel in silence down this section of the Trans-Canada highway to Millcroft Lane, we're both wondering whether Julia's reference to the mine has any bearing on her disappearance or on Danny's, for that matter. Both of them apparently knew something was happening at the mine.

A swing gate blocks the lane; signs indicate the mine is private property, and trespassers will be prosecuted. This doesn't deter Scott. He gets out of the driver's seat, walks to the gate, pulls off the chain with the rusty, broken padlock, swings the gate wide open, and drives down the main access road to the mine. During the two-minute drive to the main entrance of Millcroft Mine, we encounter No Trespassing signs as well as Danger and Do Not Enter signs. At the end of the lane, barbed wire caps the locked chain link fence. There's no way to get into the complex.

"She couldn't have gotten any farther. So, what did she see?" Scott muses, hands on his hips, surveying the area.

Trees line either side of the road. Past the gate, several outbuildings are visible, and the headframe of one of the mineshafts towers in the distance. No one else is around, as far as we can see. There's no sound of activity. If Julia thought something was going on here, there's no evidence of that now.

"Is there a break in the fence somewhere?" I make my way along the wire enclosure through the forested area to the right of the vehicle, with Scott following.

The chain link fencing appears to be intact. After following the treed fence for several minutes, we head back the way we came and try the other side of the roadway. If Julia got in through here, we don't know how.

"We need to find out if she mentions the mine anywhere else in her journal," I suggest. "Maybe there's a clue how she got in."

"Hold on. I'm going to take down the phone number on the sign." The sign he's referring to reads: **North Group Maintenance 705-385-3976**.

Once we're back at the house, Scott indicates it's time to return to Lake Kipling. It's getting late and we both have other things to do besides sit on Julia's sofa and read her journals.

"I'd like to take these home with me and read through them," I state, gathering them up before he has a chance to say no.

But he takes them from me and insists I can't do that.

"Why not? Are you taking them into evidence?"

"No. I think we've found as much as we're going to."

He sets the journals back on the coffee table, and I say I need to use the bathroom before leaving. I make a detour to Julia's room to speak to her mom in private. "Mrs. Brenner, how are you? It's Cheryl MacGregor. I'm at Julia's house."

"Have you found out something?" Hope comes through in her voice.

"No, not yet. But Detective Evans and I found Julia's journals and we think they may help us locate her." I pause to let this sink in. "And I was wondering whether it would be okay if I took them home to skim through, to see if there are any clues about where she might have gone."

Mrs. Brenner doesn't respond at first.

"It could really be useful to know what she was thinking in the weeks and months before she disappeared," I continue, in my attempt to convince her. "I know you want to do everything possible to get her back home, where she belongs."

"Well, I don't know...Julia's private journals..." she protests, sounding unsure.

"If there's a clue in there, we don't want to take a chance and miss finding it. Your daughter's life could depend on it." I appeal to the mother in her.

Mrs. Brenner consents to my taking Julia's journals. The door to Julia's room glides open. Scott stands on the threshold, a frown on his face. He strides toward the bed and I get up to leave, but he takes my hand and pulls me back down to the bed, asking what the phone call was about. I'm not sure whether I trip over his feet or lose my balance, or both, but the next thing I know is we're lying on the bed, and I'm sprawled out on top of him.

Chapter Thirty-Four

Scott

I don't know what just happened, but she's got me pinned down on the bed. While I don't mind being in this position, it only lasts a few seconds and results in a lot of embarrassment. Cheryl scrambles to get off me and off the bed, apologizing. "I'm so sorry, I didn't mean to..." Her cheeks are a rosy red. "I must have lost my balance." She makes a quick exit out the door.

I follow her to the living room and tell her it's my fault. "I shouldn't have grabbed your hand like that. I'm sorry."

After an uncomfortable silence, she says, "I guess we're both to blame."

It's time to leave. We obviously can't be alone together. I help her scoop up the journals from the coffee table and place them on the passenger side of her car, knowing it's unlikely there's anything of use in them. "Let me know if you find something." I extend my hand to give her the business card with my extension at Northeastern headquarters. "Just a minute." I write on the back. "You've got my cell. Here's my home number."

The ball's in her court. I wonder how long she'll wait to call this time. Her Toyota heads down the road, and I follow her to Lake Kipling. From there, she goes home, I presume to make dinner for her family, while I stop to pick up my Camaro and set off to my apartment in Timber Lake, a good hour and a half away. I need to get my mind back on track, on to the other cases needing my attention, and off Cheryl MacGregor, married woman and mother.

Chapter Thirty-Five

Jim MacGregor

Jim MacGregor sits opposite his newest clients, a young couple just starting out, looking for their first house. They're getting married in December and want to purchase and furnish their home before the wedding. Not only are they on a short timeline, they're also on a tight budget.

"Are you willing to look at properties outside of town?" Jim explains the real estate values in the smaller communities around Lake Kipling are significantly lower.

They gaze at each other and seem to come to a consensus without speaking. "Sure," Lily Thompson says at the same time her fiancé nods his assent. "As long as it's within a reasonable driving distance for work."

Work for both is on the west end of town. Jim has the perfect property in mind, but with one glitch. "There's a house available immediately in West Kipling. Now, it does need some TLC. It's been empty for about a year, but I'm sure the owner will be willing to take a reasonable offer. If you don't mind doing some work, it could be a good investment as well as a nice starter home."

He pulls out the MLS listing for the house on Clapton Ave. and goes over the description with his clients. The property is listed with another agency, so the commission will be split. What matters most to Jim, though, is that his clients find a home that will be right for them.

"It's a charming little story and a half, perfect for two or a small family." Jim wants to be sure he covers all the bases. If they're planning on starting a family right away, there's the second bedroom and room in the basement to expand the living space. "And the price is right."

William and Lily agree it's worth a look. Jim calls Foster Showalter and asks if it's okay to drop by to pick up the keys for 59 Clapton Ave. With his clients in the back seat of the Jeep, Jim makes a quick stop at Showalter Realty, then turns left and drives toward West Kipling. Fifteen minutes later, the three of them stand in the short gravel driveway beside the small house with a For Sale sign out front. That's not where Jim's attention is focused, though. His gaze is riveted on Julia's house and the Rav4 and unmarked police vehicle in front.

First, she tells me he's dropping the case, and she won't be seeing him anymore, then she has him over for pizza, and now they're alone together in Julia's house.

It takes some effort for him to compose himself and get back to business.

"It's kind of cute, but overgrown," is Lily's first response. The shrubs and weeds in the front flower bed, along with the grass that hasn't been cut for some time, don't make for a good first impression. "But I can see what it might look like if the lawn was looked after and with some nice flowers growing in the flower bed."

"I could build a small porch for us to sit on. It looks like it's a quiet street," William adds. "Nice for sitting out with our morning coffee."

"It's definitely quiet here. There's a path at the dead end that leads to a small lake out in the woods. Nice place for a walk. You'll find there isn't much traffic anywhere around the village, and this end of the road is especially quiet. The other end connects with the highway, so it's a second route out of town. At the intersection, there's a small convenience store where you can pick up essentials without having to drive to Lake Kipling for everything," Jim says, seeing their interest.

Fighting his way through the overgrowth blocking the front door, Jim inserts the key into the lock, turns it, and gives the door a shove. The stale air assaults his sense of smell as he enters the small living room. The space is empty, its hardwood floor in need of refinishing, and there are some holes in the drywall. Two small windows overlook the street. As they walk straight ahead, they enter the dining area with a door leading out to the deck and a compact kitchen to the right. The kitchen cupboards are white, and old blue and white tiles make up the floor. There's a double sink with a small window above it.

Lily opens and closes some of the cupboards and checks out the outlets for the fridge and stove, as though trying to visualize herself cooking in there, while William opens the door and steps onto the deck, probably imagining himself barbecuing and the two of them enjoying a nice meal on their patio furniture after work.

"We'll have to fix the holes and give the walls and cupboards a fresh coat of paint," William says to Lily. "Some new flooring will do wonders for the place. The deck looks like it needs some shoring up, but it'll do with a bit of patching and some paint."

Jim leads the way back toward the entrance and up the rickety stairs on the left-hand side of the main floor. "You'll want to replace some of these boards," he says, not wanting to sugar-coat the place.

When they reach the small hallway on the landing, they find two doors on the wall facing them, and one door on the opposite wall. Jim opens the door to the bathroom, which is straight ahead and slightly to the right. It's a small room, but has a combination shower/bathtub, which seems to please Lily, although it's obviously in need of a good clean. There's a bath towel hanging over the bathtub and toilet paper in the roll. The door next to the bathroom opens to a small dormered bedroom. "A nursery, someday," William says, smiling at his fiancée.

Across the hall is the master bedroom. Jim opens the door and is shocked by what he discovers. William and Lily gaze past him to find the room isn't empty, as they all expected it to be.

A sleeping bag lies on the floor with snack food wrappers and an empty ginger ale bottle next to it. "I'm sorry," Jim says. "It looks like a squatter's been here. I'll notify Showalter Realty so they can deal with it. These things sometimes happen with abandoned houses."

William and Lily don't seem too upset by this. "We'll change the locks, of course," William assures Lily. "And make sure the windows are all secure."

Jim wonders how the squatter got into the house. The doors lock from the inside and were secured when they got there. Downstairs, he checks the windows, but they're locked as well. Jim tells his clients to wait on the main floor until he makes sure no one is hiding in the basement. As soon as he gets to the bottom of the stairs, he notices the partially open window facing the back yard. It isn't very big, but large enough for someone to have gotten through. Scanning the unfinished basement, and determining that there's currently no one in the house, Jim calls up the stairs for William and Lily to join him.

The showing goes as well as it can, considering the condition of the house and the fact that someone has been living there temporarily. No damage seems to have been done to the house, as far as Jim can tell. Maybe some runaway kid, he thinks. Jim secures the basement window. Before leaving the house, he notices his wife is still busy detecting with her friend, Detective Evans.

When they arrive back at the real estate office, William tells Jim they'll need more time to talk it over, but they'll definitely get back to him.

"Sounds good," Jim responds. "There are some other properties we can look at if you decide against this one, but the price won't be as good."

Once his clients leave the office, Jim drives out to Showalter Realty to return the key and inform Foster that someone has been in the house. "We'll need to call the police. A woman has gone missing from that street in the last couple of weeks. I doubt there's a connection, but still, it should be reported."

Foster says he will take care of it.

When Jim comes home from work at the end of the day, he asks Cheryl what she was doing at Julia's house that afternoon.

"Detective Evans and I were going through Julia's journals and found she mentioned Millcroft mine, so we went there to check it out."

"Find anything?"

"No, but I'm going to read through the rest of her journals to see if there's more to it. I think the clue to her disappearance is somewhere in them." Cheryl narrows her eyes. "How did you know we were at Julia's this afternoon? Are you following me?" Her tone is teasing.

"I was showing a property. It looks like someone's been sleeping in the abandoned house on Julia's street."

Cheryl's face lights up. "I wonder... What if Julia was staying there? Maybe just for one night? Or two? That might explain how she managed to disappear into thin air."

Chapter Thirty-Six

Cheryl

I think I've solved this case. Julia ran away because she's pregnant and didn't want to tell her parents, especially since they made her get an abortion years ago. Not wanting people to know she ran off with her boyfriend, she made it appear that she disappeared under mysterious circumstances. They decided they should wait a while, until things cooled down with the search, then Danny would join her in Northern Bay, after which they were probably going to head to Montreal to get lost in the city. But with Detective Evans asking too many questions, Danny was getting worried he might be charged with her disappearance. That's why he's suddenly taken off, too.

The abandoned house down the road was the perfect spot for Julia to hide the night she left her house and Danny reported her missing. He probably went back for her the next night and drove her out of the area, to Northern Bay, getting her settled in a motel, with some supplies and cash. Sometime over the last few days, he packed a few of her belongings and joined her.

It's a romantic love story, kind of like mine and Jim's. Two people run away together to leave behind their old life and start a new one. I confide in Jim what I'm thinking.

"It's possible, I suppose," Jim says, although I don't think he quite believes it. "Why didn't she just pack her stuff and leave a note...? I don't know. It just seems like an odd way to leave your family."

He's right, of course. It's just too weird, all of it.

Still, the abandoned house is another clue to this mystery. I've spent the day jotting down the clues so far and trying to connect them without success. My second article about Julia's disappearance will be in this week's paper. Once again, no details that would interfere with the investigation will be released. It's more a plea for anyone who has information to come forward. I'm hoping at some point Detective Evans will allow more details to be made public so I can write my exclusive. Right now, though, the important thing is to make sure Julia is safe.

I'm going to spend some time tomorrow reading more journal entries. So far, I haven't found anything in her Grade 9 year that could be a clue. I find myself thinking of Scott, and whether he's followed up on calling the company in charge of Millcroft mine.

Tonight, Jim and I are going to spend some family time in the back yard with our kids. A barbecue and ice cream, followed by a game of catch. Later, I'm going to show my husband just how much I love him.

* * *

July 15

Jim leaves the house later than usual this morning. We stayed up late last night and slept past eight o'clock. Brent and Jamie are already in the family room, watching TV. I'm still in pajamas as I make coffee, scrambled eggs, and frozen waffles. "I'll just skip breakfast." Jim kisses me on the cheek and grabs a cup of coffee when he comes down, fully dressed and ready to go.

A few minutes later, the kids and I gulp down our breakfast, and I scoot them upstairs to get dressed for camp. By nine-fifteen, I'm back home, cleaning up the kitchen and making the beds, anxious to settle down with Julia's journals.

It's a nice day again, so I take a couple of journals with me and head to the front porch with a second cup of coffee, immersing myself in Julia's high school years. She continued her friendship with Sheila, Rachel, and Nell from Grade 8 through high school. Rebecca comes up a couple of times—she talks about being pen pals. I'm almost at the end of the Grade 9 school year when I read something that would ordinarily be normal for a teenage girl but in this situation, sends up a red flag.

He asked me out today! We were at McDonald's, and he sat down next to me when Sheila went to the bathroom. Finally, after a couple of months! I knew he liked me.

There's no mention of a name. No description. No details. A few days later, she writes about meeting up with him, but doesn't say where. There are several references to the mystery guy, but never a name or anything to indicate his identity. This surely can't be the guy who got her pregnant. She didn't have the abortion for at least two years after the end of that school year, when she was seventeen. Still, I'm curious to see whether she mentions him in Grade 10. There are a lot of journal entries to go through, and it's not exciting reading, so it's easy to miss something important. I decide to set aside the high school years for now and pick up where Scott left off at the entry that mentions something is happening at the mine.

I read backwards, like Scott did. May 4, the date he stopped, is where I begin and work my way into April of this year. By the time I get to March, I still don't see anything about a possible pregnancy. I go inside to check the time and find it's already one o'clock. In the kitchen, I pour myself a cold glass of lemonade and fix a salad for lunch. I've been putting on weight the last couple of weeks with all the fast food.

As I'm munching on my salad, it occurs to me that if Julia had been pregnant before the beginning of March, she surely would have been showing by July when she went missing. Yet, I've seen no mention of a pregnancy. I wonder if I've missed something. Unless... What if there's something in her most recent journal? What if she wrote about being pregnant after the May long weekend? Maybe she wasn't far along when she made the decision to leave.

Both Scott and I have been through that journal and didn't see anything about a pregnancy, but then, we weren't thinking of a baby. Once I've finished my salad, I take Julia's latest diary to the deck and read it again, word for word this time.

I still don't find anything about a baby. Why didn't she mention it? I understand she was keeping it a secret from her parents, but why keep it secret from her diary? Julia did tend to write vague references to things that were private. Perhaps she was worried someone else would read it. That's something I can relate to. I've never specifically written about what happened to me years ago. Writing is an excellent outlet for venting one's problems, but in my case, I've had to disguise facts. I can't risk anyone finding out what I've done.

No matter how many times I read over the entries from mid-May to the first week of July, I can't find anything remotely associated with pregnancy or a baby. Something does catch my eye, though. I wonder why Scott didn't mention it. On June 8, Julia wrote:

> **I went back again. I talked to some of the neighbors along the road, and they said they heard motorcycles at night. I checked it out and saw tracks. Probably just some kids goofing around. Danny keeps saying I should mind my own business, but I'm curious.**

Then on June 28, she wrote:

> **I was back there today. It was a nice day for a walk. Nothing much going on.**

Now that I've read these two entries several times, I wonder whether Julia was talking about the mine. She referred to going 'back there' twice. Danny warned her at least twice to mind her own business. The more I think about it, I'm almost certain she's talking about something strange happening at the mine.

The Millcroft mine entrance is quite a distance from Julia's house. Scott read her journal entry from May 5, and we know she was at the mine that day. We assumed she drove. It would have taken her almost two hours to walk to the main gates of Millcroft. She's young and fit. But what if she found another way into Millcroft?

Chapter Thirty-Seven

Scott

I need to tie up a few loose ends on the Julia Brenner file before I set it aside and work on other cases. First on the list is the abandoned property across from Julia. Cheryl thinks Julia might have hid there the night she left her house. Since the house was broken into, I have it swept for fingerprints and any other signs that Julia was there.

The second thing I want to revisit is the possibility that Rebecca knows where Julia is. Another call to her confirms she hasn't seen Julia since last summer. I consider that maybe I'm asking the wrong questions. "What about Danny? Do you know where he is?"

Again, she tells me she has no idea. I strike out with Rebecca.

Unless I find evidence of foul play in Julia's disappearance, or until I find Danny, I'm going to make the assumption that they're together, safe, and not wanting to be found.

My phone rings.

That didn't take long. I knew she'd call.

"Cheryl, what's up?" It's about two-thirty, and I'm in the middle of some paperwork.

"I need to see you. Today, if you've got time."

I'm not sure how to respond, so I say, "Okay," and wait for her to take the lead.

"I think I found something in Julia's diary. About Millcroft mine."

"I'll meet you at West Kipling in a couple of hours."

I have no idea how long I'll remain in Lake Kipling this time, so I stop at home to grab my overnight bag, which I keep packed just in case.

By four-thirty, I pull up in front of Julia's house.

Cheryl gets out of her car and strides toward my Camaro. "I don't know if it's anything, but in her diary, Julia talks about going for a walk. It made me wonder if there was another entrance to the mine, closer to her house."

This is what she called about? This is so urgent she needed to see me right away? Julia walked to the mine instead of taking the car. Before I can respond, she starts walking down Clapton Ave. with a purpose. "Are you coming?" she shouts, turning around to see me rooted in my spot.

It takes about five minutes to reach the intersection of Clapton Ave. and Governor's Road. The traffic is light on this section of the Trans-Canada highway. The variety store, gas station, and post office are on the corner. West Kipling's business section.

"What's straight ahead?" Cheryl asks. A No Exit sign stands on the gravel road that continues across the highway. When I shrug, she says, "Let's go have a look."

The road leads to a forested area. Brush and trees surround us as we walk side by side down the middle of the road. Why Julia would walk down here, I have no idea. I voice my opinion to Cheryl, who doesn't have an answer other than maybe Julia liked to explore. "Remember how Danny and Sheila said she liked going to the lake in the woods across from her house? Maybe she enjoyed nature walks and liked to find new spots."

After fifteen minutes of wandering through the forest along the gravel, I'm surprised to see signs of civilization. People actually live out here. We pass houses on both sides of the road. Five houses, to be exact. But it's what's up ahead that gets Cheryl excited.

"Look! There's a mine shaft elevator!" She points, running toward it. As we approach, more of the mine comes into view. Up ahead, the headframe of a mine shaft and several buildings are visible. Trails lead off to other areas of the property. A locked swing gate blocks access to vehicles, and signs warn people to stay out.

The Millcroft property takes up a large area of the forest outside of West Kipling. I hadn't realized there were two shafts—one on the north end at the main entrance and one on the south end where we now stand. For some reason, this end is not as fortified as the other. Perhaps it's because of its location on a dead-end road, with no signs indicating it leads to the mine. In any case, we've found the back entrance to the mine complex.

Cheryl clangs the gate back and forth, but it's clearly locked. She moves to the post on the right, shoves aside the brush, and exposes a chain link fence, blocking access to the property. Following her lead, I examine the left post. And I find a gap. Between the gate post and the start of the chain link fence, the brush covers an access spot. It appears that the brush has been pushed aside to allow entry.

Cheryl steps next to me. "It's a motorcycle track!" She points to the ground. "Just like Julia said. She saw motorcycle tracks going through here, and she said the neighbors had complained about motorcycles running up and down the road."

I'm not sure what this means, but since Julia went missing after she wrote about the mine, it warrants further investigation. Cheryl suggests we slip through the opening and enter the complex.

"No. If there's something illegal going on, we need to do this properly. I'll call the maintenance company and get access to the property tomorrow." I want to proceed with caution for two reasons—to ensure Cheryl's safety and to cover my ass in case there's evidence to be found.

"What about asking the neighbors here if they know anything?" Cheryl waves her arms toward the houses behind us. "Julia said she talked to them."

I can't argue with that. If I don't talk to them, she'll come back herself. We walk back down the road a few hundred feet, approach the first house on the right, and knock on the front door. The houses are small, white-sided bungalows or story-and-a-half buildings. A woman in her forties answers. I show her my ID, and she motions us into the living room without hesitation.

"It's about time they sent someone," she says. "I called three times to complain about the noise."

When I ask what noise, she tells us about the motorcycles that have been roaring down the road in the middle of the night during the last couple of months.

"How often does this happen, and how many motorcycles are there?" Cheryl butts in to take over my investigation again.

"Two or three times a week. Different days, different times of the night. Two or three bikes each time usually, from the sounds of it."

I ask whether she has seen them or just heard them.

"By the time I look out the window, they're gone. But of course, there's nowhere for them to go. This is a dead-end road. I hear them go by, but they don't turn around and come back. I don't know what they're up to out here. Nothing good, I imagine."

Disappearing motorbikes. An image of alien spaceships beaming up motorcycles on the end of this country gravel road flashes through my mind. Then I give my head a figurative shake and consider that the bikes entered the complex here and probably came back out at some later time, and simply weren't heard. Or maybe they found some other exit. Probably kids out on a joyride. But then again, maybe there's a connection to the other motorcycle complaints we've been receiving.

"Does anyone else live with you?" Cheryl asks. The woman confirms that her adult son lives here. "Could we speak with him?"

The woman goes down the hall and returns with a tall, skinny man in his early twenties, sandy hair cascading down to his shoulders. He seems nervous when I show him my badge, eyes darting around, like he's looking for an escape. "We're investigating the disappearance of a young woman from West Kipling. We have reason to suspect she's been in this area. Have either of you seen her before?" I show them a photo of Julia.

"Yes, she asked if we had seen anyone going onto the mine property. She had seen movement around the buildings one day," the woman says. "I told her people come to check on the place sometimes. And I told her about the motorcycles at night. Are you going to charge them?"

"We'll look into it."

"Humph! That's what the other officers said."

"Did you talk to Julia?" I address her son.

He denies having seen her before.

We thank them for their help and leave. As we walk toward the highway, Cheryl stops. "Did he seem nervous to you?" When I agree that I noticed it, too, she continues. "I think he knows something he's not telling. We need to talk to him, away from his mother."

She tells me to wait here, turns around, and runs back toward their house. Several minutes later, Cheryl and the guy drive up alongside me.

"Where's your car?" he asks, rolling down his window.

My car is back at Julia's house. I'm not sure why he's asking.

"I told Mike our car battery died and asked if he could give us a boost," Cheryl explains. Clearly, we don't have a car here. Turning to Mike, she says, "I'm sorry, I didn't tell you the car's back in West Kipling. I hope that's not a problem."

Getting into the backseat, I wonder what she's up to. Mike drives in silence while Cheryl chatters casually about the weather and the scenery. When we pull up next to my Camaro, Cheryl tells me to pop my hood. She knows damn well the battery's fine. I don't like anyone messing with my car, and I'm about to protest when she says, "Why don't you try to turn it over one more time?"

Mike and Cheryl stand to the side while I turn the key, and my brand new 2010 Camaro comes to life like a dream, as it always does. I take very good care of my baby.

"Perfect! It started!" Cheryl exclaims, as though she's surprised. "We should take it for a run, though, to make sure the battery gets charged properly."

I remain quiet, not understanding my role in this game.

"Hand me your keys," Cheryl says. Then she turns to the scraggly-haired guy. "Do you want to take it for a spin?"

The guy's mouth falls open, as I'm sure mine does. No one drives my car, except me.

"Can I?" he asks.

I shout, "No!"

Cheryl opens the passenger door. "Sure! Scott, why don't you sit up front, and I'll squeeze in the back?"

The guy walks around my car like he's buying it, admiring the metallic silver paint, polished aluminum wheels, black hood stripes, and, of course, the decklid spoiler. "Cool!" he exclaims. Cheryl tells me once again to get in the passenger seat. I want to say no, but the look she flashes me makes it clear that's not an option. I toss the keys to the guy.

Before I know it, he's got one hand on my leather steering wheel and the other on the leather shift knob.

Does this guy even know how to drive a stick?

A few rough gear changes, and minutes later, we're roaring down the highway, exceeding the speed limit, the scenery a blur.

Jesus! I hope he's got a valid driver's license, and we don't get pulled over by an overzealous cop.

"Maybe you could turn around up there." I point out the car dealership ahead. He hits the brake, the tires squealing as he makes the left turn, mercifully avoiding the vehicles on the lot, and guns it down the highway back to West Kipling.

To my relief, all four of us make it back to Julia's house in one piece— Cheryl, Mike, me, and my baby. As Cheryl gets out of the back seat, I realize she's been uncharacteristically quiet during the whole trip. No doubt praying this guy doesn't wreck my car.

Her voice shakes. "That was good driving, Mike. Do you want to come in for a Twinkie, maybe a beer?"

I open my mouth to protest, but again, she gives me that look that warns me to shut up, so I walk toward the front door, Julia's key in hand. The police tape is gone, so as far as Mike knows, this is my house. We enter, and I go to the kitchen looking for snacks, while Cheryl sits on the sofa with Mike and starts up a conversation.

Fortunately, I find both beer and Twinkies in Julia's kitchen. I'm about to bring them out when I hear Cheryl ask Mike if there are ever any good tailgate parties out at the mine. She tells him we just moved to the area, and it's so boring in West Kipling. She's looking for some fun. I stay in the kitchen, pretending I'm still rooting through the refrigerator.

He responds with, "What about your boyfriend, the cop?"

"He's not my boyfriend. He's just my brother. Don't worry about him."

How does he not notice her wedding ring?

"Oh, I thought you two were...you know."

She laughs at this as though it's implausible. "Eww...no. Gross. He's my brother, although he acts like my dad sometimes. He's trying to find my friend Julia. Her parents think she's missing. Anyway, I wondered when Julia, that's my friend who's probably off on a bender with her boyfriend, told me about the motorcycles and people around the mine, well...I thought maybe there'd be some partying going on there."

He doesn't answer. I use the lull in conversation to bring in the beer and Twinkies. "Here we go." I set them on the coffee table. "And I heard that, Sis. I'm nothing like dear old Dad. Don't believe anything she says." I open a bottle and take a large swig of beer, putting my feet up on the table, playing the role of big brother. "If she wants to party, that's her business."

"So, do you ever go to any of the parties?" Cheryl asks. "Maybe I could come with you next time? I'll bring the beer." She laughs again and opens a bottle, taking a good-sized swig herself.

Mike cracks one open as well. "No parties. Nothing ever happens around here, sorry."

"Oh, that's too bad," Cheryl says. "I thought maybe that's why people were hanging out by the mine." After a few more gulps of beer, she continues, "But if that's not it, I wonder what's going on there. Scott, maybe you should get the cops in there with a warrant to check out the mine and the neighborhood, make sure everything's okay."

"Yeah, maybe," I agree. The guy seems nervous again. "I'm sure your mom will be happy to know we're going to keep an eye out in your neighborhood."

"There's nothing going on there," he insists. "Just some guys riding their bikes."

Cheryl asks if he knows them, and he claims he doesn't. "But, I think Danny knows them."

Cheryl and I exclaim, "Danny?"

"Yeah, I've seen Danny talk to them."

143

"Who's Danny?" I ask. This can't be a coincidence.

"Just a guy I know."

"Last name?"

"Don't know."

"How do you know him?"

"He's just...I don't want to get into trouble or get anyone else in trouble." Mike gets up to leave.

"You won't get into trouble. In fact, there might be a reward for helping the police if there are trespassers at the mine," Cheryl intervenes. This gets his attention and he sits down again.

"How much of a reward?

"I don't know, but probably a lot. The people who own the mine are rich and I'll bet they don't want anybody wrecking the place. So if you know something..."

"I don't know Danny's last name. Sometimes we meet inside Millcroft."

"What's the meeting about?" Cheryl asks.

"We're friends. He sells weed," Mike confesses, fidgeting with his hands. "Not to me. I don't do that kind of thing. Maybe the motorcycle guys buy some from him. Maybe that's why they go there. Look, am I in some kind of trouble? 'Cos if not, I'm heading out."

"No, you're not in trouble," I assure him. "As long as you tell me everything you know."

"That *is* all I know," he says. "Will I get a reward?"

"I'll get back to you on that."

As Mike drives off, we wave goodbye. I turn to Cheryl. "Well, Sis, that was an unorthodox way of getting information. What's your husband going to say when he finds out you're bored and want to party?"

Cheryl's cheeks turn a shade of bright red. "Well, at least you got what you wanted."

My eyes move up and down the length of her body and give her a wicked smile. "No, I haven't got what I wanted. Yet. But I will."

She gets so flustered at my teasing, I can't help but laugh out loud.

Chapter Thirty-Eight

Cheryl

I move my rings from my right hand back to my left to remind him of my marital status. My marriage is no joke to me. "I meant that you got the information you wanted about what's going on at the mine. It's obviously something to do with drugs, and Danny's involved."

"Now we know how he's able to afford going on the run with Julia. I'm going to get in touch with the maintenance company tomorrow to get permission to have a look around the premises." He's all business again. Then he tips up my chin and makes me look directly into his eyes as he chuckles. "I love my car. You're lucky it's still in one piece, or I'd make you pay."

It is a nice car, no doubt about it. I'm sure it attracts a lot of women. None of my business, though. I need to get home to my family and figure out what we're having for supper.

"Can I come with you tomorrow?" I ask, pulling away. But he's already shaking his head before I complete the question. "Well, can you at least let me know what you find out?"

He agrees to call tomorrow, and we go our separate ways. I stop to pick up a bucket of fried chicken, fries, and coleslaw. I should be watching my weight, but it's quick and convenient, which will leave me more time to go through Julia's journals tonight. I want to find out if the guy she met in Grade 9 is the guy who got her pregnant. I need to know if she was still secretly seeing him.

Jim and the kids are in the back yard when I get home just after seven o'clock. Jim says he was about to put burgers on the barbecue, and he's glad he waited. While he takes plates out of the cupboard, I remove the food from the paper bag and set it on the counter. He doesn't say anything more until we're sitting at the table on the back deck. "How was your day? Anything new?"

"It was good." I choose not to fill him in on unnecessary details. "Scott and I went back to the mine this afternoon."

"Scott?" His frown tells me he's not happy to hear I'm spending more time with him. "I thought he'd all but given up on finding Julia. From what I understood, he thinks she ran off with Danny. But apparently, the two of you are still working on the case."

I wait till the kids are done eating and off playing in the yard to explain the new developments, cautioning Jim not to tell anyone. "One of the neighbors who lives close to the mine said Danny was selling drugs there. Scott thinks that might be how he got enough cash to run away with Julia."

"Does that mean you won't be seeing Detective Evans, that is Scott, again now that the mystery is solved? He must have other cases to work on."

"I'm not sure the mystery *is* solved," I say, picking up another piece of chicken. "I think there's more going on at the mine, and it has something to do with Julia's disappearance. The other thing I'm still wondering about is the abandoned house on her street. Do you think Julia could have been there the night she went missing? Maybe it was a temporary hiding spot. Maybe she and Danny planned it out ahead of time. What if they wanted it to look like she mysteriously vanished?"

Jim says he doesn't know why they would do that. I don't either, but it's a theory. There must be some explanation as to why she left her bedroom looking like she was about to return.

After supper, I'm eager to get back to Julia's journal. Jim takes care of the dishes and sets the kids up with a video in the family room. Retreating downstairs, I settle into the glider rocker in the rec room. I don't know what exactly I hope to find in Julia's journals, but they'll give me some insight into her frame of mind.

"What does she say about the guy she used to date?" Jim asks, coming down the stairs. "Any clue to his identity?"

I'm glad to see he's interested in my investigation, but I remember Scott doesn't want me sharing confidential information with anyone. I've already told Jim too much. Besides, Julia's journal was meant to be private. "Nothing concrete. I'm not even sure it's relevant. She obviously left with Danny, but I want to see if there's anything here to tell why she left so suddenly."

Jim seems to accept my vague response and heads back upstairs, leaving me to my reading. "Don't stay up too long. I'll be waiting in bed."

Chapter Thirty-Nine

Scott

July 16

When I call North Group Maintenance early Thursday morning, Lisa Fleming, the manager, seems surprised to hear from me. She says she has sometimes spoken to the local police about break-ins at the various properties they take care of, but she's never had a detective contact her.

When I inform her that I have good reason to suspect there are motorcyclists trespassing on the property, and there's the possibility of drug dealing, she's more than happy to have me accompany her to the premises. For safety reasons, as well as insurance concerns, her firm has been entrusted by Northwood Trust to ensure the premises are secure. After obtaining my warrant to search the property for the suspected drugs, I head out to meet her and wait at the mine entrance.

I show my badge when she pulls up outside the main gates and exits her vehicle. She's a nice-looking blonde, but she's no Cheryl. "I appreciate your taking the time to let me have a look around."

Lisa unlocks the padlock that secures the gate to the 2000-acre property and leads the way into the northwestern end of the complex. The headframe from the mineshaft is clearly visible up ahead, as are several other buildings. We drive through the entrance to the empty parking lot. Continuing down the road, the gravel crunching underneath the wheels, we stop beside the mineshaft. From there, we continue on foot to examine each of the buildings.

Lisa points out the cage, which serves as the elevator to bring workers and equipment underground. "It won't be in operation now. The electricity isn't connected. And over here is the hoist room." She unlocks it. "This is where the cage is lowered and raised." The compressor sits silent.

"Are all the buildings locked?"

Lisa confirms that's the case.

"So, it's unlikely anyone could have gotten in anywhere?"

"We do a check of the premises every week, and none of the locks have been reported broken."

A check of 'the dry,' the room where workers would have changed their clothes and showered, reveals nothing. The lockers are open, their contents long gone.

We make our way methodically through the offices, warehouses, maintenance buildings, and equipment storage shed full of heavy mining machinery, finding nothing out of the ordinary. The storage magazine has been emptied of explosives. Old equipment stands idly by on the roadway as though awaiting its drivers and operators.

"Everything's left as though they expect to come back," I say. "Are they planning on re-opening?"

"They're hoping the property will be sold once the price of gold goes back up. Before the owners closed, they were working on starting up another shaft on the other end of the property. Apparently, there's still lots of life left in this gold mine. The problem is the cost of extracting it is too high in the current market. But, with the right investors, new owners might be able to turn things around."

There's no sign of activity as we walk through the northwestern section of the complex. It's a miner's ghost town, the remnants of the once bustling gold mine left behind as a testament to the glory days. I'm particularly interested in the large reservoirs in the surrounding area.

We return to my car and drive past the gray pond where, according to

Lisa, the tailings were deposited. I can't help but wonder what else might lurk beneath the murky surface. At the southeastern section of the complex stands the headframe Cheryl and I saw from the back entrance. As in the northwestern end, there's no sign anyone has been here recently. We walk to the entrance, backing onto the gravel country road where Mike lives. I point out the tire tracks between the gate's end post and the fence to Lisa.

She nods and asks, "So where do they lead?"

All I can tell is that the tracks in the grassy brush area lead to a dirt and gravel open area, which is dry, as it hasn't rained for some time. I'm able to follow the trail for only a short distance before it disappears. With the road veering off in more than one direction, it's impossible to tell where the motorcycles might have gone.

As we return to the main entrance of the complex, I'm once again drawn to the machinery that has been abandoned. "Does anyone check the inside of the trucks and excavators, the rest of the equipment? Are they kept locked?"

"They're locked for safety and security reasons, of course," Lisa assures me. "We don't keep keys on the premises."

What is it I'm missing? The grounds are locked, except for that section at the back entrance that allows for pedestrians or bikes to get through. The buildings and vehicles are secured. The property is checked weekly by maintenance and security crews. There's no sign of activity or problems on site. Yet, Julia wrote about something happening at the mine. The neighbors reported motorcycles going up the road leading to the mine's back entrance. The tire tracks are there. Mike confessed he and Danny were inside the gates, and he witnessed Danny selling drugs on the premises. Is that all that is happening here, or is there more to it? I get out of the car again, and gaze around, trying to figure out what's going on.

"What about those pieces of equipment sitting over there? Why aren't they in storage?" They stick out like a sore thumb.

"They're non-operational. Derelict pieces left behind for parts or for scrap."

"Do you mind if I take a look inside, assuming they're unlocked?"

Lisa tells me to go ahead at my own risk, but to be careful. We walk to the open area where a large haul truck stands beside a small reservoir. Climbing the access stairs on the side, I ascend to the platform, walk to the door of the cab, and pull the handle. The interior of the cab holds two seats, with the gear shifter on the floor between them. There's nothing out of the ordinary here, just a dashboard filled with controls. Exiting the cab and standing on the platform, I glance at the metal box sitting to my right. It's likely some sort of cargo box or toolbox, approximately three feet long and two feet tall. There's a padlock attached for some reason.

"Is there a key for this box?" I shout down to Lisa.

Lisa takes out her numbered list, indicating which key fits where, and her eyes skim it up and down a few times. "No! Can't find one!"

I climb off the haul truck and stand next to Lisa. "Could you get the maintenance crew to pry it open?" I'm curious to know what type of tools require this kind of padlock.

"Do you think there could be drugs in there?"

"I'd like to check things out thoroughly while we're at it, if you don't mind." I suspect a box on an old piece of equipment wouldn't be locked if there was nothing to hide.

"I'll call my people and get a couple of them out here with a crowbar. If there's a chance we've got drugs on the property, the trustees will want it dealt with immediately."

Lisa makes the call while I put in my own request to Judge Brown, knowing she's as eager as I am to shut down the drug problem in the area. We're in luck. Two of Lisa's guys are available immediately and will meet us on site with their equipment in about half an hour.

Although it's a long shot, I've got a hunch there's something hidden in that toolbox. How it connects to Julia's disappearance, I have no idea.

* * *

If this turns out to be a wild goose chase, I'll have wasted my time and the maintenance company's time as well. The motorcycle tracks could be from kids goofing around. Maybe Mike's story about Danny selling drugs on the property was a one-time thing or maybe it was a story he made up. And Julia's journal entry could be absolutely nothing. If that box comes up empty, it's going to make me look foolish.

"It could turn out to be nothing," I preface my concerns, "but there have been complaints from neighbors about the motorcycles during the last couple of months. If they've been getting into the mine, you'll want to make sure the access is completely blocked, for safety reasons if nothing else."

We pull up to the parking lot to wait for the maintenance crew. The silence of the abandoned mine, the forest wrapped tightly around it makes me wonder what secrets the buildings hold, what stories lie deep under the ground beneath us, and what lies at the bottom of the open reservoirs. Although we've done a quick check of the buildings and a drive through the property, that doesn't mean the place is free of criminal activity. There are too many hiding spots here. I tell Lisa that I'm going to take another drive around the property, and I leave her alone in her vehicle to wait for the maintenance crew.

Suddenly, I'm struck by the color that dominates the area. The buildings themselves are almost gold, with slate gray roofs matching the pavement in the parking lot and the deposits on the roadways. It's literally a small town built of gold and gray within a green wilderness. I drive past the green-blue reservoir and the gray tailings pond when something catches my attention. To the left, a narrow clearing through the forest extends farther than I can see. Railway tracks run through the property leading to the main mineshaft area, so I shouldn't be surprised to find this as well—a landing strip, in the middle of the mine complex. Stopping the car, I walk along the grassy dirt runway, and find something surprising considering the mine has been closed for almost two years. Tire tracks cut through the swath in the forest where a plane has recently landed.

There are several offshoots from the main road, none of which I've explored. Continuing to the southeastern edge of the property, I end up at the back entrance where the motorcycle tracks began. One thing I'm certain of is there's been more traffic through Millcroft than just the maintenance crew. I'm not sure what's been going on here, although I have a pretty good idea. Before calling in the task force, I need solid proof.

As I travel back through the gray landscape, sludge surrounding me, I'm anxious to find out what's in the locked toolbox on the abandoned haul truck. By the time I return to the main parking lot, two men stand alongside the truck, talking to Lisa.

"I thought you'd want us to wait for you," she says. "If you're ready, I can give them the go-ahead to open the box."

After introductions have been made, the bolt cutters come out. Corey tries to maneuver the cutter blades around the shackle without success. "It's no good. The shackle's too thick."

Someone's gone to a lot of trouble to keep something locked up. It confirms my suspicion that something valuable is inside. Tony says he's got the tool for the job. He puts on his safety shield and work gloves, hands over protective equipment to his partner, then removes an angle grinder and a fire extinguisher from the van. "This should do it."

I'm wondering how that's going to work considering there's no electricity. But Tony knows his stuff. He plugs one end of a long extension cord into the grinder and the other into an inverter box inside the van. Once he and Corey climb onto the haul truck's platform, Tony tells Corey to be ready with the fire extinguisher, just in case. Not being an expert in power tools, I get a bit concerned when he mentions the fire extinguisher. Powering up the grinder, he sets to work on the padlock. The noise slices through the silence and pierces my ears. Sparks fly in all directions.

It takes a while—it seems longer than it really is. When the noise and the sparks finally cease, Tony triumphantly holds up the lock. I join them on the platform, and pull open the lid of the storage container, fully expecting to find something that shouldn't be there.

It all adds up—the bike tracks, the motorcycle gang complaints, increased drug possession charges, Danny selling drugs, the landing strip recently used, Julia's observations. I'm about to make a drug bust.

What I find inside the utility box is not what I expected. A bunch of rags sit on top, covering an assortment of hand tools, such as screwdrivers, wrenches, hammers. No drugs. Nothing illegal. It's a bust, all right.

Lisa shouts up to me, "What did you find?"

I feel foolish. I've wasted her time for nothing.

Chapter Forty

Cheryl

The gate's unlocked, so I'm not exactly breaking in. I know he's here. Even though I suspect he won't be happy to see me, I need to talk to him.

Once I open the gate wide, I drive through to the other side, getting out to close it behind me. I pass a huge parking lot and several buildings; the headframe of the mine shaft serves as the focal point. Bleak and gray is my impression, apart from the yellow-gold siding on the buildings. The road continues between the structures and a couple of small ponds, with a large reservoir ahead. I spot Scott's cop car and park behind it.

No sooner am I out of my Toyota strolling up to the dark Explorer when I notice the thirty-ish blond woman leaning against the front of it. For some reason, a pang of jealousy shoots through me. Scott didn't want *me* here, but he's brought some other woman. I can't leave him alone for a minute. He's two-timing me. I thought we were in this investigation together, him and me. Apparently not. Who *is* she, anyway?

The woman stares at me, obviously wondering who I am and why I'm here. I introduce myself and tell her I'm with Detective Evans, hoping she knows him in a formal capacity, not as Scott.

"He's on the truck," she indicates the road ahead with a sweep of her hand. "Looking around."

My attention turns to the monster truck. Brent would love this! Two men are packing up their tools and getting into a maintenance van as I approach and greet them.

I climb the steep steps of the huge truck when Scott hollers from above. "Stay down there!"

I keep climbing. If he can be up there, I don't see any reason why I can't join him.

"What's going on?" I ask when I reach the top.

"Nothing, that's what's going on," he responds, irritation etched into his face. "Why are you here?"

"I wanted to tell you something."

"It couldn't wait?"

"I guess it could have waited." I'm disappointed in his reaction to my unexpected appearance. "But I thought you'd want to know."

"Know what?"

"I was reading more of Julia's journal. She wrote something that I thought was strange."

"What was that?" He seems a little more interested in what I have to say now.

I explain she was bothered by noise in the middle of the night several times. "It sounded like the roaring of an engine just above her rooftop. One night, she went out on the front lawn to look at the sky. She saw lights heading in the direction of the highway. Then they disappeared from the sky. I think they could have been planes landing on the Millcroft property."

Scott's eyes are on me. "What else did she write?"

"She decided to check it out the next time she heard the planes. Julia drove out to the back entrance of the mine one night. She didn't see anyone, but she was sure the plane was landing somewhere inside the gates. When she told Danny, he said it was probably some of the bigwigs who own the place, checking out the property."

The more I talk, the more I have his attention. I wish I had something else useful to say, but that's it. "So, what are you doing up here?" I turn the conversation around, to make him forget I'm not supposed to be here. "Thinking of trading in your Camaro for a real man's machine?"

That gets a bit of a smile out of him. Finally.

"I thought I found something, but it was nothing." Scott points to a large utility box close to the cab of the truck. "It was locked up tight. Turns out there's nothing worth locking up in there."

Curious, I open the lid and look inside to find a bunch of dirty rags and some tools. I suppose that makes sense. What else would you expect to find? "It's a big box. For a few tools. It looks bigger from the outside than on the inside. What were you looking for?" I dig around the container and touch the bottom, although Scott tells me he's already checked the contents.

"Drugs."

"Oh." I should have figured that out. We step away from the toolbox and stare at it for a few seconds. He tilts his head, looking perplexed.

"You're right." Scott begins removing all the contents of the box. The dirty rags and rusty tools pile up on the floor beside him. "It *is* a big box."

Once the container is empty, he grabs a flathead screwdriver and digs at one of the inside edges. "There's a false bottom," he says excitedly. Prying out the flat metal, he sets it aside. Below, rows of white bricks wedge against each other. He's found the drugs he was looking for. Oddly, though, he's also found some stray coffee beans.

Scott grabs me in a hug and kisses me smack on the mouth. "I'm glad you decided to drop by, partner," he says when he breaks away.

So am I.

Chapter Forty-One

Scott

That evening, just after 11 pm., we stake out Millcroft mine. Two unmarked cars sit stationed outside the back gate on a neighboring driveway, hidden by trees. Officer Murphy and his partner wait in one vehicle; Officer Parker is with a rookie in the other. I've instructed them to listen for vehicles coming down the dead-end road, motorcycles in particular. The gate's closed and, at first glance, appears to be locked, but the padlock is unsecured to allow the officers quick entry.

Two more vehicles with four officers from Northeastern headquarters wait inside the complex at the end of the landing strip, hidden next to the forest. The main gates are locked up tight. One of my trusted colleagues, Detective Tremblay, and I are armed and ready underneath the large haul truck that holds the drugs. We're in contact with the other officers through our radios.

It's going to be a long night with no guarantee of success. That's the way it usually goes with stakeouts. It's not glamorous work, nor is it exciting. Employing this much of the police force for one stakeout might be a bit excessive, but I need to ensure the criminals don't have the chance to take off if they smell something fishy. Having enough officers on scene to ensure we're not outgunned is critical to the success of this operation.

Detective Tremblay has a wife and kids at home. I don't want to be the one responsible for setting him up to get shot. "Let's hope they show up tonight." He voices my own thoughts. "I don't want to spend too many nights underneath this monster truck."

Without external lighting, it's almost pitch black in the complex. The air is still and quiet. If anyone approaches the haul truck, they'll be heard. Just the same, we keep our conversation to a minimum and speak in hushed tones.

"Maybe we'll get lucky." Although I doubt it. "And they'll be in custody by morning."

Several hours pass with no sign of anyone attempting to gain entry. "This has to be one of the most boring stakeouts I've been on," Mark Tremblay remarks. We each have a thermos of coffee to keep us awake. Apart from that, we've got each other to pass the time.

Six hours later, when it's apparent there's going to be no action, we leave our position and are picked up by one of the cars from the airstrip. The night's a total bust.

Chapter Forty-Two

Cheryl

July 17

The knowledge that Danny was selling drugs and Julia's journal entries about the mine indicate the drugs Scott found might have something to do with her disappearance. According to Julia, Danny told her to stay out of whatever was going on at the mine. What if she didn't? What if Julia was as nosy as me? Did she put herself in danger? Was Danny responsible for whatever happened to her?

My other train of thought involves the old boyfriend. What if Julia was still seeing him, against her parents' wishes? The journal entries indicate she was in love with him. There's a reference to the fact that she may have seen him recently. Did she leave behind her family and friends to start a new life with this guy?

Or did she take off with Danny to begin anew? The drug money he made would have given him the opportunity to leave everything behind and offer her a fresh start. Maybe he suggested that, and she went for it. She could have been hiding in the abandoned house across the street the night she went missing.

As I'm mulling over the possibilities, Scott calls. "Nothing happened last night. We're going to try again tonight. Did you find anything else in the journals?"

"She mentions this guy from high school a couple more times. It sounds like she was seeing him for more than just a while. I think they were secretly dating from when she started Grade 9 until the end of Grade 11, but not in Grade 12. There's no more mention of him after that time. She wrote that he was older, and her parents wouldn't approve. But I still wonder if the guy she wrote about seeing again recently is the same guy. And Danny said she thought she was being watched and followed. What if it was him, the guy from high school?"

"What does that have to do with the mine and the drugs?"

"I don't know. Maybe nothing. But what if she found out about Danny dealing drugs and broke up with him? Then, this other guy came back into her life, and Danny found out. Maybe he got jealous and hurt her."

Too many possible scenarios explain Julia's disappearance, and we aren't much closer to finding out the truth than we were two weeks ago.

"Maybe this missing person case is going to remain a mystery," I admit. "Maybe there's no conclusion to the story." No one's found me. Maybe no one will find Julia. That could be the way she wants it.

Chapter Forty-Three

Scott

The second night of the stakeout, everyone's in place again. Humidity presses in through the darkness, my T-shirt sticking to my back like a wet rag. Quiet permeates the ghost town, and time stands as still as the buildings and machinery that hover in the black night.

Mark Tremblay doesn't have anything new to say, and I'm too absorbed in my own thoughts to start up a conversation. Those thoughts include the drug ring, Julia and Danny's disappearance, and Cheryl. If there's no resolution to Julia's disappearance, it's going to leave behind more than an unsolved mystery and a cold case. A family will be left shattered, never knowing what happened to their daughter, granddaughter, niece, cousin. Friends will always wonder whether she's alive or dead. There's nothing worse than not knowing. I've been involved in cases involving homicide as well as missing persons. Although dealing with the murder of a loved one is unbearable, at least the families have some closure when the killer is locked up, not free to inflict pain on others. There's a funeral and a grieving process.

In cases where the killer isn't found, it's tougher for those left behind to continue with their own lives. But when someone simply disappears, never to be heard from again, it's more than tragic. The unknown is what's most frightening. The possibilities of what might have happened to a missing loved one are too horrific to live with. I've seen more than my share of despair and despondency in my years on the force. Hollow eyes of parents, spouses, and children who've had their lives ripped apart when they lost someone they treasured. It's made me question whether I want to start a family of my own and risk the possibility of losing them someday. It's so much easier to live alone. There's no heartache in that. But, meeting up with *her* has made me consider there may be more to life than a series of casual encounters.

While I'm lost in my thoughts, Mark sits quietly, probably thinking of his own family. We both nearly jump out of our skin when a voice comes over the radio.

"The show's starting; they're on their way. Motorcycles at the back exit," Officer Murphy reports from his post outside the gate. "Two guys on two bikes, plus one left behind, probably as a lookout."

Once I confirm receipt of the message, Mark and I crouch behind the huge tires, our guns drawn. The roar of motorcycles in the distance, coming our way, increases as the seconds pass. Not knowing whether the bikers are armed or not, or whether they're expecting more men to join them, we sit and wait.

The thunder of bike engines stops, and silence follows, although the bikers aren't close to the haul truck yet. I'm sure both of us have the same thought— we've been made. The bikers must have spotted one of the unmarked police vehicles parked on the property.

"Shit!" I manage to keep my voice to a whisper. The whole operation is about to fall apart if the bikers suspect cops are on the property. Having no other option, we wait it out. Either the bikers will leave the drugs behind and exit the property the way they came or through some unknown exit, or they'll approach quietly on foot, under cover of darkness. Either way, we need to be ready.

Carefully peering around the huge truck tire, I check out the darkness in the direction where I last heard the motorbikes, watching and listening for signs of life. Off in the distance, a light cuts through the pitch black. Nudging Mark, I whisper, "Someone's down the road. Let's just hang tight for now."

We don't radio the other officers because we might be heard by the bikers. Sound travels well at night, especially in a deserted mine. If we come out from under cover and head toward the light, we could be heard or seen, making us sitting ducks. There's no way to outrun the motorcyclists. Our best course of action is to wait. Once the bikers restart their engines, I'll radio the officers in the landing strip to pursue the bikes off the property to the back entrance gate, where the other unmarked cars have the road blocked. That is, assuming they have no alternate exit. We may not catch them with drugs in their possession, but we could bring them in for trespassing and questioning.

We don't need to wait long. The bikes roar to life and head down the road. To my surprise, they don't head toward the exit. They zoom directly toward the two of us. We crouch lower to keep ourselves concealed.

Once again, the bikers cut the engines before they reach the haul truck.

What the hell are they doing? What's up there, on the road, worth stopping for? The drugs are here.

I watch from my post as a light shines through the darkness, not far down the road from our hiding spot. Several minutes later, the engines come to life again. Then it occurs to me—there are other pieces of mining equipment sitting along the road.

There must be drugs hidden elsewhere. This is a bigger operation than I realized.

"This is it; they're heading our way," I tell Mark. He notifies the waiting officers that it's about to go down. Our Glocks are ready as the motorcyclists close in on the haul truck. Shutting off the engines and dismounting their bikes, they scan the area with flashlights. Hopefully, we're well-hidden underneath the truck, hugging the tires. The steps clank as one of the bikers climbs the steps of the monster vehicle.

Then, several things happen almost simultaneously.

The guy on the platform above shouts, "What the fuck?" He's discovered the padlock has been cut and the toolbox opened.

"What's going on?" The other biker shoots up the steps to join his buddy.

"Freeze! Police!" I bellow as I emerge from my hiding spot and stand alongside the steps, gun pointed upward.

Mark swings around to the outside of the tire and aims a bright flashlight onto the truck's platform, commanding, "Hands in the air! Now!" With his right hand, he's ready to fire off a warning shot.

The two unmarked cars from the airstrip race toward the haul truck.

"The cops are here! Get out of there!" The motorcyclists' lookout shouts into a walkie-talkie as his bike roars down the road away from the mine.

The crunch of stones and bones breaking cuts through the night as one of the bikers jumps off the other side of the haul truck onto the crushed gravel roadway. The other biker freezes with his arms in the air when he hears his friend's screams.

Chapter Forty-Four

Aaron Parker

A t the back exit, two police vehicles pull out of the driveway, ready to block the road leading from the back gate. The third motorcyclist who had been staked out at the exit zips around them as they maneuver their cars into position. Upon receiving confirmation that the bikers at the haul truck have been handcuffed and escorted to the back of a police car, Officer Parker makes a split-second decision.

"Go join the other officers," he says to the young rookie who's riding with him. "Let Detective Evans know I'm in pursuit of the third biker."

Once his partner exits the vehicle, Officer Parker spins the car around and goes after the runaway biker. He waits until the bike is out of sight so as not to alert the biker that he's coming after him. To keep tabs on the motorcycle, he lowers his window so he can hear the bike's engine up ahead.

Once the motorcycle reaches the stop sign at the end of the back road, there are three directions the rider could take. A left turn leads to Lake Kipling, a right turn connects to the highway that leads south to Northern Bay, and the road ahead ends up at West Kipling. There's little to no traffic on the Trans-Canada highway. When Aaron reaches the intersection, he looks in all directions and listens carefully. The motorcycle's roar slices through the night air.

He's gone right, probably going to head down south. If I get this right, it might be just the break I need to get closer to that promotion.

166

As Aaron is about to make the left-hand turn onto Highway 11, which leads south to Northern Bay, he receives a radio message from Detective Evans requesting his location. He's instructed to proceed with caution, no sirens or lights. "Backup is on its way."

Aaron is already twenty minutes away from Millcroft. Northern Bay is two hours down the highway. Aaron hits the gas on the open highway and keeps his eyes open for tail lights.

Ten minutes later, he lucks out. Red lights are visible ahead on the straight stretch of road. The biker must have decided he was far enough away from the mine and no longer in danger of being pursued. Careful to maintain his distance, Aaron keeps his eyes and ears open. He's surprised when, fifteen minutes later, the lights seem to vanish. Speeding up, he still sees no sign of them.

Fuck! Where the hell did he go?

Having just passed the sign for Eagleheart a few minutes ago, with a turnoff to the left leading into town and a dirt road to the right, Officer Parker pulls over to the side of the road and listens. Hearing nothing, he looks out the window in both directions and decides to turn around. When he comes to the intersection in Eagleheart, he cruises through town. Three streets run north to south and six east to west. The village backs onto railway tracks. The only exit out of Eagleheart is back onto the highway. Everything seems quiet in town. Making his way back to the main road, Aaron swears as he's about to radio Detective Evans to tell him he's lost the suspect.

Then he figures he might as well have a look down the dirt road on the other side of the highway.

He doesn't need to travel far down the road before he spots it. On the left-hand side is an old white two-story farmhouse set back from the road. Parked to the side are a half dozen motorcycles. He drives past the house and pulls over on the gravel, turning off the engine and the lights. Once he calls in his location and details to the detective, he sits and waits.

* * *

Scott

I secure a search warrant immediately due to the urgency of the situation. About fifteen minutes after Officer Parker calls in his location, a backup car joins him. Together, they continue surveillance of the farmhouse until I can get there with the warrant and more backup.

Six officers cover the back and side exits of the farmhouse as Officer Parker accompanies Detective Tremblay and me to the front door. "Police!" We pound on the door, guns drawn.

All six sleepy occupants are apprehended without incident. A search of the premises results in the seizure of 46 grams of cocaine, 104 grams of marijuana, 52 grams of methamphetamines, five 9mm handguns, and $63,000 in cash, which I assume to be procured from drug trafficking.

By the time the sun comes up, eight bikers are in custody at Lake Kipling station for possession and trafficking of illegal substances, among other charges.

"Great job, Aaron." I commend Officer Parker for his role in the discovery of the bikers' hideout. Thanks to excellent teamwork, the stakeout proved to be a total success.

Chapter Forty-Five

Scott

July 18

That was a helluva good night's work, if I do say so myself. But it took two nights without sleep. What I need now is a good day's nap. But I won't get it. Too damned much paperwork. I need to crash for a couple of hours before I can get my head around it, though. I'm beat and not up for the trip home. I could get a motel room, but that would hardly be worthwhile. It's eight in the morning, and I just need to lie down and close my eyes for a while.

For some insane reason, an image of Cheryl's lilac and gray guest room pops into my mind. Before I can think through the implications of what I'm about to do, I pick up the phone and dial her home number. "Hey, it's me."

She recognizes my voice right away despite my fatigue and asks how last night's stakeout went.

"I've got quite a story for you. But not now. I'm about to keel over and fall asleep on the floor." Hoping she'll extend an invitation, I politely wait for her response.

"So, I guess I'll talk to you later, then?"

Not the response I wanted. Looks like a more direct course of action is required. "Any chance I could pop over to your place and rest for a couple of hours?"

The silence on the other end of the line tells me this was a bad idea. I may have ruined our relationship with that question. I quickly try to take it back. "Sorry, I'm really tired. What I meant was, is there any chance you could pop over to the station after I get a couple of hours rest on the pull-out cot in my office?"

"Our guest room is available if you need some peace and quiet for a while. Jim's still sleeping, but I could pick you up in half an hour, if you want," she kindly offers, taking pity on me for making a fool of myself.

It suddenly occurs to me it's Saturday morning and she was probably sleeping in, but regardless, I don't hesitate to take her up on the offer. At eight-thirty, she walks into my office and finds me with my head on my desk.

"You look like you haven't slept for days," she comments, her face makeup-free for the first time since I've met her. Still beautiful, though. "Let's get you home to bed." God, she's an angel.

Any other time, I would have jumped at her invitation to go to bed, but right now, I can barely get myself upright. "Sounds good," I mumble.

Her Toyota is parked out back in the visitor's area. Climbing into the passenger seat, I'm tempted to close my eyes and doze off right then and there.

"I take it you had a rough night?" she asks as she gets behind the wheel. "Think you can stay awake for another five minutes? I don't think I can carry you out of the car up to the guest bedroom."

* * *

The next thing I know is it's after six o'clock in the evening. I only know this because the digital clock radio on the nightstand beside the bed reads 6:12 p.m. I'm fully clothed underneath the lilac and gray duvet in a room I don't recognize. Slowly, it all comes back to me, and I sit bolt-upright. I've just slept through the entire day. A note on the nightstand next to the clock reads: **Gone for groceries. Jim's working in the back yard if you need anything before I'm back.**

I'm assuming Cheryl's back from the grocery store by now. I need to get out of here before her husband decides to kick me out. After straightening the duvet over the bed and fluffing up the pillows, trying to make it look unslept in, I tiptoe through the door into the hallway and bump into Jim.

"Cheryl says you may as well stay for dinner," he says curtly. "Unless you've got other things to do." Jim looks me up and down, probably trying to size me up and hoping I'll say no.

Despite his cold stare, I accept the invitation, "No, nothing else. Dinner sounds great."

He tells me Cheryl's in the kitchen, getting burgers ready for the barbecue. He heads into his own bath for a shower while I use the main bathroom to slap cold water on my face and rinse out my mouth.

When I join Cheryl in the kitchen, she comments that I'm looking a lot better.

"Listen, I'm really sorry about this." I apologize, embarrassed at having imposed myself on her family.

"About what?"

"Taking advantage of your hospitality. I shouldn't be intruding on your personal life."

"Don't be silly. You're not an intrusion. Friends look out for each other."

"Friends? Is that what we are?"

"We work together. We see each other a fair bit. I'd like to think we're friends." Cheryl grabs some romaine out of the refrigerator. "Even though we haven't known each other that long."

"I'm glad to hear that." I don't mention that my feelings for her cross the friendship line. "Thanks for letting me crash in your guest room all day. I guess I was a lot more tired than I realized."

When I ask if there's anything I can do to help with dinner, she tells me to have a seat out on the deck. Brent's outside entertaining Jamie in the sandbox with construction vehicles. The three of us engage in a conversation about diggers and dump trucks, with me telling them about the gigantic mine equipment.

Jim comes out to throw burgers on the barbecue and watches me play with his kids. I'm thinking maybe the cozy little family scene might not be so bad, after all. With the right woman, one that isn't already married, I just might go for it.

* * *

July 19

This morning, I'm back in my own bed in Timber Lake. I managed to drive home last night after a nice dinner with Cheryl and her family. Today's agenda is all about tying up the drug case, crossing the t's, and dotting the i's. I need to get the paperwork done after wasting yesterday sleeping like a baby in Cheryl's bed.

The shower spray feels good on my face, and I stay in it longer than I should. After shaving and brushing my teeth, I change into fresh clothes, grab a cup of coffee, then head out the door of my apartment.

It's less than a ten-minute drive to my office at Northeastern headquarters, back to my own personal space, not just a room assigned to me at another location. It's comfortable to be back home, but I'm beginning to become attached to Lake Kipling for more than one reason. The officers are good to work with, but it's a certain nosy reporter who makes life there more interesting.

After filing my reports, I give my other files a quick go-over once again. These cases have been put on the side burner. Now that I'm reasonably assured the evidence points to Julia running off with Danny, I can focus my attention on these other issues.

That suspicious transactions case is still active. The amount of money coming and going through Northern Lights Raceway has dramatically increased in the last year. I haven't made any progress in this case, partly because I've been occupied with Julia and now the drug takedown and mostly because there are no leads to follow.

Northern Lights Raceway is owned by the Northern Entertainment

Group. I've already done a check of them. It's a subsidiary of Hamilcorp, a Hamilton-based corporation with diversified interests. Run by CFO, Andrej Simcic, Hamilcorp oversees its various businesses at arm's length. I imagine there are a lot of layers to go through to get to the person who's actually in charge. My concern, though, is what's happening locally in the north.

A few weeks ago, Northeastern police were contacted by a major Canadian bank to check into the operations at Northern Lights Raceway concerning several large deposits and unexplained withdrawals in the last few months. The general manager of Northern Lights, Lou Jagas, declined an invitation to speak with me when I initially called. His receptionist said he was busy with the racing season in full swing and the lake overrun with tourists this time of year.

It could be that business is booming, and that's the reason for all the extra money flowing through the bank, but I'm sure there's more going on than meets the eye. At some point soon, I'm going to have to pay a surprise visit to the raceway and have a look around.

Right now, though, I'm more concerned with tying up the motorcycle and drug case. With the eight people we have in custody, along with the drugs, money, and arms, we've broken the surface of a major drug operation involving that well-known biker gang. Now, we need to find out who else is involved. There are bigger players here than a small houseful of bikers.

My phone rings as I'm considering my next course of action. It's Officer Murphy, letting me know what's happening with said bikers. "Bail's been denied. Looks like we've got a possible talker in the group. Young guy, seventeen, acted as a lookout at the mine. Says he might be willing to tell what he knows in exchange for complete immunity."

"I'll be there in a couple of hours," I say, already packing away the files on my desk.

* * *

As soon as I arrive at Lake Kipling station, I ask for the kid to be sent to the interrogation room. And he *is* just a kid. Black hair, a bit too long, falling across his eyes, baby smooth face. He looks like he's trying to act cool, sitting at the table, his fingers drumming out the rhythm to some rock song. The tough act disappears when I inform him that trafficking large quantities of cocaine can result in a life sentence.

"I didn't do anything," he claims.

I remind him that he was apprehended in a houseful of drugs, guns, and a large sum of cash, along with the fact that he's already confessed to being a lookout at the mine.

"I want complete immunity," he responds, to which I inform him I can't make promises. This isn't like TV or the movies, but things will go better for him if he cooperates.

"I want a lawyer." Then he shuts up completely.

* * *

A couple of hours later, he's back in the interrogation room with a Free Legal Aid lawyer. "My client wishes to disclose what he knows about the drugs at the mine. He was not involved in any form of trafficking. Keep in mind he's legally not an adult."

Robbie Simard tells me he recently moved into the farmhouse when he ran away from home in Northern Bay. His cousin, Tyler Johanson, told him he could stay with him for a while. Turns out his cousin shares a house with some members of the biker gang he belongs to.

"I knew they had drugs at the house. They gave them to other bikers and drug dealers and got money from them," Robbie explains, his voice shaky.

"What about the drugs at the mine? Where did they come from?"

"I don't know." He shrugs.

"Did you know there were drugs on the mine property?"

"Yeah."

I lean across the table and ask him to please elaborate.

He says he overheard some of the bikers talk about picking up drugs from the mine, but he doesn't know how the drugs got there. "This was my first time going with them. They said I could tag along and be their lookout in case the cops showed up."

I know there's more to this story. The quantity of drugs we seized indicates this gang is part of a larger operation. "Where did they take the drugs after they took them out of the mine?"

He squirms around in his seat. "Some went to the farmhouse. But most of it went somewhere else."

"Where else?"

"I don't know. I saw some bikers load up their bikes and head down the highway, toward Northern Bay."

The information I've received from Robbie doesn't get me to the source of the drugs, but it gives me a lead. Robbie will likely end up spending some time in juvie hall for his association with the biker gang, and hopefully learn a life lesson.

When I finish with Robbie, Officer Murphy hands me a folder. "Here are those phone records from the farmhouse that you requested."

There's a long list of incoming and outgoing calls for the past month. I skim through to see if anything stands out and find one number appears more than others. When I check out the name associated with the number, it rings a bell. The number is registered to Lou Jagas, manager of Northern Lights Raceway.

Suddenly, everything becomes crystal clear.

* * *

Northern Lights Raceway, a major employer in Northeastern Ontario, has been under new ownership this past year. A large entertainment complex situated halfway between Lake Kipling in the north and Northern Bay to the south, it sits on the northeastern shore of Lake Temagami, just off the Trans-Canada highway.

I've been here many times over the last few years for music concerts, weddings, and work conferences. I'm not really into the thoroughbred racing and bingo that Northern Lights hosts, and I can't really afford the luxury hotel rooms, rustic cabins, or fancy restaurants, but I have brought women here on more than a few occasions, hoping to impress them. Tonight, though, I'm here to lead a takedown of the people who manage this fine establishment. I don't expect I'll be welcomed back to enjoy the amenities any time soon.

With a search warrant in place, we storm into the locked office at Northern Lights Raceway. Lou sits behind his solid oak desk, going over the proceeds from the day. By the time his security gets wind of our presence, the complex is surrounded by unmarked police cars, and every entrance is covered as provincial police officers from Northeastern, aided by the Lake Kipling and Northern Bay detachments, storm the buildings in a coordinated takedown.

On this particular evening, at about 10:15, patrons are still enjoying themselves in The Northern Lounge, which provides an intimate setting for musical entertainment and comedy routines and is well known in the north for its selection of wines and signature cocktails, alongside a world-class dining experience. It's The Coffee Bar, however, which overlooks the race track and is famous in its own right for specialty blends and fresh baked goods that's the focus of our search. The coffee beans that we found mixed in with the drugs seized from the toolkit in the mining equipment have convinced me that the coffee shop is connected to drug dealing.

As a team of drug enforcement officers sweeps through the now-closed coffee shop, Lou Jagas is handcuffed, led through the hotel lobby, and deposited into a waiting police car. He's apprised of his rights and opts to remain silent. Nine million dollars in cash is found in the office safe, which was left open while Lou was counting. I have my doubts about the entertainment business being that lucrative. I order the money to be seized and taken into evidence. Then I head to the coffee shop to see what other valuables might be hidden on these premises.

Several officers go about their methodical search. Rectangular wooden tables with leather benches are set along the wall of floor-to-ceiling glass, overlooking the racetrack on the other side. Brown paper bags filled with coffee beans, as well as bags of ground coffee, sit behind glass doors under the sales counter. Each row is labeled with the name of the blend, as is each bag. Behind the wooden-topped glass counter, wooden shelves hold mugs with the Northern Raceway logo. Underneath these shelves hang clear canisters, which dispense a variety of specially prepared coffee blends. The top of the counter holds a variety of coffee machines and various dispensers for flavored syrups, milks, and creams. There's nothing here other than what you would expect to find in an upscale coffee joint.

But appearances can be deceiving.

One of the narcotics officers seems extremely interested in what's inside the brown paper bags in the locked drawer underneath the glass counter. Upon examination, she points out these bags are labeled differently from the ones behind the glass. What differentiates them is the letter added on after the 'best before' date—M, C, or W. The officer opens some of the bags and finds ground coffee inside.

Digging deeper into one of the bags with a C affixed to the end of the date, she discovers a small, sealed plastic bag containing white powder. As the bagged coffee from the drawer is taken into evidence, my presence is requested in the kitchen. Several bricks of drugs, like the ones seized at the mine, have been found in a locked cupboard with specially marked Coffee Bar bags. It looks like we've found the packing facility.

When I notify my boss, he secures a warrant authorizing police from surrounding municipalities in Northern Ontario to search the other twelve Coffee Bar locations.

This case is going to put my career on an upward trajectory. Detective Staff Sergeant, hopefully. I know who to thank for that. Without her, I'd still be scratching my head over the case files, wondering where on earth to start. She's the one who pointed me to Millcroft. And she's going to get quite the exclusive story. Hopefully, it'll give Cheryl that big break she's been looking for. It's tough to make a name for yourself in a small town. Maybe this will make her famous.

Chapter Forty-Six

Cheryl

July 20

When it rains, it pours. That may not be the best adage to use at this time, but it's definitely apropos. I'm going to get my story, just not the one I was expecting. Julia's disappearance may not be the headline of the decade, but the drug bust is certainly a big deal. Scott's going to meet with me to provide all the details now that the arrests have been made. It's the most sensational news I've ever covered. The presence of illegal drugs in the north is more widespread than most people think. We assume we're immune to these types of problems, living in small communities. The reality is, we're not. The fallout from drug use is extensive, ranging from mild addiction and financial difficulties to the breakdown of families and even death. It's a scoop for me, but a tragedy for so many.

But, like I said, it's begun to pour. Figuratively, that is. I'm going to have more than one exclusive to cover in the next week. Bad news seems to come in threes. Another idiom to suit the circumstances. I'm more inclined to think it comes in numbers larger than three. The good news is that bad news feeds the newspaper business.

A good downpour would be welcome right now, in the literal sense, that is. Forest fires have broken out northwest of Lake Kipling the last few days.

The weather has been too sunny and too warm for too long. That, coupled with irresponsible campers, has created a potentially disastrous situation. The Ministry of Natural Resources claims everything's under control, but I'm worried it could escalate.

Then, of course, there's the fact that no one has heard from either Julia or Danny. Scott says they're probably fine, but I just don't know. You'd think they would have the courtesy to let her parents know she was alive and well, especially when they must have heard the media reports about their disappearance. And why has no one spotted them? When Jim and I left Hamilton, we notified our parents and made sure they understood our lives were in danger should they let our new identities and location slip, even though we didn't confide in them why we needed to be so secretive. As far as anyone else who knew us was concerned, we simply moved away. And if the police wanted to question us about the shooting…we'd left no clues behind as to our whereabouts. But, of course, the police weren't the main threat to our existence. No, the real danger came from the man from whom I took everything.

Scott wants to meet and I suggest my house would be as good a place as any to get together. It's quiet and comfortable. No one will disturb us. He arrives around eleven o'clock, and I've brewed a pot of coffee to serve with the cinnamon rolls I baked last night.

He greets me amicably and we settle on the back deck with our late morning snack. "So, you've got yourself a story." A big grin spreads across his face.

"And you've made a big drug bust. Must be a real feather in your cap."

"I can't disagree with that. Killed two birds with one stone, as they say. Maybe three. I solved the case involving suspicious transactions at Northern Lights Raceway, put an end to the complaints about motorcycles and planes in the area, and brought down a huge drug operation. All in a good couple of week's work," he boasts. "With your help, of course," he adds, almost as an afterthought.

"Too bad we couldn't figure out what happened to Julia," I remind him as I open my notebook, ready to record the facts. "But I appreciate you coming by to give me the full scoop on the drug story."

"I owe it to you. You were the one who pointed me in the direction of the mine in the first place."

I can't believe he's actually giving me credit.

He proceeds to tell me how the manager at Northern Lights Raceway and his son, a member of the bike gang, were importing illegal substances inside coffee bean sacs from South America. The bags arrived in Millcroft Mine by private plane. Once the crew separated the drugs from the coffee, they resealed the burlap and unloaded the narcotics into the old mining equipment. The coffee beans were then sent onto the raceway.

"And Julia noticed the planes and saw the motorcycle tracks. What if they saw her? What if they thought she was a threat?" I interrupt, trying to get his focus back on Julia.

"There's no evidence of any connection between the bikers and Julia other than her journal. It's unlikely she approached them."

Scott ignores my suggestion that Julia's disappearance may be connected to the drugs and continues with the story. "The idea was to distance the raceway from the original source of the drugs. Once or twice a week, in the middle of the night, drugs were transported by the bikers from the mine to their farmhouse, then to the raceway. In the coffee shop's kitchen, they were packaged for consumer purchase. Not only did they sell in the raceway cafe, they were also distributed to their other twelve locations. They used the coffee packaging, but with a special code marked on the bags. C for coke, M for meth, W for weed."

"So people could have their caffeine fix and their coke fix at the same time," I joke, though it's no laughing matter. Not for victims of addiction.

He flashes a brief smile. "You could say that."

"What about Danny? How was he involved?"

"The bikers kept some of the product for local distribution. It was repackaged at the farmhouse, then distributed to dealers who sold the drugs for them. The bikers were like wholesalers. Danny was one of their dealers," Scott explains. "They provided drugs for their network of biker members and drug dealers in the northeastern area. Stan made sure the profits returned to the Northern Lights coffers, and everyone was paid for their services."

"So the whole drug operation was orchestrated by Lou and Stan Jagas?"

"And distributed by the bikers and their dealers, as well as managers at the coffee shops."

I'm curious to know how the general manager of a raceway comes up with enough money to finance a drug ring of this size. And where does he get the connections? Through his son's biker group?

"That's the whole story, then?" I suspect it's not.

"There could be more to it."

"Such as?"

"I don't think it's a coincidence that the raceway is owned by a company in Northern Bay that, in turn, is owned by a corporation based in Hamilton. Said corporation allegedly has ties to the Mafia, although it hasn't been proven. And the biker gang is also based in Hamilton, coincidently. But it'll be up to the Hamilton area provincial police to investigate the Mafia family's potential involvement in this drug organization."

The mention of Hamilton and the Mafia brings out an anxiety attack, and my world fades. Scott asks if I'm okay and kneels in front of me, taking my hands in his. "You look white as a ghost. Are you sick?"

I manage to shake my head. "No, no, I'm okay. Maybe I should lie down for a while." The palpitations in my chest and the throbbing in my head overwhelm me, and I'm about to pass out. Scott helps me into the house and lays me down on the family room sofa.

"You're hyperventilating." He sounds worried. "Take a deep breath in, let it out slowly. In…and then out." He's got one hand on my forehead, and the other holds my left hand, his thumb gently rubbing my palm.

I need to pull myself together. The Mafia he's talking about can't be the same Mafia I got myself involved with. It's not possible. Surely there must be more than one Mafia group in a city that size.

"I'm okay," I try to convince both of us. "I must have gotten too much sun." After a few minutes, I attempt to sit up. The panic attacks occur every so often, as do the bouts of insomnia. What keeps me on an even keel most of the time is my family. Jim and the kids are my saving grace.

"You should probably go now," I say, needing some breathing space. "I'll be fine. I just need some rest."

"Are you sure?"

"Can you see yourself out?" I don't trust my legs to take me as far as the door. "I'll call you if I have any questions about the story."

He seems hesitant to leave. After I reassure him that I'm all right, he agrees to go. "Okay, but I'm going to call later to check on you."

Once he's gone, I wonder how this could happen. Does Stefan know where I am? Does he have Mafia members running things here? Is it a coincidence that he's got business dealings at the raceway? Up north where I escaped? Up north, where I thought I was safe from him and his goons?

One of the most important things I've learned in life so far is: Do not take something precious from a Mafia godfather. I hope to God I live to learn more lessons.

Chapter Forty-Seven

Scott

I feel good about what I've accomplished in the last few weeks. A bit of quiet on the work front might not be such a bad thing. Maybe I'll take a few days off and go see my folks up in the Kap, visit old friends, have some fun, then come back to work with a fresh perspective. I've been spending too much time working and too much time obsessing about Cheryl MacGregor, married and unavailable woman of my dreams.

The news comes on the radio as I'm heading back to the station. Several small forest fires are burning northwest of Lake Kipling, but officials are confident they're contained. I'm glad to hear that. With this dry, warm weather and the amount of campers and cottagers in the area for summer, there's always a danger of wildfires. Currently, there are flames southeast of Timber Lake as well. If things were to get out of control, they might shut down the highway that runs between the two towns.

Officer Murphy greets me as I come through the doors of Lake Kipling station. His expression tells me I won't be taking a vacation any time soon.

"We've got another one," he says, shaking his head. "A baby this time. Missing from his cradle."

The third missing person in two weeks. My hopes for promotion go down the drain.

Logan Murphy gives me the details and says a search has been initiated. The mother was the only one home with the three-month-old boy. She fed and changed him, then placed him into his cradle in the nursery with the baby monitor turned on. As it was a nice day, she hung up the baby's laundry in the hot sun, then went out to the covered front porch swing with a book. The back door to the house was unlocked. She also left the baby's window, which faced the back yard, open to let in some fresh air. Neither Officer Murphy nor I think of that as negligence. In small towns, people tend to keep their doors unlocked and their windows open, sometimes even when they're not home.

The young mother, Lacey Stromberg, waits in my office. Her pretty face is red from crying and she's pacing around the small space like a caged wild animal. When I walk in, she glares at me. There's a moment of expectation, maybe hope, when she first sees me. Then, it fades and becomes a look of disbelief. Maybe she expected someone older, with more experience. "I'm Detective Evans. I'm very sorry to hear about what happened."

She probably remembers meeting me before, that's what it is. But I've encountered so many people in this line of work that after a while, all the faces look familiar.

"We've issued alerts for your baby, and officers are out looking for him right now." I attempt to calm and assure her. "I know you've already gone over this with Officer Murphy, but I'm going to need you to explain exactly what happened again." My notepad is open to take down the details by the time she begins to talk, hysterically repeating that her baby's gone.

"What time did you last see him?" I try to get her to focus. It seems to help. She becomes more coherent.

"About eleven o'clock. Then I went in to check on him before lunch."

"Before noon, then?"

"No, it was closer to one o'clock. I dozed off for a little while, I guess. But I had the parent end of the monitor outside with me," she adds, somewhat defensively.

I'm not here to judge. I know of cases where parents have gone out to the barn to do chores while they left the baby sleeping in the house, without a monitor. Parents have other things to do besides watch the baby 24/7.

It's just before two o'clock now. That means the baby went missing at least an hour ago, probably more like two. "What about the baby's father? He wasn't home at the time?"

"His father doesn't live with us. He didn't want anything to do with the baby."

Perfectly understandable. No man wants to be trapped into being a father. Still, there's the issue of responsibility.

"What's your ex-boyfriend's name?" Maybe he changed his mind about wanting the baby. "Is he local?"

"It wasn't him. He wouldn't take Christopher."

She's reluctant to implicate the father. "It's important that we have all the facts if we're going to find Christopher."

"He's not from around here. It was just a weekend fling when I went to visit my friend in residence at Northern University last year. I never saw him again."

An alarm bell goes off in my brain. Something's off with her story. The university wasn't open in the summer, which would fit the timeframe for when she became pregnant. "Could you give me his name?"

"I don't know his name."

How did she contact him to let him know she was pregnant if she didn't have his name? "What about the baby's grandparents? Where are they?"

She tells me they live in town. "Oh, no…I need to call my mom!" she exclaims, as though she's suddenly remembered she neglected to notify her parents.

I wait for her to make the call. "What about other family members? The baby's other grandparents? What about brothers and sisters? Any other boyfriend in the picture?"

She has two younger siblings and no boyfriend. She has no idea who the baby's other grandparents are.

About ten minutes after Lacey phones her mom, a forty-something heavy-set woman bursts into my office, followed by Officer Murphy, who appears apologetic, shrugging his shoulders as if to indicate he couldn't hold her back.

She runs to her daughter and hugs her, then pulls away and asks what happened. Lacey breaks down in tears again as she explains the circumstances of her baby's abduction to her mother. Mrs. Stromberg turns to me, no doubt wondering what I'm doing to help the situation.

I assure her we're doing everything we can. "We have officers doing a door-to-door search in town. There's an alert out for the whole northeastern area. We're preparing posters for the public and a media release for the radio station." Every minute counts when a child is missing. The baby could be two or three hours away by now.

I ask Mrs. Stromberg if she has any idea who might take the baby, and she responds in a similar fashion to her daughter. Lacey has two younger brothers who live at home. The baby's father is unknown to her, and there is no boyfriend in the picture.

"When Lacey told us she was pregnant and planned to raise the baby on her own, we said we would help her out. Our house has only three bedrooms, and Lacey wanted to have space of her own to raise the baby." As a Christmas present, Lacey's parents put a down payment on the small home where she now lives with Christopher. They live several streets away, close enough to help with the baby. Lacey is planning on going back to her dental receptionist job in the fall and has daycare already lined up. "Whoever took Christopher, it's not family or friends," Mrs. Stromberg insists. "We're all supportive of Lacey. She's a good mom."

With both women crying and shaking uncontrollably now, I don't think they're going to be able to offer more insight into what's happened.

Once the Stromberg women leave the station, Officer Murphy has some news for me. "The team's finished going over the house for evidence. They found something while they were doing a sweep of the house."

He holds up a plastic baggie with a couple of joints in it. "Some recreational marijuana. It was in her bedroom, tucked away in a drawer. She probably didn't think to get rid of it when she called 911 to report the baby missing."

"Not a major offense." We can hardly go around arresting every person who smokes a joint now and then. I did it myself when I was younger.

"Then there's this." He pulls out another baggie with a small quantity of white powder. "It was found in the baby's room."

186

I'm guessing it's not baby powder. I can't ignore that. As much as I hate to do this, I tell Officer Murphy to bring Lacey back in for questioning. It's all she needs right now, with her baby gone. She's just another victim of the drug trade.

Remembering I told Cheryl I'd call her, I check if she's okay. Cheryl says she's perfectly fine, but she's going to stay out of the sun for the rest of the day and work on her drug bust article inside. When I tell her what's happening at the station, she lets out a squeal that nearly shatters my eardrum.

"A baby! Oh my...!" She stops and seems to consider something, then continues. "You don't think...?"

"Think what?"

"This has something to do with Julia and Danny?"

"Why would it?"

"Well, it seems clear to me. Think about it. First, Julia goes missing. Then Danny disappears. He buys some baby stuff. Now, a baby's missing. There's obviously a connection here. Anyone can see that. Which one of us is the detective here, anyway?"

"Sometimes I wonder," I joke. But she's got me. I can't argue with her logic. It's bizarre, though. "But, why on earth would they take someone else's baby?"

* * *

Lacey Stromberg is back at the police station again, this time against her will, causing quite a scene. Officer Parker is one of the two accompanying officers. He's trying his best to calm her, but she keeps kicking and screaming as they lead her in.

"I didn't do anything! Why aren't you looking for my baby? I want my baby back!" She glares at Officer Parker. "What happened to him? Where is he?"

"Don't worry. We'll find him. Officers are out questioning the neighbors right now," he says. "Someone may have seen something."

She's brought to the interrogation room. The lawyer her parents called shows up and joins us. Throughout the questioning, Lacey maintains the cocaine found in her house isn't hers, and she has no idea how it got there. "Let me take a drug test," she offers. "I'll prove I'm not on drugs."

The tests are carried out and Lacey is sent home with her parents, who remained quiet throughout most of the ordeal. Lacey more than made up for their silence with her insistence that the drugs were planted, and the police are trying to frame her for doing something to her own baby.

I call the crime unit at Northeastern headquarters. "I need a rush on the fingerprints in the Stromberg case. Notify me as soon as you have something." If it turns out there's no sign of anyone having been in Lacey's house, I'm going to have to consider the possibility that she harmed the baby herself.

There was a missing baby case once before during my time with Northeastern. A few years ago, a newborn was taken from Northern Bay Hospital, out of the cot in the hospital room while the mother was sleeping. The baby was found within twelve hours, in the home of one of the nurses who worked in the obstetrics unit. After questioning the hospital staff, it was discovered that the nurse recently had a stillbirth and suffered from depression. When the police came to her home, the nurse returned the baby without incident, saying she just wanted to know what it felt like to be able to bring her baby home. Because of the extenuating circumstances, the nurse was granted probation and had to attend mandatory counseling.

Considering whether someone in Lacey's neighborhood recently suffered the loss of a baby, I call Judge Brown to procure a warrant to check hospital records. She recognizes the urgency of the situation, and I head to Lake Kipling General Hospital.

The three-story red brick building sits in the center of town. The sign at the entrance announces it's a 74-bed facility serving the residents of Lake Kipling and the surrounding villages and cottages. A 24-hour emergency department provides the community with exemplary health care. The obstetrics unit is on the third floor.

I ride the elevator and follow the signs to the nurse's station. Chief of staff, Dr. Ken Lowrey, has instructed the head nurse to provide me with information about stillbirths, miscarriages, and abortions going back six months.

Linda Solomon is only too happy to assist me. "I'm a mother myself. I couldn't imagine what I'd do if my daughter, Casey, went missing." According to Linda, there were two stillbirths in the last six months and several miscarriages and abortions.

I take note of the addresses of each of the women involved. "Did any of these women stand out as being emotionally unstable? Was there anyone who you remember as having difficulty with the grieving process, maybe denying the baby was gone?"

"It's always difficult when a woman loses her baby, whether it's early in the pregnancy or later. But of course, a full-term baby…, you can imagine how awful that is for the mother. For the father, too." Empathy is evident in Linda's expression.

I dread having to question the poor women who've lost their babies. There are parts of this job I would prefer to let someone else handle. As I leave the hospital parking lot, I consider how to approach these women. How am I going to ask them if they know anything about a missing baby?

Chapter Forty-Eight

Aaron

April Campbell, the occupant of the house to the left of Lacey's small home, is taking laundry down from the line when Aaron Parker rings her doorbell. He peers through her screen door straight down the hall and through the back door as she drops clothing in the basket and runs inside to find a police officer on her front porch. Her initial expression is one of fear—understandable. She probably wonders if something happened to her husband, who works at the Beaverton Sawmill. The young officer assures her everything is fine, that they're just canvassing the neighborhood, looking for information about a missing baby.

He explains that Lacey's baby has been taken from her home by an unknown person. "Did you happen to hear or see anything unusual next door earlier today between eleven and one o'clock? Anyone lurking around you didn't know?"

"Oh, my, how awful for Lacey! That's terrible! In this neighborhood? It's so safe here, except for the motorcycle gang that's been coming through lately. Do you think they have something to do with the baby being taken?" She glances to the right and left, as if the baby might suddenly show up. "I wish I could help, but I was inside with the air conditioning on. I wouldn't have heard anything. And I can't see Lacey's house from my front window." She gestures to the neighboring house. "Who would do such a thing?"

"We're going to do everything we can to find out," Aaron promises. "We want the baby to be safe, where he belongs. If you remember anything that might help, give us a call at the station."

Officer Parker continues to the neighbor on the other side of Lacey's house, then across the road, back and forth down the street, repeating his questions with the residents who are home. Several of the houses are empty, their occupants at work or out shopping, maybe away on vacation. So far, no one has seen anything. No one has heard anything. Satisfied that the neighbors on Lacey's street have no information to assist with the case, he returns to the police car and joins up with his new partner, rookie Jerry Chapman, who has been canvassing the street behind Lacey's. "Anything?"

Jerry shakes his head. "Except some little kid playing outside. Said a man with a hoodie ran through the yard next door. Do you think he might have cut across the back yards to get to Lacey's place and taken the baby through the back door?"

"Did the kid see the man with the baby?" Aaron wonders how credible the kid's observations are. Is he a possible witness?

"No, no baby."

Aaron brings his hand up to his mouth and drags it down over his chin. "Well, that's too bad. Maybe he was just making it up. Kids do things like that to get attention sometimes." Aaron thinks that if no one else has seen anything, it's probable the kid didn't either. The man he saw wasn't carrying a baby. That is, if he actually saw a man with a hoodie at all. "We better keep going through the neighborhood. Every minute we waste is a minute farther the baby could be."

The two officers continue their door-to-door questioning, as do another half dozen officers from Lake Kipling and Northeastern provincial police. If they don't find the baby soon, they likely won't find him at all.

Chapter Forty-Nine

Scott

"Hey, I wondered if you could give me a hand with something. In an unofficial capacity." I hate to ask her to do a job that makes me uncomfortable, but if anyone can get these women to talk, it's her.

Following a moment of silence on the other end of the line, Cheryl says it depends on what I need. "What is it you want from me?"

That's a loaded question.

"You have a way of getting people to open up." I try to convince her through compliments. "Like I said before, you're good at what you do. Think you could question some women who've lost their baby recently? I'm sure they'll be more comfortable talking to you than me."

After I pick up Cheryl at her house, I fill her in on the situation. "It's possible the baby was taken by one of the women who lost her own baby. There was a similar situation a few years ago. Tragic. For both the mothers involved, the one who lost her baby and the one whose baby she took."

"I can't imagine how hard it must be to lose your child."

"The woman who took the baby was a nurse who had a stillbirth. She was suffering from depression after the loss."

"That's terrible. There needs to be a better system in place to help people with mental health issues. I did an article on that a while back. There just isn't enough support in place for people. The health system is so focused on physical illnesses. It's tough to get medical professionals to acknowledge an illness when there aren't blood and lab tests available to make a definitive diagnosis," Cheryl empathizes, shaking her head.

We pull up in front of a two-story gray and white house. A woman in her early thirties answers my knock. From inside the house, we hear children fighting over their toys. "Mine! Mine! Mine!" A toddler hollers from the living room.

The woman apologizes for her children's behavior. When I show my ID and explain that I'm investigating the abduction of an infant, she invites us in. "That's awful! What a terrible thing to happen! But what does it have to do with me?"

The three children in the living room are all very young, and the place is a mess.

Cheryl butters her up. "What a beautiful family and lovely home you have. It's so nice they have each other to play with. My husband and I have two. We'd love to have more, of course."

The toddler throws a stuffed animal at her oldest brother. "No! No teddy! Want car!"

"It's my car!" The boy holds it behind his back, out of reach. His mother tells him he needs to share with his sister, to which he responds by running down the hall, screaming, the toy car protectively clutched to his body. The toddler responds by banging her head on the wall. Meanwhile, the three-year-old brother is drawing a picture on the opposite living room wall with a red crayon.

This is why I've never wanted kids.

"The police are doing a door-to-door check in case anyone has seen the missing baby or noticed anything odd in town this afternoon." Cheryl works on getting her sympathy. "The baby's mother is frantic. I'm sure you understand how terrible it is to have your baby taken away, being a mother yourself."

The woman nods, scooping up the bawling toddler and trying to soothe her. "I don't know what I'd do if someone took my babies. I hope you find him or her. A baby needs her mother." As she kisses the toddler's forehead, the kid gives her a swift kick in the thigh, hollering for all she's worth. The woman calmly sets her down and turns to the other kid. "That's a lovely drawing, sweetie, but Mommy would really like to have the next one on a piece of paper so she could make it into a book."

Like I said, no kids for me.

When we leave the house, Cheryl comments, "She didn't do it."

"How do you know she didn't?"

"She has her hands full. She loves her kids, but she wouldn't steal someone else's to make up for the one she lost. I just don't see it."

Ten minutes later, we arrive at the home of the other mother who gave birth to a stillborn. This time, there's no sound of children.

Once we introduce ourselves, Cheryl apologizes for bothering her. "We're visiting homes in town. There's been an abduction of a child." She explains once again that a baby has been taken from its home, and they're checking as many homes as possible to see if anyone might have information that would help the police bring the baby back home where he belongs.

"I can't help you. I don't know anything."

But Cheryl knows just how to handle her. She places her hand over the woman's hand and sits quietly for a few minutes.

"I'm sure you know how the mother feels. She needs her baby back. The baby needs his mom." Cheryl speaks softly. "If you do hear anything, please call the police station."

"Yes, of course."

Back in the Ford, I ask, "Well? What do you think?"

"I think she needs help."

"But did she take the baby?"

"I don't know. But I don't think so. I sensed her sadness as soon as she opened the door. She'd be happier if she had a baby to look after. But I don't get the feeling she'd try to replace her own baby with someone else's. She wouldn't want to inflict the pain she's feeling on another mother."

I inform Cheryl there are about a half a dozen more women on my list that I want to check out. "The others lost babies, but not near to full-term. We won't get to all of them this evening. Are you free tomorrow?"

Cheryl turns to me and says she can be free if I need her. Not sure if there's an underlying meaning in her words. "But I think you're overlooking the obvious."

"And what's that?"

"Julia went missing. Julia lost a baby. Danny went missing. Danny bought baby supplies. Put two and two together. Julia now has a baby. Are you sure you're a detective?" She narrows her eyes, shakes her head, and laughs.

Chapter Fifty

Cheryl

The town's overrun by police cars all afternoon, searching for Christopher Stromberg or information leading to his whereabouts. I'm worried that it's too late, that he's been taken far from his hometown, or worse yet, that his lifeless body has been disposed of in the forest or a lake.

I imagine everyone is talking about the missing baby—that and the forest fires burning not far from Lake Kipling. The missing persons bulletins about Julia and Danny are still being circulated, but most people probably think they simply ran off together. I know Scott does. The news on the local radio and television stations is centered on these three major stories. But I've got the inside track on all these situations—A.K.A. Detective Scott Evans and my husband Jim, who's a volunteer firefighter. No information has been officially released about the drug bust. That story's going to break open the day after tomorrow. By me. Things are certainly heating up in this small Northern Ontario town where nothing of note ever happens.

I spend all night writing my article about Northern Lights Raceway and the drug bust. I've got a lot of information to work with, much of it firsthand, and I want to be sure it's ready for the front-page headline of the weekly paper. The next day, I'm exhausted, but ready to once again assist Scott with his interviews of local women who've lost a baby. Finding Christopher is more important than getting my name in the headlines.

Chapter Fifty-One

Scott

July 21

No one has come forward with information about Julia and Danny. If Cheryl's theory that they have Christopher is right, they've gone to a lot of trouble to stay hidden. None of the neighbors saw anyone around Lacey's house at the time of the abduction, and the door-to-door canvassing hasn't resulted in any leads so far.

Cheryl meets me at the station just after nine o'clock, ready to talk to the other five women on my list. Five more women who have suffered a loss, five more women who may be desperate to replace the baby they lost.

"You look tired." Maybe not the best way to greet a woman, but I'm concerned about her. She's been doing her own job, caring for her family, and helping me with *my* job. That doesn't leave time for her to look after herself.

"I was up late getting my article written." She suppresses a yawn. "I need to go over it today, so it's ready to hand in later this afternoon. It comes out tomorrow."

"I want to thank you again for your help with the drug bust."

"I'm just excited I could be part of it. My story is going to be a full-page feature, with my personal account of how I was involved in discovering the drugs. I should be thanking *you* for giving me the exclusive on the story."

"I guess we make a good team."

She agrees we do.

Knowing she has a busy afternoon, I want to get these interviews done in the morning and let her get back to her own job. We find two of the women at home. One lives with her parents, and one with her husband. The first young woman is upset when she hears I'm here to see her about the baby she lost.

"Mom and Dad don't know about the abortion." She whispers, even though her parents are at work. She's a teenager who clearly had no interest in having a baby. We stroke her off our list of possible suspects.

Our visit to the second woman's home is a short one as well. She's expecting again after miscarrying five months ago. "The police were already here yesterday. I was hoping he'd be found by now," she says, her concern appearing genuine.

"What now?" Cheryl asks as we get back into my car.

"I'm going to talk to Lacey's parents. I want to find out more about the ex-boyfriend, or one-night stand as she called him."

Cheryl raises her eyebrows. "You still think the father took the baby? She said he didn't want anything to do with him."

"That's what she said. We only have her version of the story. I'd like to hear what the father has to say for himself."

I drop Cheryl off at the station so she can collect her car. "Good luck with your article. And get some rest. I'll call you tomorrow, let you know what I find out from Lacey's mom."

Mrs. Stromberg is home with her teenage sons. All are off for the summer. Mrs. Stromberg plans on returning to her teaching job in the fall, and the high school boys work part-time at McDonald's to earn extra spending money. She invites me in, eager to see if I have any news about Christopher.

"Lacey's just beside herself," she says, wringing her hands. "I told her to come stay with us until they find Christopher, but she insists on staying alone. She wants to be in her own home when he's brought back."

Neither of us mentions the drugs found in her home. If it's her first offense, she may get off with a fine and a slap on the wrist. I hope that's the case. I hate to see people's lives ruined over one stupid mistake. We've all made them. Besides, she claimed the cocaine wasn't hers. Maybe it wasn't. Maybe it belonged to a friend of hers. If, on the other hand, she's an addict, then I want her to get the help she needs to put her life back on track so she can raise her child properly.

Laura Stromberg wonders what she can do to help find her grandson. "What if we offer a reward? My husband and I will do whatever it takes to get Lacey's baby back."

I ask about the baby's father. "In most child abduction cases, it's not a matter of money. Usually, it's one of the parents who feel they should be given more access to the child. Sometimes, they think the other parent isn't doing a proper job. Unfortunately, there are cases where the child becomes a pawn when the relationship sours."

Laura doesn't know who the baby's father is. "To tell the truth, I'm not sure Lacey knows."

I'm not one to judge. I've had my share of one-night stands. "Is there some other man in her life? Or someone from her past? Maybe someone who has a jealous or possessive streak?"

"I can't think of anyone like that. She hasn't dated for a long time, not since she found out she was pregnant. Lacey's been concentrating on raising the baby.

"Is there anyone else you can think of who might want to hurt Lacey or take the baby?"

I leave the Stromberg residence with no leads. As I drive back to the station, I'm hit by a sudden brainwave. What if Danny is the baby's father? Cheryl is convinced there's a connection between the three missing people. I've got to admit, it does make sense, but I couldn't imagine why Danny would steal someone else's baby. But, if it's *his* baby, then it's possible he took him. He came to town last summer—the timeline fits.

Did Julia tell him about her abortion? Did she say she wanted to keep the baby, but her parents wouldn't let her? Is it possible Julia can't have more children? This new train of thought gets me excited that I'm on to something. Something Cheryl hasn't thought of first. Another thought enters my mind even as I head toward Governor's Road and Danny's apartment. What if Danny was supplying Lacey with drugs? Did *he* leave the cocaine in her house?

Danny's superintendent accompanies me to his apartment. "I haven't seen him for over a week," he says, offering to do what he can to help. "Some lady came around a couple of days after he was gone, looking for him."

Cheryl.

I glance around the place; everything is just the way Cheryl described it. If I didn't know better, I would assume Danny was coming back at any time. I contact Judge Brown again, requesting a search warrant ASAP, to cover my ass. Given the fact Danny went missing under strange circumstances much like his girlfriend, that he purchased baby items, and a baby is missing, she agrees to my request. I tell her that I also have information tying him to the drug ring. He was a known dealer, and drugs were found in the missing baby's home. Judge Brown says she'll send the warrant my way immediately.

The super has no problem with me having a look around. Danny's rent is paid for this month, but he says once the month is up and the last month's prepayment is used, he's going to have to get rid of his stuff and rent the place to someone else.

Donning gloves, I start going through drawers and closets. "Does Danny have many visitors? Any parties?"

"No, he's pretty quiet. Keeps to himself, mostly. Except for his girlfriend."

"Any other friends?"

"Not that I know."

The living area and kitchen are one combined room. There's nothing incriminating here, as far as I can see. The entry closet holds a couple of coats, some accessories, and shoes. In the kitchen cupboards, I find about a week's worth of groceries, an odd assortment of dishes, cutlery, pots, and pans. The counter holds the remnants of his last lunch preparation. My search of the bathroom and bedroom reveals nothing other than what one would expect in a man's apartment. His clothes are here, along with a couple of suitcases; some toiletries sit on the bathroom counter. None of Julia's things seem to be here. Unlike Julia, Danny doesn't have family photos or journals. One thing gets my attention—an open box of condoms in the nightstand drawer beside his bed.

Did he and Julia *not* want to get pregnant? Why, then, does he need baby supplies? His credit card was used for over two hundred dollars' worth of baby stuff last week. Because Julia's pregnant or because he took Christopher? There's a discrepancy here. Why the birth control? Why the baby stuff? Why abduct a baby?

And another thing. Where are the drugs? Mike said Danny was selling drugs at the mine. Standing in the small hallway, I glance around the apartment, thinking he must have them well hidden in some secret hiding spot I haven't noticed. There's a small balcony, but it's empty. I do another quick scan of the apartment, opening cupboards and drawers and closets one more time, rummaging around.

New shoes.

A shoe box sits on the floor of the closet underneath his winter boots. I open it and find several baggies packaged in the same manner as the drugs we removed from the motorcyclists' farmhouse.

The super, who stands behind me, seems shocked. "I didn't know anything about that! If I had known, I would have kicked him out. We don't tolerate drugs on the property."

Before leaving with the drugs, I ask whether Danny had provided any references before renting the apartment.

"His employer, that's all. He said he was new to town and didn't know anyone, but he had a job offer."

"That would be MacGregor Realty?"

He confirms that his reference was Jim MacGregor.

After thanking him for his cooperation, I stop at the fast-food joint at the other end of town for lunch. I'm surprised to bump into Sheila Gray at the counter. We exchange greetings, and I ask if she has a few minutes to chat about Julia and Danny. No sooner do we sit down in a booth and unwrap our burgers than Cheryl enters the restaurant and walks up to the counter.

Once I catch her eye, I smile and wave. Her gaze goes from me to Sheila and back to me again. She raises her eyebrows, unsmiling, and turns away without acknowledging me.

"You said you wanted to talk about Julia and Danny." Sheila touches my hand in an attempt to regain my attention.

"I was wondering whether they ever talked about having kids. Did they want a baby?"

"A baby? Why on earth would they want a baby? They weren't even talking about getting married, as far as I know. I don't think Julia would have wanted to have a baby without being married, not after the way her parents reacted to her first pregnancy." Sheila's face pales. "Oh, I shouldn't have said that." She puts her hand over her mouth as if that action could shove the words back in.

"I know about the abortion." I try to quell any concerns that she may have broken Julia's trust. "Was Julia able to have more children after that procedure?"

As far as Sheila is aware, Julia wasn't expected to have any problems with future pregnancies. "I'm sure she wants to wait for the right time, though."

"Do you believe Danny and Julia have run off together?"

"Maybe they did. But I don't understand why they wouldn't tell anyone."

When I ask whether she's thought of any place they might be, she has no idea. Then, after some thought, she adds, "But I guess it makes sense they're together. It can't be a coincidence they're both missing. Maybe they went back to Montreal. They went there for a vacation a couple of months ago. Julia said she loved it there."

After lunch, I head to MacGregor Realty, a few streets down from the restaurant, to talk to Danny's employer. When I enter the main office, I notice Jim's door is closed. An older woman sits behind the receptionist's desk. When she asks how she can help me, I say, "I'm looking for Jim."

"He's having lunch with his wife," she answers, then hesitantly adds, "Maybe you could come back later? I don't think now is a good time."

I'm not one to interrupt a man having lunch with his wife, so I tell her it can wait. "I'll be back in a while. Tell him Scott was here." I figure we're on a first-name basis now that I've dated his wife several times, played trucks with his kids, and had a sleepover at his house.

In the meantime, I need to see Lacey again. It's a short drive to the other end of town. Lacey is at home alone, and it's evident she's been crying. When she sees me, her expression takes on a look that's a cross between hope and despair.

"Did you find him?" She steps aside to let me in.

"No, there's been no news." I hate to disappoint her. "I just wanted to check something with you."

"What?"

"Do you know this man? Is he Christopher's father?" I pull out the photo of Danny that Cheryl gave me. I can tell immediately that she recognizes him.

"No. No, that's not his father. I've never seen that man before."

"Take another look. Are you sure you don't know him?"

After hesitating, she casts her eyes back to the photograph. She bites her lower lip and seems to be considering what to say. "Why? Is he the one who took my baby? Does he have Christopher?"

"Do you know him?"

"No, no, I don't know him. Why would he take Christopher?" She's getting more and more agitated. "You need to get my baby away from him. Please."

I tell her we're doing everything we can, and I will keep her informed of any developments. Walking back to my car, I can't help but wonder what she was holding back.

Why is she lying? Who is she protecting?

Back at the real estate office, Jim's door is still closed. I tell the receptionist I'll wait and pick up one of the real estate magazines from the stack on the table centered in front of four leather chairs arranged in the waiting area.

I'm starting on my second round of flipping through the same magazine, feigning interest, when the door to Jim's office swings open. Cheryl's on her way out, her face flushed. "Oh! What are you doing here?"

"I need to talk to Jim."

I turn from her and focus my attention on Jim as he comes up behind her, putting his arm around her waist.

"Can we have a word in private?" I ask him. "In your office?"

"My wife and I don't keep secrets from each other." He glares at me, then motions to one of the leather seats in front of his desk. "Come in."

Cheryl appears a bit disheveled, and it doesn't take a detective to figure out what exactly was going on behind closed doors. Not that it's any of my business.

"So what's this about?" He gets right to the point as I lower myself into the chair, Cheryl taking the other one.

"I wondered if you could give me more information about Danny. Is there anything in his employment file, references perhaps, or maybe you could tell me about some of his acquaintances?"

"If I had any information, I would have already shared it with you, but I don't know much about his personal life. What specifically are you looking to find?"

"Did he provide phone numbers for you to contact as references?" There must be someone who knows this guy. Super, employer, co-workers, girlfriend, drug clientele… But does he have no family or close friends? Why is no one looking for him?

"He gave me a reference letter from his former employer and his old landlord, along with his real estate certification. This was his first job selling properties. I thought I'd give him a chance to prove himself. Prior to that, he was a mailroom clerk in Toronto." Jim's eyes flit back and forth from me to Cheryl.

"And did he prove himself?"

"I had no complaints with his work. He seemed like a nice guy and got along with the clients. Why are you focusing on Danny suddenly? What about Julia? Have you found out anything more about where she might be?"

"I still think they're likely together. But I'm considering Danny may have been involved in the abduction of Lacey Stromberg's baby. I'm wondering if he's the baby's father." Maybe Jim will be able to tell me whether Danny was ever involved with Lacey.

There's an audible gasp from Cheryl and she joins the conversation. "That would explain everything! The two of them had to go on the run if they were planning on taking the baby. That's why they left separately—they didn't want the police to connect them to the abduction."

She voices exactly what I'm thinking.

Chapter Fifty-Two

Cheryl

It's all coming together. I can see the front-page story now. Julia and Danny ran off together to start a new life with his biological son. Julia wanted a baby for years after having an abortion. Of course, I wouldn't include that in print. It's too personal. Danny was dealing drugs to save up enough money for the three of them to run away together. Not that real estate doesn't pay well, but this isn't the big city. There are only so many properties and so many buyers. He needed extra cash in a hurry, got desperate, and turned to selling drugs as a second job.

"What about Montreal? Do you think they were scouting out a place to live when they went there in May?" I turn to Scott as the pieces come together in my mind.

He agrees it's possible. "I'm going to alert Montreal police that Danny and Julia might have the abducted baby with them. Then I'm going back to interview the women who weren't home this morning when we went to see them. Cover all the bases."

Jim raises his eyebrows. "I thought you were busy with your article. How did you have time to conduct interviews with Detective Evans?"

I should have told Jim I was with Scott this morning. Now it looks like I've kept it from him. "I was only out of the house for an hour or two this morning. I'm going to hand it in later today. Just a bit of fine-tuning yet. I'd better get back to it now."

I don't know why I'm trying to justify my time spent with Scott. It's not like there's anything going on between us. Still, if the tables were turned and Jim was spending time with some other woman pretty much every day, I'd be more than a little suspicious, too. Not to mention extremely jealous. In fact, I wouldn't like it one little bit. I'd put an end to that in a hurry.

Scott gets up to leave when I do. My heel catches the chair leg, and we bump into each other as we extricate ourselves from the chairs. It's an awkward moment. We apologize at the same time, then Scott thanks Jim for his time and walks out the door. I kiss Jim to assure him he has nothing to worry about. He doesn't look convinced, his eyes following Scott as he heads out the main door.

The rest of the afternoon is spent going over my article, making sure it's ready to print, and driving to the office to hand it over to Darren.

I wait in his office as he reads it over. "Perfect!" he exclaims when he's done. "A first-hand report of what happens in a drug operation. I love the details you've been able to add, with your involvement. It reads like a mystery story. People see something suspicious going on at the mine, and your investigation leads to Northern Lights Raceway. The mine, the planes, the motorcycle gang, the drug dealers, The Coffee Shop, the raceway—people are going to love this. I couldn't have done any better myself. I want to see more of this type of story in the paper. A personal account of the events that affect the people in our small town, not just a factual news report. Anybody can recount the facts. But this…this is real writing."

I'm thrilled he loves the way I approached the article. I wasn't sure what he would think. "I'll keep that in mind for future stories, then."

"Just one thing, though," he says, deflating my balloon. "What about the owners of the raceway? I see you haven't mentioned them. This must be a bigger operation than just a manager distributing drugs. Who's behind it all?"

I feel the room fade away, and I grip the sides of the chair. Please don't let this happen now. I can't have a panic attack in front of my boss.

"Cheryl? Are you alright?"

Closing my eyes for a moment, I tell myself it's okay. I'm safe. Stefan can't reach me here. "Yes, I just had a bit of a dizzy spell, that's all."

"You're not pregnant, are you?"

"No, no, I think it's just the excitement of this story. And to tell the truth, I didn't get much sleep last night. Detective Evans said it'll be up to the city police to take the investigation from here."

"What city? Montreal...Toronto...Ottawa...Hamilton?"

Darren's arms reach out to catch me as I slump toward the floor, and everything goes black. A while later, something cools my forehead, and Darren is calling my name.

"Cheryl? Are you okay? Do you want me to take you to the medical clinic?"

"No, I'm okay. I just need to get some rest. I've been running on adrenaline, and I guess it's finally run out."

He seems to accept this and congratulates me once more on a job well done. Darren makes me sit in the air-conditioned office until he's sure I'm okay to drive. When I get back home with the kids in tow, excitedly telling me about their day at camp, I decide to order pizza for supper. I'm way too tired to cook. The drug case is solved. Detective Evans has a firm lead in the missing persons cases. My family needs me to spend more time at home.

Away from Scott Evans.

Chapter Fifty-Three

Scott

July 22

Last evening's interviews with the women who lost their babies don't lead anywhere. I'm almost 100 percent certain the abduction can be connected to Julia and Danny at this point. The Montreal police have been notified of the situation, and there's nothing more to do except wait to see what they uncover. If they're hiding out somewhere else, someone will recognize them from the media reports or the police bulletins. People will sit up and take notice of anything odd when a child is involved.

When I arrive at Northeastern headquarters, a faxed report waits for me. The Forensic Crime Unit has identified the fingerprints from Lacey's nursery as belonging to Lacey, her parents, and her brothers. The family was more than willing to be fingerprinted to assist the police in finding out who was in the nursery other than themselves.

Their cooperation is going to pay off. A set of fingerprints taken from a snow globe on the baby's dresser is not a match to family members. I set out to Lake Kipling to find out more about the snow globe.

Lacey is at home with her mom when I arrive unannounced. It looks like the two of them have been crying, which isn't unusual, but I detect something else in their demeanor. Clearly, they've been arguing or at least heatedly disagreeing about something.

"Sorry to bother you again, Lacey, but if you don't mind, I'd like to have another look at the baby's room."

Laura Stromberg stands in the living room, with her arms crossed, her face stern. Lacey looks like she's almost afraid to see me. Both women are flushed from crying, their eyes puffy.

I'm escorted to the nursery, with Lacey asking if I've found out anything about Christopher. When I tell her I'm working on some leads, but have nothing to report to her right now, she starts sobbing again. "What if you don't find him? What am I going to do? My poor boy, my sweet little boy. Why would someone do this?"

The snow globe sits where it was when the room was initially searched for evidence. Upon examination, I notice it's a souvenir globe made specially for Lake Kipling. It's not something you'd find in just any gift shop. Rather, it's very specific to the town's main claim to fame. In the center of the glass globe, sits a model of Millcroft mine with its headframe as the focal point. It's a night scene, with the moon and stars lighting up the dark sky. The ceramic bottom is engraved with holly and ivy and the words 'Merry Christmas'. With my gloves, I pick it up and turn the globe over. The switch is in the off position. When I turn it on and wind the key, it begins to play soft music. The bottom has a label stuck to it—Millcroft Mine. As I set it back down, white snow falls gently to the sound of Silent Night.

"That's a nice globe. Where did you buy it?" There can't be many of these around. It's unique. Something tourists might buy. Not that there are many tourists who venture up here, especially in winter.

"It was a gift," Lacey answers. "From my real estate agent when I bought the house."

A red flag goes up in my brain. "Which real estate agent? Do you remember the name?"

"Yes, it was MacGregor Realty."

"And it's been in the baby's room all this time? A Christmas souvenir in July?"

"Christopher likes the music. It puts him to sleep." She begins a fresh bout of bawling, no doubt resulting from the confirmation that her baby is gone and I can't find him. I'm not intentionally insensitive, but this job does tend to harden you.

Her mother comes up behind her and puts an arm around her daughter. "You need to tell him," she says quietly.

My eyes sweep from one woman to the other, waiting for some revelation that will break open the case. Lacey remains silent.

"You need to put Christopher first. Once you get him home, we'll deal with the rest of it," Laura says, supporting her daughter emotionally as well as keeping her physically upright.

"It's him," Lacey finally says. "I lied."

Now we're getting somewhere. "What did you lie about?"

"The photo you showed me yesterday? I did recognize him. It's Danny."

I knew it. "Danny is the baby's father?"

"What? No! He's the guy who sold me the weed." She vehemently denies Danny is the father. "Of course, he's not the father!"

Laura Stromberg takes her daughter by the shoulders and leads her to the living room. Then she proceeds to tell me what she knows about Danny.

"Lacey said you showed her a photo of some guy and wondered whether she knew him. When she told me she lied, and why, I came right over to talk her into confessing."

Now I understand why they were arguing when I arrived.

"Why did you lie?" I ask Lacey.

"I didn't want you to know I bought the marijuana from him. The coke isn't mine, I swear. I've been clean for months now..."

Laura picks up where Lacey left off. "Lacey was involved with a bad crowd a few years ago. She got swept up in the party lifestyle—drinking, sex, drugs." She stops when Lacey gives her an accusing look. "I'm sorry, Lacey, but it's for the best. We need to tell the detective the truth."

I nod slowly, not wanting to intimidate Lacey, and choose my words carefully. "Every bit of information you give me will bring us one step closer to getting Christopher back. Help me find him."

"Mom's right. I did get mixed up with the wrong crowd. But I'm not anymore. Since I found out I was pregnant with..." She begins a fresh wave of heaving sobs, tears streaming down her face.

"When she found out she was pregnant and didn't know who the father was, we encouraged her to seek help. She's been getting drug counseling for the last ten months," her mother continues. "Everything was going so well, then..." Laura loses control and joins her daughter in uncontrolled sobbing. It leaves me uncomfortable and unsure of what to say next.

"Just get him back," Lacey manages to say.

I assure her I will do everything I can.

Leaving the two women to grieve the missing baby, I drive back to the station with a purpose. If Danny's fingerprints are on that snow globe, maybe it's because he picked it up when he was taking Christopher. What if it suddenly began to play, and he turned it off so Lacey wouldn't hear it and come running to the nursery? What if he thought about taking it with him, then changed his mind and set it down? But then again, his prints could be on it from when he gave it to Lacey in the first place, when she bought the house from him. Or maybe when he gave it to her as a gift for Christopher.

I'm certain that fingerprints are crucial to the solving of this case. Danny connects to the missing baby as well as to his missing girlfriend. Lacey initially refused to acknowledge that she knew Danny or that the marijuana was hers. She also refuses to acknowledge who the baby's father is. I'm betting that they could be one and the same person—Danny Anderson.

Back at the station, I spread out all the fingerprint reports from the missing persons cases. The prints from Julia's house have all been identified as family and friends, except for one. The report from the abandoned house brought back many prints. Prints from Lacey's house are accounted for, except for the ones on the globe.

Picking up the phone, I call Ted Clement from the forensic unit at Northeastern. "Hi, Ted. I need some info on prints from the missing persons cases here in Lake Kipling ASAP. Have a look at the ones from Julia Brenner's house and the abandoned house across the street, along with the prints from Lacey Stromberg's nursery. I'd like to know if there's a set of prints found in all three locations." If I can find concrete proof that Danny was in each of those places, my theory that he accompanied Julia to the abandoned house and that he took Lacey's baby from his crib may have some credibility.

I have my answer later in the day. There's a match. Fingerprints from the same person have been lifted from all three houses. They're not Danny's. In fact, they don't match any of the known players in the missing persons cases. I'm left hanging with one question. Who is the mystery person belonging to the fingerprints in Julia's bedroom, Lacey's nursery, and the abandoned house across from Julia?

Chapter Fifty-Four

Cheryl

I am so excited to open today's newspaper. My exclusive will be on the front page—in fact, it will be the whole front page and more. This is my first big break. It's the story of the decade, at least by Lake Kipling standards. And my name will be in the byline: Cheryl MacGregor.

I can't wait. The *Gazette* is normally delivered door to door. It's a free periodical published weekly. There isn't enough local news to publish more frequently than that. Our news of the world comes through the big papers that people buy at the news stands of variety stores.

The *Gazette* can also be found in the various kiosks around town. My paper delivery boy is not all that reliable. Sometimes, he delivers in the morning, sometimes in the afternoon. There are times I have to wait until evening to get the news. I'm not waiting today. As soon as I drop the kids off at camp, I go to the nearest kiosk and grab a copy of the free paper out of the cubicle.

What I see on the front page almost brings me to my knees. This isn't what I expected. It never occurred to me he would do this. Exposed to everyone—clear as the nose on my face—is me—or rather an image of me. Darren has taken the file photo from human resources and printed it under the headline next to my byline.

I can't deal with this. Somehow, I manage to get back into the car and calm down enough to make it to Jim's office. Barging through the front door with the paper firmly rolled up in one hand, I head straight into his office without saying hello to the new receptionist and throw myself into his arms, blubbering.

"What's wrong? Are the kids okay?" He pulls away to search my face for answers.

I hand the paper to him. His face drains of color as he sees my photo. For nearly twelve years, we've been hiding under assumed identities. Now I'm plastered on the front page along with the biggest story to come out of the north in some time.

Along with details about the local drug operation, the article states Northern Lights Raceway is controlled by Hamilcorp, based in Hamilton.

How could Darren do this to me? Put my photo in the paper? Go behind my back and research the ownership of the raceway? Publish their connection to Hamilton for all to see? But, of course, Darren doesn't realize the implications of what he's done.

I'm ready to pack up and make a run for it. Jim is quiet, trying to compose himself, I'm sure. When he speaks, it's not what I expected him to say. "It'll be okay. He's not going to read the *Gazette*. We're still safe."

"But Scott confirmed the raceway is connected to the Mafia in Hamilton. They're bound to find out how their drug ring got busted and who was behind it."

"You're just the reporter. They're not going to be reading a news story in a local paper. And it doesn't mention the Mafia."

I'm not convinced. If *he* finds out I'm involved in bringing down this operation, he'll come after me. He already has reason enough to want me dead. That's why we ran. We've been keeping our eyes and ears on news from the city, knowing the day would eventually come when he'd find us, especially after my visit to Hamilton last fall. My parents' car accident, my trip to Croatia to find out more about their history, Stefan lurking in front of my childhood home—it all comes rushing back to me.

Jim insists that Stefan won't be reading the local paper, and the city paper is unlikely to mention me. "And it's the police who are responsible for the drug bust, not you. We're not running again. This is our home."

It *is* our home. But the head of the Serbian Mafia has the means to destroy it. "I don't know. I don't think I can ever feel safe again if we stay here. I'm still not convinced he wasn't behind the truck crash at the *Gazette* when I came home from Croatia."

"The police found no evidence of it being anything other than an accident. And besides, nothing has happened since. We can't spend our lives running away on the off chance that he might see a photo of you. Besides, you look different now. And you've changed your name."

"Not that different. What if he recognizes me?" What if he comes for us? I changed my hairstyle and color, ramped up the makeup, and I'm older now, but you can still tell it's me in the photo. All I can do is hope he won't remember what I look like, that his memory has faded with the passing years. It's not like he met me more than twice, and only briefly at that.

Jim's arms offer safety despite the terror I've been feeling since I opened today's paper. "We need to stand our ground. We're not the criminals here. He's the one who was convicted of killing his own son."

And got out after serving ten years for manslaughter.

What started out as a terrific day, full of expectation, has become a nightmarish morning. I don't think I'll ever be able to shake this feeling that he's going to come after me.

Chapter Fifty-Five

That evening, a mailbox is opened. Inside is a typed note reading: **I have photos of what you did. Leave one kilo of coke on the climbers at Teck Park at midnight tomorrow or they'll be public.** The note's recipient now knows for certain this isn't a game. The note that was sent earlier was a teaser, a prelude to this open threat. Something needs to be done.

Chapter Fifty-Six

Cheryl

July 23

As if I didn't have enough to worry about, now Jim's going to leave me.

This morning, the smaller fires that began about twenty-five miles northwest of Lake Kipling combined into one big fire. The forest and small lakes make a great spot for people who enjoy the wilderness. But, careless hikers neglected to fully extinguish their campfires, and the warm temperatures, along with the lack of rainfall are contributing to the spread of flames. Firefighters from the town have already joined the Ministry of Natural Resources fire rangers in battling the blaze.

Until today, they had things under control. This afternoon, the wind changed direction, pushing the fires southeast toward town. Volunteer firefighters are being called upon to assist the department with taming the inferno.

But nothing tempers the firestorm in our household this morning caused by my husband's altruism.

As a member of the auxiliary volunteer fire department, Jim's eager to step in and aid his full-time colleagues, who've been working around the clock. I'm terrified of losing him to the raging fire, but there's no point in continuing to beg Jim to stay behind. Lord knows, I've tried, exhausting my vocabulary of plaintive entreaties, and it's fallen on deaf ears. At times like this I wish that Jim wouldn't put others ahead of himself. He's too good for his own good.

"Our own home is in the line of fire," he reminds me, calmly justifying his leaving. "It's not just the townspeople. I need to do my share to protect my family and keep us safe."

I want to suggest we simply grab the kids and leave everyone else to fend for themselves, but I bite my tongue.

"Please, please, be careful." My arms wrap around him, and I've almost convinced myself he won't go if I hold onto him tightly enough. I don't want the kids to see how terrified I am that something will happen to their dad. I also don't want Jim to worry about the kids and me after that newspaper fiasco. I need to let him go, knowing we'll be okay. "Stay safe. I love you." I repeat the last three words, my eyes holding his.

The kids take their turn to give Jim a big hug, and Brent tells him he's a hero. "Be careful, Dad. I love you," he says, following my lead, and Jamie follows her brother's. Jamie, I'm sure, has no idea the danger we could be facing.

"I love you guys so much. Don't worry, I'll be fine." Jim holds onto them for dear life, his eyes on me, a tear in one corner. "Don't get upset if you don't hear from me for a while. I don't know about cell reception. We'll probably be staying at the fire camp and I'm sure they'll have some way to communicate, but the lines will be busy. I'll try to call whenever I can," Jim says. "If there's any problem, call the police." I know he's referring to Stefan, not just the wildfires. "If you need help, call…" He hesitates, then adds, "Call Scott."

Before he leaves, Jim gives me one last passionate kiss to see me through till his return. My hand slides down his arm into empty space as he slips out of my grip on his way to the hellhole.

***

I need to be brave. I need to be strong. It's what Jim would want me to do.

According to the radio, the residents of West Kipling have been put on alert. I'm sure they must be getting more anxious by the hour as they wait. I turn on the local television station and see the Millcroft headframe splayed against a backdrop of dark, ominous clouds of smoke. The surrounding forest lies between the mine and the fires, a source of fuel for the rapidly advancing flames. Over a hundred people in the surrounding area have already been forced to leave their cottages as a result.

At about two o'clock, the TV news shows police cruisers driving up and down the short streets of West Kipling, knocking on doors, advising the occupants to pack a few belongings and leave their homes. A temporary relief shelter has been set up in the Lake Kipling arena for those who don't have relatives or friends in town.

I tell the kids we're going to help a friend and buckle Jamie into the back of the Rav. Brent rides shotgun, keeping his eyes trained to the right, staring at the oncoming white and gray mass of smoke. I don't want the kids to be any more frightened than they already are. "It'll be an adventure. Daddy's out fighting the fire to make sure it stays away. Our job is to do what the firefighters and police tell us. Some people have to leave their house for a while and stay someplace else till the fire's put out. If everyone does their part, everything will be just fine."

My destination is Mrs. Kaufman's house. I'm worried about the poor older woman who lives by herself. When I pull up in front of her house, the door and windows are closed tightly, and her vehicle is parked in the driveway alongside the house. I bring the kids with me and ring the doorbell.

After a short wait, Mrs. Kaufman comes to the door. "Oh, it's you. Brent, Jamie, my, how you've grown. What are you doing here?"

I explain we've come to check on her. "I wanted to make sure you have somewhere to go. If not, you should stay with us."

"That's so kind of you, dear. I was expecting to go to the arena in town. I've already packed some things, but I don't know what to do about Muffy. I can't leave her. I was wondering whether they would keep her at the animal shelter till this has all settled down."

"She can come with us, no problem, as long she's okay with our pup. I can get her stuff, if you want to finish packing your own things. Just point me in the right direction."

Mrs. Kaufman tells me Muffy's stuff is kept in the back kitchen. As the kids and I pack up the food and bowls, litter and litter box, scratching post, cat bed, along with a few toys, Mrs. Kaufman goes upstairs.

"Here, kitty kitty," I call, shaking a bag of cat treats. The fluffy cat scoots out from behind the closed curtain of the living room window. Muffy allows herself to be petted while she munches on treats. When she's done, she rubs against my legs, and I take the opportunity to pop her into the pet cage, locking the door securely. As Muffy yowls at my betrayal, I go through the main floor, making sure the windows and doors are locked. I check that the stove is off and the tap isn't running, then unplug the television, DVD player, and computer. Mrs. Kaufman comes downstairs.

"Have you locked the windows and checked everything upstairs?" I ask.

Mrs. Kaufman confirms that she has but needs help with her two suitcases. Brent and I haul them downstairs and into the back of the Toyota with the cat paraphernalia. "Make sure you have the key and lock up," I tell Mrs. Kaufman as I go back for Jamie and Muffy.

Mrs. Kaufman settles into the front seat as Jamie joins Brent in the back. Wide-eyed, he comments that the fire looks like it's getting close.

We take one last look at the encroaching smoke and head east, away from the danger, toward Lake Kipling.

Chapter Fifty-Seven

Julia Brenner

The baby's crying again. Still. It seems like he's always crying. There doesn't seem to be any escape from it in the small three-room cabin in the middle of the woods, next to a lake. Julia's comfortable enough on the recliner rocker with a couple of large fans, keeping the rooms cool during the day. A radio tuned to the local station and an assortment of books and magazines keep her entertained. The kitchen is fully stocked, including baby formula. An infant travel cot and other baby essentials take up one bedroom, and the other is where she retreats to get some peace and quiet at night. Julia keeps the bedroom doors open so she can tend to Christopher when he wakes up.

Outside, a couple of lounge chairs sit on the grass, facing the lake. This is where Julia likes to relax during the day, sometimes with a book on her lap, sometimes with the baby on her chest, depending on whether he's awake or not. A path follows the lake's shoreline, and she enjoys walking and dipping her toes into the water when Christopher is asleep in his cot, but she doesn't stray far.

It would have been a nice little vacation spot, if she wasn't trapped there. She has no vehicle, no phone, no nearby neighbors. She doesn't dare wander far off because she doesn't want to leave the baby. Not that it would do any good. She's deep in the forest, many miles from civilization. Her only visitor comes once a day. He already checked in earlier today.

Now, as she looks off in the distance, she's worried she'll never get out of here. She senses something is wrong before she sees it. Above the tree line, beyond the lake, smoke billows out from behind the greenery.

The forest is on fire.

Chapter Fifty-Eight

That evening, he's ready to follow the blackmailer's demands. The park and playground are dark, except for the light of the moon and the stars. Having obtained the kilo of cocaine as requested, he carefully makes his way through the grass and shade trees, past the benches and picnic tables, his cargo wrapped in a simple plastic bag. Once he reaches the wooden climber, he ascends the steps and places the bag on the landing. He scans the area but can't see anyone in the darkness.

His car waits on the road, visible in front of the area where he entered the park. His plan is to leave the drugs, walk back to his vehicle, and drive off. At least, that's what he wants the blackmailer to see.

That's exactly what he does. The last thing he wants to do is spook the blackmailer and have him go to the cops with what he knows.

Less than an hour later, a silhouette jogs from the street, into the park, toward the playground, then steps up the climber. Seconds later, it's gone, running back onto the street. It happens so quickly he can't see the face of his blackmailer as he crouches behind the hedge bordering one side of the park. He had driven his car to the next block and walked back to the park, thinking he might catch a glimpse of the blackmailer in hopes of identifying him. No such luck. All he sees is a figure in jeans and a hoodie. Springing from his hiding spot, he takes off in the direction the man or woman has disappeared, taking care not to be heard. He's come prepared, wearing running shoes with quiet soles and black clothing.

With any luck, he'll get a license plate number once the blackmailer reaches his getaway car. He's fit and catches up with the dark figure as it's getting into a vehicle two blocks down from the park entrance. Not wanting to be seen, he hangs back at a safe distance and watches as the driver pulls away from the curb. The dark vehicle has no license plate. It's been removed.

He's lost them. With no clue to the blackmailer's identity, he's out a kilo of stolen coke and still in danger of being exposed for what he's done. All he can do is wait to hear from his blackmailer again.

Chapter Fifty-Nine

Scott

The forensic reports stare me in the face. Ted explained the results to me, but I'm still perplexed. Three sets of matching unidentified prints were taken from the three houses in question. Who would have been in both Lacey's and Julia's bedrooms? A boyfriend? I was so sure it had to be Danny. The problem with that theory is the prints taken from the drug shoebox and other items in Danny's apartment don't match the prints on the snow globe or the prints from the abandoned house. There is, however, a set of prints taken from Julia's bedroom, specifically on the clock/radio on the nightstand, that matches the snow globe and matches prints from the empty house across from Julia. I'm stumped.

More information about the origins of that snow globe could shed light on this mystery. There are several places in town that might sell globes. Lake Kipling Jewelers is the first place I check out. Very quickly, I rule it out as the source. The jeweler tells me they don't sell globes of any sort. He suggests the gift shop down the street.

When I enter the shop, I see racks of gift cards, and shelves displaying various statues, artwork, photo frames, calendars, mugs, candles, jewelry, and yes—they have a few water globes. Of course, none of them are Christmas globes. It's the middle of summer.

The clerk behind the counter asks if I need assistance. "Yes, actually, I'm looking for a very specific snow globe." I provide a full description of the one in Lacey's nursery.

She knows the one I'm talking about. "We sold a few at Christmas," she says, and my ears perk up. "There are none left."

When I ask if she would happen to know who bought one, she tells me they don't keep records of their customers. I've hit another dead end.

"I know where you might be able to find more of them, though," she continues. "A Bit of Everything, the surplus store on the edge of Governor's Road, heading out to West Kipling. That's where ours came from. You can't get them anywhere else."

The surplus store is a two-story large white brick building situated away from the downtown core. The small parking lot is full, and I have to wait for someone to pull out and compete with a couple of others for a spot. When I enter through the glass doors, I see immediately how it got its name. There's everything in here, but the kitchen sink. Oh wait, I'm wrong—there are a couple of kitchen sinks on the far back wall. There's no way I'm going to locate a snow globe amid all this merchandise and paraphernalia.

Not seeing a salesclerk around, I get in line and wait in front of the counter, behind half a dozen other impatient shoppers. While I'm waiting, I browse through the merchandise displayed in the aisle beside me. Something catches my eye. It's a sky-blue journal with flowers and butterflies decorating the edges. In the center, the script reads: **I'm Basically a Detective.** I can't resist it. This is the perfect gift for Cheryl, to thank her for helping with the drug/money laundering case.

When I finally get to the head of the line, I explain what I'm looking for. The clerk tells me where they are located. "Down aisle twelve, Christmas surplus," she says, motioning somewhere over to the far side of the store.

"I'm wondering if you could give me a list of people who've bought one of those," I say, showing my ID.

She tells me they don't keep a list of who buys what. When I ask to see her manager, she makes an in-store call, and before long, a middle-aged woman comes along and asks what the problem is. Upon seeing my ID, she asks how she can help.

"We don't keep records of every customer," she repeats. "But I can tell you where they came from. The Millcroft mine had these made for their employees the Christmas before they closed. The manufacturer made an error in the quantity and shipped out several hundred extras. They ended up here."

"I understand you don't keep the names of all your customers, but is there anyone in particular you remember purchasing one of these?' Maybe someone stood out.

"I do remember one person who bought quite a few of these. He's been back a couple of times for more."

When I ask if she knows who it was, she gives me a name—Jim MacGregor, the real estate guy.

Chapter Sixty

Jim

With the fire getting closer to West Kipling, the higher-ups have made a decision. Heavy equipment needs to be brought in. Until now, the fire rangers have kept the fires under control. Thanks to the multitude of small lakes in the area, the pumps and hoses are effectively put to use. Pickaxes and shovels are employed to create fire lines, and along with controlled fires, they're helping to maintain boundaries.

But suddenly, things begin to worsen. When the wind shifts, the water bombers are brought in, as are all available trained volunteer firefighters. Jim MacGregor dons his protective equipment, and along with his fellow crew members, he listens to instructions. The fireproof suits and helmets protect somewhat, but there's always a danger from falling trees, and entrapment, along with smoke inhalation and heat-related injuries. Jim, along with a few others, is given the job of wetting down fire lines that have been created by the fire rangers.

The mayor of Lake Kipling, in consultation with the Ministry of Natural Resources, has rounded up bulldozers and their operators from local construction companies to take down the trees fueling the fires. He also contacted the owners of Millcroft Mine, asking them to donate the use of the mine's bulldozing equipment and qualified personnel to run the heavy vehicles. The machines assist in creating a series of fire breaks, by taking down trees and vegetation in the path of the out-of-control blazes.

To keep the public safe and allow firefighters to do their job unencumbered, the main highway heading north between Lake Kipling and Timber Lake is now closed. With the unpredictability of the course of the fire, officials have decided it's best to keep people from unnecessary travel. Things are burning out of control.

Chapter Sixty-One

Cheryl

From my front yard that evening, the thick wall of gray/black smoke and red/yellow flames billows in the distance, threatening to envelop the town. The radio station announces that people should stay indoors and keep their windows closed. West Kipling has been evacuated, and the residents of Lake Kipling are advised to stay tuned for further news. Although the ministry is assuring everyone the town will be safe, people are being put on alert. Things could change at any time.

I carry Mrs. Kaufman's suitcases to the guest room, then fix pasta and salad for supper. Mrs. Kaufman and the kids watch a video in the family room. As worried as I am about Jim, it's best to keep my mind off what he's doing right now. It's pointless pacing around the house, getting myself into a panic state. I need to stay calm for the kids.

To keep busy, I go back to reading Julia's journals. They don't offer any more information that might lead to Julia's whereabouts. I flip through the pages, looking for any mention of the boyfriend from high school, and find a few more references to him. It sounds like she's talking about the same guy from Grade 9 right through to the end of Grade 11, when she got pregnant.

Something catches my eye as I'm reading about the boyfriend. The summer after Grade 11, about the time Julia would have been pregnant, he told her that he was going to change. **He said he wants to go back to**

school and have more than just a dead-end job. Something respectable. Then maybe my parents will accept him. We could get married and be a family. I wonder whatever happened to him and his plans.

* * *

July 24

The next morning, I stand on my lawn again and watch smoke threaten the town. The radio station is now telling people to be prepared to evacuate. Lake Kipling police have contacted the station at Northern Bay, asking them to be ready to set up temporary shelters if and when necessary. I call Scott to check in with him. "Did you hear the news? The fire is getting out of control." I try to sound as calm as possible, given the current danger.

"I heard. I've got the radio on here. Sounds bad. Are you okay? And the kids, Jim?"

"Jim's gone—he's a volunteer with the fire department. He left yesterday afternoon to help out. Do you think they'll evacuate the town?" My voice sounds panicky to my own ears.

"I think there's a very real possibility of that happening. Best to be ready. Pack some bags, just in case. I'm here if you need me. I'll check on you later."

Brent calls me over to the window and points out the water bombers in the distance. "Is Dad okay?' He's picked up on my anxiety.

I try to reassure him, and then my thoughts turn to Lacey Stromberg. As worried and upset as I am, I can't imagine what it would be like to have my child go missing during all this turmoil. Maybe she'll appreciate a visit from someone who's concerned about her. I tell Mavis I'll be back within the hour, and drive to Lacey's home. Approaching the front door, I prepare to ring the doorbell, thinking of what I'm going to say.

Lacey answers the door on the first ring. "I know you! You're that reporter who busted up the drug ring. I saw your picture in the paper yesterday. Are you here about my baby? Did you find out where he is?"

I explain that I'm a friend of Detective Evans, and I'm here to make sure she's preparing to evacuate, if necessary. "I'm sure you'll be going with your parents, but I thought maybe you could use a friend. Is there anything I can do? Help you pack some stuff, maybe?"

Lacey says she isn't going anywhere. "I'm waiting for Christopher. I want to be here when he comes back."

"You need to stay safe, so you'll be ready for him when he comes back. He's going to need you to be strong and healthy. That means you need to take care of yourself. You have to be ready to leave if necessary."

Several seconds pass before Lacey decides to invite me inside. "You're right. I need to do whatever it takes to make sure I'm okay when he comes back. I'll pack a few things. Do you really think they'll evacuate us?"

"My husband is out fighting the fires right now. He's a volunteer firefighter. I'm sure they're doing everything they can to contain the danger. But I'm going to pack some bags for myself and my kids just in case we need to leave. I don't know how I'm going to leave my husband behind, but if I have to, I'll protect our kids, and we'll leave town without him." A lump forms in my throat. "Sometimes it's hard to leave, but it's necessary. Detective Evans told me there's a real possibility we might be evacuated, so I'm ready for the worst."

"Have you known Detective Evans very long?"

"No, just a few weeks. I've been helping him with a couple of cases. Don't worry, he'll find Christopher. He's good at his job."

"I met him once before under different circumstances. We were at a bar. He didn't say he was a detective. He mustn't remember me, because he didn't say anything when he questioned me. But I remember him."

Another one of his conquests, obviously. I'm surprised he doesn't remember, though. I wonder if he'll remember me when this case is over.

Lacey goes to her room to remove a suitcase from the closet, while I peek in the baby's room. Maybe there's something of Christopher's that Lacey could bring along to keep a part of him with her if she's forced to leave home. I notice the snow globe on the dresser. I've seen lots of those—Jim gives them to his clients as gifts, a little memento of the town where they're making their new home. I call out to Lacey. "Did Jim sell this house to you?"

"What? Jim? Who's he?"

"Jim MacGregor, my husband, MacGregor Realty?"

"Oh! Yes, that's right. I remember now. It was Jim. He's your husband?"

"Yes."

"Oh, I didn't know that. Yes, he did sell the house to me. Why are you asking?"

I can hear Lacey going through her drawers and closet, packing clothing into her suitcase.

"I just noticed the snow globe. It's his signature gift to clients this year. Danny works for Jim. Do you know Danny Anderson?" I'm fishing for information to see if I can find some connection between Danny and the baby.

Lacey walks into the nursery, hesitates, then says, "A little. Not that well."

"He's Christopher's father, isn't he?" I blurt out the words before I can stop myself.

"What? No!"

She denies it so vehemently, I don't believe her. Something else on the dresser catches my eye. "Oh, that's cute." I point to a soft-cloth police car. "Is it special?"

"It was a gift. From someone I used to know."

"Maybe Christopher will grow up to be a police officer. Like Detective Evans."

"You mean just like his... God, I hope not."

Something in her tone leads me to believe there's more significance to the police car than a baby gift from an old friend.

"Maybe you'd like to pack this with you in case you have to leave, something of Christopher's to hold onto till he comes back."

Lacey doesn't respond right away. Then she quietly asks, "You don't think he took him, do you?"

"Who?"

"His father."

I let out an audible gasp. "I thought you didn't know who he was."

Lacey tries to take back her words. "No, I don't. What I mean is…well, he didn't want a kid in the first place. He wouldn't take him now."

"Who is he?" I'm hoping to get Lacey to confide in me.

"I can't say."

I have no choice but to leave it at that. "I'll give you a call tomorrow to check in with you, if that's okay. I need to get back home."

When I turn the key in my front door, the kitchen phone begins to ring. Running to answer it, I step on a toy car and slip onto the tiles, the receiver dangling toward the floor. "Ouch!"

"Cheryl? Are you okay?"

The alarm in Scott's voice comes through. Assuring him I'm fine, I rub my sore leg. Scott says he's calling to check up on me and let me know the police are going around town flashing lights and blowing the air horn to warn people to be prepared for a possible sudden evacuation. The mayor has just declared a state of emergency.

"What about you? I heard the highway's closed heading north. Where are you staying?"

"I just crashed at the office last night. The motels are full of evacuees from the surrounding area."

"That's not good. Why don't you come stay here?" I realize that's not a good idea as soon as it slips out of my mouth.

Scott says exactly that. "I don't think Jim would appreciate me moving in with his wife while he's out in the forest helping to keep the fire under control. I don't want to impose."

"Don't be silly. We've got lots of space. There's no need for you to stay in your office all night. You'll be a lot more comfortable here and a lot more rested to do your job properly. I'm sure you'll need to be alert with everything that's going on." Scott says when I put it that way, he can't refuse.

What could possibly be wrong with having a friend stay over? Mavis is here already, after all. One more won't hurt.

235

Chapter Sixty-Two

Jim

With another shift in the wind's direction, the fire turns northeastward to the area of Emery Park. A brief rainstorm brought a welcome relief, but with it came a lightning strike east of the park, sparking another major blaze. To prevent the two fires from converging, the mine's bulldozing equipment and crews are being sent to create firebreaks to the west and east of the park. Water bombers are still dropping fire retardant and water to the west and north of Lake Kipling, in an effort to keep flames from consuming the town, and crew members use drip torches to burn away brush to keep it from feeding the fire.

It looks like a war zone. It sounds like a tornado roaring through the forest.

Jim has been working with a crew northwest of Lake Kipling, establishing fire lines with their Pulaski and McCloud scraping tools. It's arduous work, digging and chopping away at the limbs and roots of fresh vegetation, destroying fuel for the fire. As he works in the oppressive heat, Jim's muscles ache from the strain of repetitive motion. Even though he's been out on occasional wildfire calls before, his toned body has grown somewhat softer from years of sitting behind a desk. Locks of black hair stick to his sweaty brow, and smoke parches his throat. Despite the discomfort, Jim has only one thing on his mind—Cheryl and the kids. He's focused on keeping them safe from danger. It gives him the adrenaline to keep going.

The ground sizzles, the smoke wafts through the air, fireballs reach the sky, trees crash to the ground, and deadwood surrounds them. The sound of chainsaws taking down large trees that have caught fire is heard above the sounds of the scraping and the roar of the flames.

But, the immediate threat to Lake Kipling has been averted, thanks to the wind and rain. Now, the main concern is the thousands of acres of greenery in Emery National Park. Not only does the natural area need to be protected, but fire crews need to prevent the park from fueling the fire that threatens the small communities in its surrounding area.

When Jim and some of his fellow crew are reassigned to the new location, he's given a brief respite from his labor as they climb into the trucks and drive toward Emery Park. The Timber Lake Fire Department joins them in the effort to prevent sparks from reaching the forested recreation zone. Circling Emery Park, along Highway 62, fire trucks and heavy equipment form a convoy to tackle the wildfire in the east before it sweeps through the park, creating an inferno when it joins up with the blaze to the west.

As Jim and the others fan out in the area, gear in tow, they trudge through the thick forest, their eyes moving back and forth between the smoke closing in from the west and the east. The area has plenty of natural deterrents to the flames. Lakes, rivers, and streams populate the park. But the fire could jump over some of these areas. What's of even more concern is the terrain. The forest is sloped throughout, which could increase the spread with the updraft. Fire travels twice as quickly up a slope.

As they're scouting out a suitable area for a firebreak on the eastern side of Emery Park, one of the men shouts, "There's something up there!"

Jim joins several others who converge at the bottom of the forested slope and look upward. What looks like someone's clothing is caught on the branch of a tree amidst the shrubbery about 100 feet uphill.

"I'm going to take a closer look." The man starts to scramble up the incline, grabbing onto the vegetation as he carefully climbs toward the object that has caught his attention.

"I think it's..." he yells as he inches closer. "It's a person!"

Chapter Sixty-Three

Cheryl

There's something about what Lacey said, or maybe didn't say, that's bothering me. I can't quite put my finger on it. I've got an icepack on the leg that hit the toy truck when I fell earlier, and it's propped up on a pillow on my bed. I'm passing the time by reading over Julia's journal entries. The kids are down in the family room being entertained by Mavis, or maybe they're entertaining Mavis. I'm not sure which, but she insisted on looking after them and shooed me off to bed to rest my leg.

I'm about to doze off when the phone rings.

"Hi, Honey." Jim, thank God! "I just wanted to let you know I'm okay and make sure you're alright."

"We're fine. I'm so glad to hear your voice. I've been going crazy worrying."

"I knew you would be. But try to stay calm. What's going on there?"

"They're telling us to be ready to evacuate if necessary. I've packed some things just in case. They're setting up emergency centers in Northern Bay."

"Okay, good. Let's hope it doesn't come to that. Things are getting under control to the west, but there's another blaze east of Emery Park, so they've sent me there. Listen, you may hear of some casualties out where I am. But I don't want you to worry if you don't hear from me. Don't jump to conclusions. Okay? Tell Brent and Jamie I love them and I'm fine. I love you. Miss you."

"I love you, too. Be careful." I'm lucky to have Jim. He's so brave. But every time he gets called out to help the department with a fire or some other emergency, I worry something will happen to him. I'm glad it's not his main job. I'd be a basket case if he was always in the line of danger. It's a good thing he's not a full-time firefighter or a police officer. Real estate is a pretty safe career choice. So is newspaper reporting. Most of the time, anyway.

Then I recall what was bothering me when I saw the toy police car in Lacey's house. I said maybe Christopher would grow up to be a police officer, like Detective Evans, and she said she hoped not. Why would she say that? She said she didn't want him to grow up like…. She never finished the sentence, but then she talked about Christopher's father. Does that mean Christopher's father is a police officer?

Or am I just reading something into it?

Chapter Sixty-Four

Aaron

The Lake Kipling Emergency Medical Unit is already at Emery Park when Officers Murphy and Parker arrive at the scene of the accident. The Lake Kipling police force is stretched to the limit with the possible evacuation and the missing baby. Everyone is working overtime. Logan and Aaron, who were manning the station when the call came in, are briefed on the situation. The accident is unconnected to the fires. It seems a hiker has taken a tumble down the side of the hill. No word yet on the condition of the victim.

The rescue crew, tethered to ropes, scale the side of the steep hill with the aid of ice picks. Ropes are secured around trees, and a system of pulleys is in place along the slope as they pull the rescue basket up with them. Once they reach the mass of clothing, they check for vitals. Shaking their heads, they relay the message to those below and prepare to lift the body into the basket and ease it down the incline.

Upon examining the body, Aaron exclaims, "It's someone we know!"

The identity of the accident victim is confirmed by Logan.

As the emergency crew awaits the arrival of the coroner, the officers drive through the park to the top of the ravine and examine the spot from which the man has fallen. They stand gazing across to the west and east, smoke and flames encroaching upon the park.

The officers scan the side of the hill, trying to locate the exact spot where the body was found. Their eyes scour the rock, dirt, and brush for any disturbance in the vicinity where the hiker has gone over. The earlier rain has washed away any tracks that might have been found. They conclude the cause of death will be attributed to an accidental slipping off the edge. With no one accompanying him, the victim probably wasn't heard if he had still been alive to call out for help.

"That," says Logan, "is the first rule of hiking—always take someone with you. It's a real shame not everyone follows the rules."

"We need to get out of here," Aaron says. "Let's split up and have a quick look around the area, then head out. I'll take that direction, meet you back in ten."

"See anything?" Logan asks as they meet up after scouting the surrounding area.

Neither officer has found evidence to indicate anything other than an accidental fall caused the demise of the hiker.

"Let's go. Those fires can jump quickly," Logan says. "I better get some photos of the scene, and we can return when it's safe, if necessary."

"That's if there's anything left to see," Aaron adds.

As they get in their police car and drive away from the accident scene, Aaron says, "Stop the car! I think I see a vehicle amongst the trees."

It's a vehicle they both recognize as belonging to the victim. Upon examination of the locked car, they find a note sitting on the passenger seat. "We'd better get it towed out of here. If the fire keeps advancing, there won't be anything left but burned-out forest in a day or two," Logan suggests. "There could be some crucial evidence in the truck."

Aaron agrees the victim's vehicle should be brought in as evidence. They turn back in the direction of the fire break to speak to the crew. "Any chance of commandeering a truck to tow out a vehicle? It belongs to the victim. We'd like to get it back to the station for examination, if possible."

Half an hour later, the vehicle is chained to one of the fire crew's pickup trucks and on its way to Lake Kipling station.

Chapter Sixty-Five

Cheryl

I'm still wondering what happened to Julia's old boyfriend. He said he wanted to get a respectable job. Where is he now? Sheila doesn't seem to know much about him, nor do Julia's parents. There's one source I haven't checked personally who might have some answers—Rebecca Collins. I know Scott's talked to her, but I'd like to speak with her myself.

Julia's mom gives me Rebecca's number, no questions asked, except whether I'm any closer to solving the mystery of her daughter's disappearance. I assure her I'm still working on it. Rebecca answers on the third ring. After introducing myself and telling her what I'm calling about, I ask if she has any information about Julia's old high school boyfriend.

"Why are you asking about *him?* Some detective called and asked me about Danny," she says.

"I'm just wondering if there's any possibility she may have been seeing him lately."

Rebecca hesitates before answering. "I didn't want to say anything to the police in case... But I'm getting really worried about her, especially now that it's been almost three weeks, and the police haven't found her."

"Are you saying you *do* know something about the boyfriend? Did she run away with him?"

"I don't know. She might have. We don't talk often, just now and then."

"So you think she might have been seeing him recently?" That would explain everything. Except, whatever happened to Danny?

"She told me she felt someone was stalking her, but she wasn't sure he was the one. When she finally confronted him, she told him to leave her alone, and he said he didn't know what she was talking about. But in her last letter, she asked whether I thought she should give him another chance, so I guess she could have been seeing him in secret, just like she did years ago."

I need to know who he is. A name.

Rebecca says she doesn't know. "I know he's older. I wondered if he was married. But Julia said he was wild, and her parents wouldn't approve; he smoked and drank, did some weed, liked to party. But she couldn't stay away from him, even when she found out he was cheating on her. When Julia got pregnant, he said he didn't want anything to do with the baby. Julia was afraid to introduce him to her parents, and they forbade her to see him again anyway when they found out about the pregnancy. They convinced her she was too young to raise a child on her own and talked her into having an abortion. But then, he changed his mind and said he'd take responsibility and look after her and the baby. Only it was too late."

I tell Rebecca I've been reading Julia's journals, trying to find some clues about what might have happened. "She wrote that her boyfriend wanted to change, to get a respectable job, and have a family with her. Do you have any idea what happened to him?"

"Oh!" Rebecca shouts so loudly I need to move the phone away from my ear. "That's right, I remember now. She told me years ago—he wanted to become a police officer someday—a detective."

Detective? The phone nearly falls to the floor, and my head spins from the shock of her words. Is it possible? The father of Julia's baby wanted to be a detective. Lacey's baby may have been fathered by a cop. Is it the same guy? Regaining control of my emotions, I ask Rebecca if there's any way she can find the name of Julia's ex-boyfriend. It's critical to finding her safe and sound. I leave her with my number and say, "Call me if you remember his name. It's important."

The minute I hang up, the doorbell rings. Mavis answers it, telling me to stay off my sore leg. Please, don't let it be bad news. Jim had better be safe. The town had better be safe. I don't know what I would do without Jim, without our family and the home we've made together.

When I hear his voice, I remember the invitation I extended to him earlier. Detective Scott Evans is here to spend the night.

Chapter Sixty-Six

Scott

I t'll be fine. I'm just going to have to be careful to maintain my distance from Cheryl. If she ever gets to the door, that is. What's taking her so long?

Should I tell her what I'm thinking? Or wait to confront Jim? Give him a chance to explain himself? If I could just put the puzzle pieces together and make the picture complete. Julia is missing, as is Lacey's baby. Both women had a mystery boyfriend they didn't want to expose. Why was that? Did he want his identity kept secret? Because he was married? There's a strong possibility the prints on the snow globe belong to Jim. Those prints match the prints on Julia's phone. Was Jim in both women's bedrooms? Is he the mystery boyfriend? Julia first met her secret boyfriend about ten years ago. What if Jim was stepping out on Cheryl? And what if he got jealous when Julia took up with Danny? Both Julia and Danny worked for Jim. Coincidence? Cheryl wondered about the possibility of Julia being kept temporarily in the abandoned house across the street. Jim had access to the keys.

Why doesn't she answer the door? I know she's home. Her car's here. I press the doorbell again, turn the doorknob, and the door swings open. I come face to face with Mrs. Kaufman. What is she doing here?

"It's that detective! Should I let him in?"

Cheryl's voice comes from upstairs. "Yes, let him in. I'll be right there."

Mrs. Kaufman apologizes for taking so long to answer the door. "I had to put Muffy in the basement so she wouldn't run out the door. Are you allergic to cats?"

"No."

"Are you sure? She's long-haired and sheds."

A minute later, which seems more like an hour with Mrs. Kaufman glowering at me and my overnight bag, Cheryl limps down the stairs.

"Are you all right?" I gesture to her leg.

She says it's nothing, just a bit of a bruise.

"I was going to take you up on your offer to stay here, but I see you've already got a house guest. I'll head back to the office."

"That's a good idea. I'm sure you've got plenty of work to do with everyone going missing and the fire coming this way," Mrs. Kaufman agrees. "And Cheryl's husband could be back anytime." She narrows her eyes at me, no doubt, to scare me back to my car. It works.

"I'll give you a call later..." I turn in the direction of the door.

"It's fine," Cheryl interrupts, but her face says otherwise. Something has changed. She squints at me, her brow furrowed, like she's trying to read me, as though she hasn't met me before. "There's plenty of room. Of course, you'll stay here. We've got a pull-out sofa in the basement. Brent will show you. Brent! Detective Evans is here!"

Brent bounds into the hall with the hairy pup following. They, at least, seem happy to see me. "Can I go for a ride in your Camaro?"

"Sure." I don't mind, as long as Cheryl doesn't tell him he can take it for a spin, like she did with Mike.

"Cool." He opens the door, ready to go.

"Maybe later, Brent. Right now, can you show Detective Evans the sofa in the basement, and help him get settled in first? He's going to stay there tonight. The highway's closed, and he can't get home," Cheryl says.

Jamie runs up behind her brother and peeks around him, assessing me. "Will you play with us, Detective Evans?"

"Enough of the detective. We're all buddies here. You can call me Scott." When I tell her I'm looking forward to playing, she jumps up and down.

"Yay!"

The fluffy pup, not wanting to be left out, runs circles around me, yipping in excitement.

Cheryl, much like Mrs. Kaufman, doesn't look nearly as thrilled to see me. I'm beginning to wonder if she was just being polite, inviting me over, not really expecting me to take her up on the offer.

"There's a bathroom downstairs. I'll get some fresh linens and towels ready for you," Cheryl says, "while you take your stuff down and get the sofa pulled out."

Her words indicate she's fine with me staying, but there's something in her tone or her demeanor that tells me I shouldn't have come. In any case, it's too late to gracefully bow out, so I follow Brent down the stairs, nearly getting tripped by a cat as it bounds up the stairs, to a nice-sized rec room with a sofa, a glider rocker, and a television set. Off to one corner is a heap of toys, and I can see the bathroom, complete with a shower, to the right.

Once Brent and I have the sofa pulled out and I unpack my stuff, Mrs. Kaufman, holding a stack of linens, hollers down the stairs. "Do you want to come up and get these, or do I have to bring them down myself?" When I reach the top of the stairs, she whispers so Brent won't hear. "Don't forget she's happily married."

"I know," I whisper back. "We're just friends. And by the way, I love cats. And dogs." I don't mention kids, but I've got to say, they're growing on me.

Brent tugs at one end of the fitted sheet while I pull on another, and somehow, we manage to get the bed made. "I want pizza for supper," he says, out of the blue. "Not fish."

"Pizza sounds good," I agree.

Brent takes the stairs two at a time. "Mom! Scott wants pizza for supper!"

I head up to join him. In the kitchen, Cheryl is taking fish out of the fridge freezer.

"But fish is good, too." Judging from Brent's reaction, I've betrayed him. "Listen, why don't I order pizza? It'll save you the trouble of cooking," I suggest, trying to redeem myself in Brent's eyes.

"He got to you, didn't he?" Cheryl asks, hands on her hips.

I've got to admit he did. The kid and I have a lot in common—we both like cool cars, pizza, and his mom. Cheryl relents and says pizza sounds good. Jamie, having heard, jumps up and down again, yelling, "Yay!" then takes my hand and leads me to the family room where a plastic town playmat on the floor holds an assortment of vehicles.

"I'll order delivery. Mavis, what would you like on your pizza?" Cheryl asks the little old lady who sits on the sofa, glaring at me.

"Oh my, I haven't had take-out pizza in ages. Pepperoni is fine with me, and ham, maybe some mushrooms. I don't care for peppers or onions. Too much spice gives me gas," she answers.

"What about you, Detective Evans?" She's being damn formal with me, considering everything we've been through together.

"I'm easy." I hand her a couple of twenties, which she turns down, telling me I'm a guest.

While we're waiting for supper to be delivered, the kids and I get down on the floor and do some serious driving on the playmat. The fire trucks head out to the fire, and the police drive through town, telling people to evacuate. Just like real life. The construction vehicles are on their way to the forest to help. The planes are in the sky, heading out to waterbomb the fire. Mrs. Kaufman is put in charge of flying the planes, a job she can do from the sofa.

Jamie and I are making siren sound effects when Cheryl hobbles back into the room. Mrs. Kaufman informs her we're getting ready to fight the fire, just like Daddy.

"Dad's a hero," Brent reiterates, as if I didn't already know.

Jim, the hero. Jim, the great husband and dad. And if those are his fingerprints in Lacey and Julia's bedrooms—Jim, the possible philandering husband. Maybe not the saint Cheryl thinks he is.

"Mom, you can be the bulldozer," Brent says as Cheryl carefully lowers herself to the ground, placing a cushion under her leg.

Guilt and remorse flood through me as I consider how it will affect Cheryl if my suspicions are correct. I don't want to be responsible for destroying this happy family. Maybe I can find some other explanation for the prints.

CHAPTER SIXTY-SIX

And we're all having a great time when the doorbell rings.

"I'll get it." I jump to my feet, not giving Cheryl the opportunity to beat me to the door. I pay for the pizza and give the guy a generous tip. It's the least I can do for intruding on Cheryl's personal life.

Chapter Sixty-Seven

Cheryl

We're having pizza and watching *Honey, I Shrunk the Kids* when the doorbell rings again.

Please don't let it be bad news, please, please.

Scott gets up to answer it. When he comes back, he says it was Officer Murphy, and he'll tell me more about it later. "I've got something I need to do, but I'll be back in a while." He wolfs down the rest of the pizza on his plate, polishes off his beer, and helps me to my feet, guiding me to the kitchen.

"Officer Murphy said the power's out in some areas of town, so there's a chance we could lose ours tonight," he says, though I'm not sure that needed to be said in private.

Hopefully, the power will stay on until the movie's over. As I open a drawer and root around for flashlights and candles, Scott adds, "There's something I need to talk to you about. But I want to wait till the kids and Mavis are asleep."

Whatever he has to tell me, I'm not sure I want to hear it. Ever since I heard from Rebecca that Julia's ex-boyfriend is an older guy who wanted to be a detective, I've had these crazy thoughts and suspicions about Scott. Is *he* the ex-boyfriend? Could he be the cop who's the father of Lacey's baby? What about Sheila? She said she was interested in some cop who was flirting with her, and I saw the two of them having lunch. And that blond at the mine? She seemed to have her eyes all over him.

Is Scott Julia's ex? Am I not the only woman he flirts with? Obviously not. The guy's a womanizer, plain and simple. What if he has something to do with Julia's disappearance? And what if he took the baby? No one would ever suspect him. He's a respectable police officer. A nice guy. A detective sergeant. Maybe it wasn't Danny at all. Maybe Scott's trying to put the blame on Danny, and Danny took off because he was afraid for his life.

If only Rebecca would call back with the boyfriend's name... In the meantime, I can't let on I'm suspicious of him. Hopefully, I'm wrong. God, I hope so.

Chapter Sixty-Eight

Scott

This changes everything. A body has been found. What started out as a mysterious missing persons case has turned into a major drug bust and a child abduction. Now, a body has turned up in the middle of a forest fire. Maybe I should go back to Toronto, where things are quieter.

With the fire destroying everything in its path, it's unlikely there'll be any evidence to explain what happened. The emergency rescue team had to leave the scene before the coroner could get there. As the fire rapidly advanced on both sides of them, they made the decision to get out of there and let the fire crews get on with building their fire break. The coroner's examining the body right now at the hospital morgue.

Leaving Cheryl's cozy little home life behind, I take the short drive to the hospital to check things out firsthand. When I arrive, I take the elevator down to the morgue. Derek Zimmerman has the body laid out on a gurney. He greets me with a nod and says he's just finishing up. I stand idly by, waiting. I've seen plenty of bodies before, but it still gets to me. It's especially sad when it's someone young. I find myself wondering how it got to this point. Hopefully, Derek will have the answers I need.

He takes off his gloves and shakes his head. "Inconclusive. Contusions on the body and a good-sized cut on the back of his head. Consistent with a fall off an embankment. He probably hit trees and rocks on his way down."

"Why do you say it's inconclusive, then?"

"There's a possibility some of the injuries may have been sustained during an altercation."

"So, he could have been in a fight with someone before he went over?"

"The blow to the head could be from hitting his head on a rock, or it could be from someone hitting him on the head with a rock."

"Are you saying it could be murder?"

"I'm saying death was likely the result of injuries sustained from the fall, but I wouldn't rule out a blow to the head," he reiterates. "Was there any evidence of anyone else being with him?"

"No. What about the time of death?"

"Again, it's hard to say with certainty. The body's been exposed to the elements for some time, obviously. I'd say about a couple of weeks."

The coroner isn't giving me much to go on. I suspect we may never find out what happened. I take one last look as I leave the shell on the examining table, hoping it will be ruled accidental, nothing more.

I don't want to have to deal with any more bodies.

Chapter Sixty-Nine

Aaron

Terry Lawrence has backed himself into a corner, though he doesn't quite understand that yet. But he will. He broke more than one law and lied to the police from the beginning.

When questioned earlier, the superintendent of the apartment building where Danny lived left out some details. When that woman came around snooping, according to Terry, he had been cordial and let her into Danny's place. But then the detective came around and found the drugs. Terry insisted he knew nothing about it.

Terry didn't mention he knew Danny as more than just a tenant. He and Danny were friends, in a way. Or at least good acquaintances. Danny was his source of cocaine.

Now, he's changing his story. Making some very serious accusations. Aaron listens to Terry's latest version of what he knows about Danny and the drugs.

The last time Terry saw Danny, they met in the hallway as Danny headed for the back door of the apartment building. "Hey, Danny. How's it going? I was just about to come see you," Terry greeted him.

"I'll see you later," Danny answered. "When I get back. The police have a lead on Julia. Someone's seen her at Emery Park. I don't know why she'd be there, but if there's a chance, I need to find her."

"Want me to come with you? I can help you look."

"No, I'm good, thanks. I just got a call asking if I wanted to join the search. The police are already there, but they were wondering if I wanted to help check out some other areas. I'm going to meet up with one of them now."

"So, I'll see you later, then?"

"I'll be back before dark," Danny said. "I'll call you."

Terry grabbed his camera and followed Danny to the park that day anyway, thinking there'd be some sort of reward in it for him if he was the one to find her. If the police questioned his presence there, he'd just say he was out bird watching.

The reward wasn't the type he was expecting. When he wandered off to a remote area, he witnessed something he shouldn't have. There was no time for Terry to run over and stop it. Just enough time for him to yell out, "Hey!" from his hiding spot. Enough time for him to snap a photo of the man going over the edge. Enough time for him to run. Run like his life depended on it. It was a good thing he ran laps every day.

He ran and hid till he knew he was in the clear. He made his way back to his car, which was parked a distance away. Once he was safely home, sure that he wasn't followed, an idea came to him. A way to get his hands on more coke.

And it would have worked just fine if he had remembered to re-attach his license plate. In the excitement of the previous night, picking up the coke at the playground, Terry forgot about it. Getting a hit was his top priority. This afternoon, he prepared half a dozen small baggies of 8 balls of coke and called some potential clients. Once the first stash was sold, he figured he could get his hands on more. He could tap into his supply chain again.

With thoughts of the wealth he was about to accumulate from drug trafficking no doubt flashing through his head, he hadn't been paying attention to his speed limit as he headed east along Governor's Road, past a cop car. Officer Parker switched on the siren and flashing lights. When he pulled Terry Lawrence over for a missing license plate and exceeding the town speed limit by 23 mph, he found him to be under the influence. Not only that, sitting on the floor of the passenger seat were several pouches of cocaine. His subsequent arrest resulted in a search warrant for his apartment, where more drugs were found.

Now, as Terry sits in the interrogation room, he's trying to plea bargain his way out of the charges, drafting a new story, knowing an additional charge of blackmail won't help his case any. A sitting duck, Terry vacillates between keeping silent about what he knows and spilling the beans to a judge. "Maybe we can make a deal," he states.

"A deal?" Aaron's not sure what to do with this information. An accusation of this sort needs to be watertight. Will Terry's story hold water? Aaron's promotion is on the line. Because of a junkie's story of what he thought he saw.

Officer Parker leans forward. "Are you sure you want to go through with this?"

"I've got proof. The photo." Terry smirks. "That should get me something."

"You've got driving under the influence without a plate. You've got possession with intent to traffic. You've got attempted blackmail. You've got holding back crucial evidence in a police investigation. Unless that photo is absolutely 100 percent crystal clear, you've got a long jail term ahead of you."

Terry squirms, eyes darting around the room, looking for escape. "I know what I saw. Where's Detective Evans?"

One thing Officer Parker tells him is certain—he's going to need a good lawyer. "Do you really think they'll take your word over that of a well-respected cop?"

Chapter Seventy

Cheryl

By the time the movie's over, it's after nine o'clock. Jamie's eyes are as wide as an owl's. She's not ready for bed, with the excitement of having guests over and the possible evacuation.

The doorbell rings again. Brent turns to me for a second, then races to the entrance. I know he's worrying about his dad, just like I am, and putting on a brave face. "It's just Scott! He says we can go for a spin around the block now if I'm allowed."

"Okay, but don't be long." I turn my attention back to Jamie and bargain with her. "If you get into your pajamas now, we can play a game for a little while."

While she goes up to change and brush her teeth, I dig out a couple of board games from the shelf by the fireplace, and not long after, Scott and Brent return.

"That was way cool! Mom, you should go for a ride in Scott's Camaro." Brent flies through the door. "I'm going to get one when I'm old enough to drive."

Scott seems absorbed in his thoughts. I wonder what's going on in his head. Mavis has started to doze off but sits up suddenly every once in a while as though she doesn't want to succumb to sleep. I tell Jamie to pick a game. *Trouble* is her choice, which is fortunate for everyone, because I don't think any of the adults can handle anything too challenging at this point.

Halfway through the game, the doorbell rings once more. Scott says he'll get it.

"Officer Parker, for me," he says when he returns, no further explanation.

By the time we're done playing, with me being the big loser, it's totally dark outside. Once I tuck the kids into bed, I return to the family room to ask Scott what he wanted to talk about earlier. Mavis is asleep, slumped over on the sofa.

"Shh…" Scott whispers, his finger to his lips. He gets up and steers me toward the hall, down to the living room.

"I'll be right back," he says after he sits me down on the sofa. "I've got something for you."

He returns with a small notebook.

"What's that? Another one of Julia's journals?" Taking it from his hand as he holds it out, I read the cover. I feel a big smile spread over my face as I realize it's for me. He tells me to open it. The inside cover reads: **To the best partner and friend in crime solving I've ever had. Scott.**

"Thank you. That's so thoughtful. It's beautiful. You've given me lots to write about, that's for sure." I give him a hug as he sits down beside me and asks where my leg hurts. "It's nothing. Just a little bruise on my thigh where I hit the floor. It'll be fine." I rub my leg where it connects with my hip.

Before I know it, he swivels me to the side and gently places my leg on the sofa with a throw cushion under it. "I moonlight as a registered massage therapist," he says with a grin.

"Really?" I'm skeptical.

"No, not really. But I can make you feel better." His hands are firm yet gentle as he reaches over and strokes my bruised hip. It does start to feel better. He's not making any inappropriate moves, and it's heavenly, so I allow him to continue. After a few minutes, though, his hands wander a little too far, and I caution him. "Careful what you're doing. I'm a happily married woman."

"Sorry, my hand slipped," he says with that disarming smile of his. But I don't believe him, not for one second. I'm not sure I can trust him. But I *am* enjoying this great massage.

Scott changes the topic abruptly. "There's something I wanted to ask you. I've been afraid to bring it up, but I guess this is as good a time as any, especially since Jim's not here."

I'm both nervous and curious about where this is leading. He moves the pillow out from under my leg and moves closer, placing my thigh directly in his lap. My muscles must tense up because he tells me I need to relax and loosen up a bit. "I'd ask Jim directly, but since he's not here, maybe you can give me the answers I need."

"Okay," I whisper, very aware of his hands on my upper leg. I'm glad Mavis is staying here. I've unwittingly put myself in a compromising situation, if not a dangerous one. I remind myself he's a respectable member of the police force.

"Is there any reason why Jim's fingerprints would be in the abandoned house across from Julia's?" he asks. That's not a question I was expecting.

When I tell him Jim showed the house recently, he nods and says, "Oh, okay." Then he continues, eyebrows raised. "And would there be an explanation for why Jim was in Julia's bedroom at some point?"

I don't know what he's getting at. "Why are you asking where Jim's been?"

"I suspect his prints are at all the crime scenes."

"What? Why would you think that? What are you suggesting? Is he a suspect? You think he has something to do with Julia's disappearance? And he took the baby?" Why would Scott think that? It's absolutely insane. My eyes focus on him, seeing him in a different light. Is he trying to frame my husband for something?

"The prints on the snow globe in Lacey's room match prints in the abandoned house and on Julia's bedroom phone. I have good reason to suspect the globe came from Jim, and the unidentified prints taken from it belong to him."

"Well, of course, his prints are on it. He gives those globes to his clients as a housewarming gift. And his prints are in the abandoned house because he showed it last week." My voice rises, though I'm conscious of the kids possibly overhearing. How dare he accuse Jim?

"What about Julia's bedroom?"

"I don't know. Jim must have used her phone for some reason. He sold her the house. She works for him. He probably stopped in to talk to her about something. That's all there is to it." I can't believe him, thinking Jim might be involved.

He nods again, saying, "I guess that explains it, then. That's good. Jim had legitimate reasons to be in all three places."

Although his words and smile tell me he's no longer suspicious of my husband, there's something in his eyes that makes me think he's just a bit disappointed. Did he honestly think he had the case wrapped up?

"Listen, there's something else I need to tell you," Scott says as he takes hold of one of my hands and keeps his eyes on mine.

Just then, Mavis walks in to see me with my leg on Scott's lap and his hand moving up and down rhythmically.

"Cheryl!" She's clearly shocked by my brazen behavior. "Your husband..."

I remove my leg quickly with a loud yelp and sit up properly. "Detective Evans was just massaging my bruise. He's a registered massage therapist."

I can tell she's not buying it. Mavis wedges herself between the two of us.

"What else did you want to tell me?" I strain forward and backwards, trying to get around Mavis so I can see his expression.

"I've got some bad news." He leans forward, trying to bypass Mavis. "Could we have a few moments of privacy?"

"Is it Jim?" My heart thumps loudly enough for them to hear it. "Is he okay?"

Please, please, please, don't let it be Jim.

Scott jumps out of his spot and kneels in front of me, putting his hand on mine, circumventing Mavis. "No, not Jim. Cheryl, no, Jim's fine. I'm sorry I scared you."

Mavis suggests we reconvene at the kitchen table. Scott helps me up, leads me down the hall, and pulls out a kitchen chair for me.

"What bad news?" I don't really want to hear it.

"A body was found this afternoon in Emery Park," Scott says. My face must register shock because I can feel the blood draining out of it. "I know you were hoping for a happily ever after for Julia and Danny, but that's not going to happen."

"Who…What…?" I try to process what he's telling me. "Is it Julia?"

"It's a male. The body was found on the side of a steep slope by firefighters. They were in the process of creating a fire break when they saw him. The coroner says he's been there a couple of weeks, so it could have been there since Danny went missing." Scott pauses to let me take it all in. "When he examined the body, the coroner couldn't come up with a definitive cause of death. Either he accidentally slipped and fell over the edge, or he was in an altercation with someone."

"So it was an accident? But it could have been murder? Is that what you're saying?'

"That was what I thought until tonight. Until Officer Parker came to the door."

"What do you mean?"

"Danny's truck was found at Emery Park. When the forensic team went through it, they found something." He goes into the dining room and brings back an evidence bag with a piece of paper folded inside.

"What is it?"

"It's a typed note, found on the passenger seat of Danny's truck." Pulling a pair of plastic gloves out of his pocket, he removes the note, careful to not leave prints, and reads it out loud:

I'm so sorry. I never meant for this to happen. When Julia found out I was dealing drugs she wanted to call it off between us. I went to her place that night but she wouldn't let me in the house so I got her to come with me in the car and go for a drive to talk things out. When I said we could run away together and start a new life she just kind of freaked out and told me to pull over and then she ran off into the forest. I think she thought I was going to hurt her or force her to come with me but I would never do that. I followed her but I lost her and she wouldn't come when I called out. It was dark and I couldn't find her. We weren't too far away from

the house. I didn't know what else to do so I went back to her place and called 911 and hoped the police would find her or she'd somehow come back home herself. I was too scared to tell the truth. I thought I'd get blamed for doing something to her if they didn't find her. I kept trying to find her myself. But the more time passed I knew something terrible had happened and it was my fault. When they couldn't find her I knew she must be lost for good or dead. The detective kept asking me questions. I knew he suspected I did something to her. I can't face knowing I'm responsible. I'm sorry. I hope you find her.

Danny

"I don't understand," I say when he looks up from the note.

"It looks like this could be a suicide note. Danny felt responsible for what happened to Julia, but he didn't want to admit his involvement. If he had just told the truth in the first place, maybe we would have had some chance of finding her."

"What are you saying? Is Julia still lost out in the forest somewhere?"

"I'm saying it's unlikely we're going to find Julia at this point. I'm sorry. I wish things were different."

Easing myself out of my chair to stand at Scott's shoulder, I peer down over the note. It's printed on MacGregor Realty letterhead. "It looks like Danny's signature."

"Clearly, it was premeditated. He planned to jump."

"But what about the baby?"

"Like I said before, it's usually one of the parents when it comes to child abductions. I don't think it has anything to do with Julia and Danny, after all."

"What about the baby stuff bought on Danny's credit card?"

"Someone must have stolen his credit card somewhere along the line. The chances are that he was already dead by the time the purchase was made."

"So Julia's dead?" I can't believe this. It makes no sense at all. She was supposed to be off with her boyfriend somewhere. I was so sure of it. "All because Danny took her for a drive, and she ran out of the car? Why wouldn't he tell the police what happened when he called 911?"

"I don't think we'll ever really understand. The only two people who know what happened are dead. Maybe he did do something to her, and he couldn't admit it, even to himself. It's surprising what goes on behind closed doors. And what goes on in some people's minds. The stress of living with what he'd done must have finally gotten to him." The phone rings. "I'll get it." After answering, he covers the mouthpiece. "Can I get you to join Mavis in the living room? It's for me. Police business."

Why are they calling my number?

As I slowly move down the hall, I notice a flash of movement, disappearing around the corner. Mavis has been listening in on our conversation.

"That poor girl. I knew something was wrong," she says when I walk into the living room.

The whole story sounds kind of fishy to me. "Why on earth would Danny not tell the police where he left her?"

"How awful, she was such a nice girl." Tears pool in the corner of Mavis' eyes. "I just knew something terrible happened when I saw the police car come and go from her house late that night. When I saw Danny pulling into her driveway later, I assumed everything was okay and went back to bed. I had no idea she was missing. And then the police were all over the place when I woke up in the morning."

"The police car came to Julia's house before Danny did?"

"Well, yes, dear. The police car was there just after Julia came home, around one o'clock. Then Danny came at about a quarter to two."

How could the police have responded to Danny's 911 call before he made it? Mavis must be confused.

"You didn't tell me there was a police car at Julia's *before* Danny got there."

"I told you I saw Danny and the police."

Scott returns to the living room; I ask who was on the phone.

"Work, like I said."

Just then, the power goes off, plunging the three of us into darkness. A sudden, crazy thought finds its way into my brain. Am I sitting here in the dark, with an injured leg, a sweet little old lady next to me, my kids sleeping helplessly in their rooms, my husband out fighting a fire, and a psychotic killer making himself at home in my house?

I guess you never know about people.

Chapter Seventy-One

Julia

Julia is becoming frantic. He should be coming for them. With the fire from the west threatening as it creeps closer and smoke now appearing from the east, they're going to be surrounded if help doesn't arrive soon. Packing up her few belongings and the baby's things, she's ready to be evacuated anytime. If he doesn't come himself, surely, he'll send someone else.

That first night, Julia was terrified when she realized what he planned to do. Even though he explained it was for the best, that she needed to leave her old life behind for them to make a fresh start, she knew this wasn't the way to go about it. It wasn't what she wanted. Her parents no longer controlled her life, and she didn't see the point in running away.

Now, stuck in this cabin, she misses her family and friends. She wants to go home. The forest frightens her, especially after sunset. Although the cabin is rustic and charming, and the lake is peaceful, the days go on and on. She's tired of reading and going for short walks. It's a vacation in hell. The fear of getting lost in the woods keeps her within eyesight of the cabin, and the romance of the situation is overshadowed by the horror of how he abducted and imprisoned her without consent.

But he's been good. He would never do anything to hurt her. He's proven his love over and over by checking on her welfare and bringing little gifts. He held and stroked her, kissed her, never expecting anything she didn't willingly give. The baby was the ultimate confirmation of his commitment. When he brought him earlier in the week, she was shocked. But when she looked at the tiny little thing with his cute, chubby face, her heart melted. This was the child she should have had seven years ago if her parents hadn't taken that choice away. That night, their first night as a family, they made love in front of the fire. Everything seemed perfect. And it wasn't like he stole the baby. He told her he meant to return him to his mother once they were pregnant with a child of their own. And although she knows it was wrong for him to take the baby, even if it is his son, in her heart, she knows he did it for her. Because he loves her.

Now, as she watches death approaching, she knows he'll come. The only question is whether he'll make it in time.

Chapter Seventy-Two

Danny

Two Weeks Earlier

A call to Danny's number comes from Julia's house. Is it Julia or someone else? Someone messing with his head? When Danny hangs up, he tries calling her. There's no answer. He runs out the door and climbs into his pickup and drives back to West Kipling. Once again, he pounds on the doors and peers through windows, looking for some sign of life inside. Everything is quiet. Danny considers breaking in to see if Julia has come back or if someone else is with her, holding her captive. Like her stalker.

Maybe this is a trap. I don't need to get arrested for a break-and-enter. Or snooping around a crime scene.

Danny decides to go home, wondering whether the phone lines got crossed or something. Maybe he should call the police.

Just as Danny enters his apartment, the phone rings again.

Is someone playing a cruel game with me?

This time, it's the police. When the person on the other end of the line identifies himself, Danny wonders what's going on now. Are they going to question him *again*?

"I thought you might want to know we have a lead on Julia's whereabouts. We received an anonymous phone call from someone who claims to have seen a woman matching her description."

"Where?" Danny holds onto the counter to support himself.

"In Emery Provincial Park. We're heading out there this afternoon, but we can't possibly cover the whole area. It could be nothing. I know if it were my girlfriend, I'd want to check it out personally."

"Where exactly was she seen?"

"On the Bog trail. But we're already checking that out. We won't be able to get to all the trails today."

"Where should I be looking, then?" Danny's eager to find out if Julia is there. Is it possible? Then who called from her house?

"If you'd like, I'm available this afternoon. I have a few things I need to do before I can leave, but if you want to head out, we could meet there later in the day."

"Yeah, that'd be great. Where should I meet you? What time?"

"At the west end of Miner's Trail, how about 5:30? There's a turnoff just off the highway, to the left, where the sign is. It's a narrow path, but wide enough to get your car through. Take a look around the area yourself first, if you want, and I'll meet you at your vehicle."

"Sounds good. I'll see you there. Oh, and thanks, man." Danny hangs up the phone and wonders what to make of this. Taking along a bottle of water, he locks up his apartment and sets off for Emery Park. If Julia's there, he wants to be the one to find her.

About two hours later, he's in Emery Park. Maneuvering his vehicle down the dirt path where he was instructed to park, he doesn't see anyone around. Leaving the windows down a crack, he steps out of his pickup and tentatively walks around the area. Ten minutes later, someone approaches from behind.

The two men greet each other, and Danny eagerly heads toward Miner's Trail.

"Hold on a minute. I think we should have a look beyond the trail in case she's wandered off and lost her way. We can cover the trail later," the other man suggests.

Danny agrees that makes sense. The two of them wander off the path, in the opposite direction of the trail, deep into the forest, following a narrow path. They get their shoes wet crossing a stream. Further along, a steep ravine cuts off the path.

"I guess this is as far as we can go in this direction," Danny observes.

"Yeah, I think this is the end."

"I don't know why she'd be in Emery Park, anyway. She wouldn't have come here on her own. And her car's in the driveway." Danny considers the possibility that someone took her against her will and brought her here. He doesn't want to think about what might have happened. "Do you think someone's hurt her? I've been thinking about the phone calls. It looked to me like the wires on the phone box outside her house might have been disconnected. I'm wondering if that's why she didn't answer the phone when I tried calling her that night. What if someone planned to take her?"

"The phone wires were tampered with? Are you sure?"

"It looked off to me." After a short silence, he adds, "Do you think she could be dead?"

"It's usually the husband or boyfriend who'd be the main suspect in that case."

Danny once again feels he's being railroaded.

They're trying to pin this on me.

"Well, I know it wasn't me," he says. "And there's only one other boyfriend Julia ever had. Do you think he could have come back and done something to her?"

"She had another boyfriend? Why didn't you mention that before?"

"It was a long time ago. She hasn't been seeing him. I got the feeling he hurt her real bad. She didn't really want to talk about him." Danny faces the other man, and something dawns on him. "I wonder if he's the one she thought was following her."

"Did she *say* he was following her?"

"She didn't say who it was, but she felt she was being watched. I wonder if she was being stalked by someone she knew. Do you think it could have been him?"

"Did she give you a name?"

"A first name, that's all. She wouldn't tell me much about him. Said he wasn't important." They're standing at the edge of the treed ravine, where it slopes suddenly a couple hundred feet down to the bottom. "Actually, it's the same as your name." Danny watches the other man's reaction.

"Well, it's obviously not me. There are a lot of guys with my name."

"Julia said he was a real scumbag." Danny knows he's embellishing, but he wants to point the cops in a different direction, away from himself. "He treated her like a piece of meat. Some older guy who took advantage of her. Knocked her up and threw her aside like garbage."

It comes out of the blue. Danny feels the blow to his stomach, and he doubles over. "What the hell?" He doesn't have a chance to say much more. Another blow connects with his shoulder, knocking him to his knees.

"Sorry, I don't like men talking about women that way," he says as he helps Danny back up. "It's not respectful."

Danny doesn't care if this guy is a cop; he's not going to put up with getting his ass kicked. He pulls himself to a standing position and looks him in the eyes. There's something dark there. Something he hasn't noticed before. Danny takes a swing at him. "You wouldn't happen to be that scumbag, would you?" His blow misses its target. He tries again, this time connecting with the man's jaw. "Are you the guy who knocked her up and ruined her life?"

His question is met with a shove. "You're the scumbag! She's too good for you. Does she know you're dealing drugs?"

The fight escalates with more shoving and punching. Another blow hits him, sending him off balance.

From somewhere in the forest, Danny hears someone shout. "Hey!"

His last thought as he goes over the edge is that he hopes Julia is safe.

Chapter Seventy-Three

Cheryl

July 25

Scott fetches flashlights from the kitchen and brings them to the living room. "I guess we should all head to bed now anyway." He hands a flashlight to me and one to Mavis. "We'll see where things stand tomorrow." That's how the night ends, with everyone going to their separate beds just after midnight.

He seems to be acting normally, not like a psychopath at all. I really am letting my imagination go wild. Scott Evans is a respectable detective sergeant with the provincial police. He wouldn't be in that position if there was any reason to doubt his integrity. Just because he likes women doesn't mean there's anything nefarious about him. I'm just trying to convince myself he's hiding something to counteract the attraction drawing me to him.

When I wake up this morning to find him in the kitchen, slathering peanut butter and jam on slices of bread for the kids and himself, I realize exactly how silly I was to think for a moment that he might be involved with Julia or Lacey. And if he wants to date Sheila, that's his business. I've got no right to be jealous.

"Want some breakfast?" He notices me staring at him. "I make a mean peanut butter and jelly sandwich. Just one of my many talents."

With the power still out, coffee isn't an option this morning, so I pour myself a glass of the orange juice he's set out on the counter. "Sounds good." I take a seat at the table where the kids are already sitting, a milk mustache formed on Jamie's upper lip.

"I'm going to the station after breakfast. There are some things that need my attention," Scott informs me. "I want to thank you again for taking me in last night." He pauses, then adds, "How's your leg?"

"Better, thanks."

"I told you I was good at massaging. Anytime you want more..."

"I'm sure you're good at a lot of things. And, by the way, I like a man who knows his way around a kitchen." He responds to my compliment with a smile as he sets plates of peanut butter and jelly on bread in front of Brent and Jamie, and heads back to the counter to make more.

"So, what do you have planned for today?" Scott joins us at the table, setting down a plate for me and one for himself.

"Just hanging out, I guess. With no power, it kind of limits what I can do around the house. Maybe I'll just read." My bigger concern is how to keep the kids entertained with no morning children's programming. Maybe we can go outside for a bit; the air doesn't seem too smoky. Hopefully, Mavis likes a good book.

Just then, Mavis enters the kitchen, and Scott asks if she would like some breakfast. Taking one look at the options, she turns to me. "Do you happen to have any cereal? High fiber, preferably?"

Once everyone's fed, Brent asks Scott if he wants to go out to shoot some hoops. My son seems to have taken a real liking to Detective Evans.

"Detective Evans has work to do," I say.

"I've got time." Scott gets up from the table and puts his plate, along with Brent's, into the sink. "Let's go."

Mavis and I spend the next half hour sitting on the deck watching the boys play, while Jamie sways back and forth on the swing set. "Have you heard any more from your husband?" I suspect that's her way of reminding me I'm married.

"No, but he said I might not hear anything for a while. So, I'm trying not to worry."

"He'll be fine, just busy. He's a brave man. I'm sure you're very proud of him."

"Oh, I am. He's a wonderful man. Jim always puts others ahead of himself. He's a great husband and father. I'm so lucky to have him."

"You must love him a lot." She says it in a way that makes me feel guilty. A woman who's deeply in love with her amazing husband shouldn't be feeling any kind of attraction to another man. Should she?

"I do. He's everything to me. I can't imagine living without him."

She nods and is about to say something, then seems to change her mind. Scott heads in our direction. The three of us sit in silence for a few minutes and watch the smoke in the distance.

"Is that radio in the kitchen battery-powered?" Scott bolts out of his chair before I confirm that it is. "I want to hear what the local station is reporting about the fire."

CBLK plays a mixture of rock, country, and pop. Presumably in an effort to please everyone. In reality, it just irritates a lot of people. Right now, they're playing "Wicked Game". It seems like a long wait until the news finally comes on at ten o'clock.

The big story, of course, is that a body has been found in a treed ravine at Emery Park, and police are investigating. The death is not connected to the fires raging in the area. Lake Kipling is still under an evacuation advisory, and residents of West Kipling are not to return to their homes yet. The highway north to Timber Lake remains closed. Although the wind has caused the flames to shift toward the northeast to an uninhabited area, that could change at any time. Emery Park is still in the path of the fire, and fire crews are hard at work slowing down the spread. There have been no injuries or deaths reported as a result of the fires.

"Thank God!" I didn't mean for it to come out so loud, but hearing someone announce it on the radio, for some reason, gives me confirmation that Jim is fine. I feel like I've been holding my breath since he left. The thought of turning on the radio and hearing bad news was something I couldn't deal with, so I kept it off until now.

"He'll be fine," Scott and Mavis both say the words, almost simultaneously. A sense of relief blankets me when I hear their assurances.

Until the phone rings. Then I nearly jump out of my skin.

"I've got it," Scott insists as he rushes in through the patio door. I follow him as quickly as I can and hear him say he can take a message. Judging from the look of disbelief on his face, I know it's not good news. He stands there, head bent, one hand on the phone and the other holding his forehead. "Yes, I'll let her know. Okay, thanks. I appreciate it."

"What is it?" I'm unable to conceal the alarm coursing through my body.

"Nothing." He still appears stunned. "Just one of those telemarketers. I'm assuming you don't need your ducts cleaned?"

Chapter Seventy-Four

He needs to get them out of there. At first, he assumed they would be safe, out of reach of the fire. But as the wind direction changed and two fires converged into one, he grew worried it might make its way to the cabin. When he learned a blaze had started east of Emery Park as well, and there was a concern it would join with the fire to the west, there was no question they couldn't stay put.

His grandparents' cabin is situated on a lake in a remote area thirty minutes northeast of Lake Kipling. This summer, his elderly grandparents weren't feeling up to spending time there. Instead, they elected to stay in town in their small bungalow, close to the health facilities. That worked out perfectly for him. The cabin was the ideal spot for the two of them or three as it turned out, to spend some quality time together alone before starting their new life together.

The night he took her, he used a penlight and a small toolkit to disconnect her phone wires before she returned home so she wouldn't be able to make or receive calls. Once he had Julia in the car, he told her he thought he heard a noise in the back yard and wanted to check it out. That was when he reconnected the wires so no one would know the lines had been tampered with.

When he brought her to the cabin, she made a run for it as soon as she got out of the car. Of course, she didn't get far. It was dark, and she didn't know the area like he did. When he spotted her with his flashlight, he convinced her it was safe, that she could trust him. For the first week, he locked the doors to the cabin from the outside and rigged the windows so they could only open so far. He told her it was for her own good, and warned that if she broke out, he wasn't going to look for her. No one was going to find her out in the wilderness except maybe the bears or wolves, the coyotes and lynx.

His threats worked. Julia stayed inside reading and waited dutifully for him to visit each day. When he knew he could trust her, he allowed access to the outside, but reminded her to stay near the cabin and out of the lake. He had gone back to her house and fetched some of her belongings when she asked for the inhaler. And almost got caught. He knew she looked forward to his visits as much as he did, but he could tell she was still lonely. That's when he thought about the baby. It was his child, after all. Although he wasn't ready to be straddled with kids, Julia wanted nothing more than a baby.

There was no reason why he couldn't take Christopher off Lacey's hands for a while. And it wasn't like Lacey was going to say anything. He had warned her that if anyone found out he was the father, he'd make sure her drug addiction would result in Christopher going into foster care while she served a jail sentence. She wasn't fit to be a mother. Julia, on the other hand, would be a perfect mother to his boy until she became pregnant herself.

It's too early to set her free. She's not ready to admit to everyone that she voluntarily left her house and ran off without notifying family and friends. There's no chance she'd stick to the story he made up to explain her absence. But the fire's just too close. That's not the only threat to their happiness, though.

Terry Lawrence. It's only a matter of time before he starts talking to everyone. He can't wait any longer. It's time to take them somewhere else. Time for him to go on the run with his family.

Chapter Seventy-Five

Cheryl

There's more to this than duct cleaning. He's acting strange, secretive. One thing I can spot a mile away is when someone's hiding something. I'm a master at hiding the truth myself, even *from* myself. I guess it's true what they say—it takes one to know one.

"I need to call the station to check on a few things. I'll be a little while," Scott says. "Why don't you go back outside?" Now I know he's hiding something from me.

Jamie's on the climbers and Mavis is keeping an eye on her. "You go ahead and make your call. I'm just going to tidy up a bit inside." In the family room, I fluff throw pillows and tidy up toys while I listen in to his conversation.

"Would Officer Parker happen to be in? That's okay. I'll talk to him, thanks." For a minute, I don't hear any more, then he says, "What? Are you sure? How the hell did that happen?"

I come running into the kitchen to find out what's going on. "What?" I whisper. Scott shakes his head and mouths for me to be quiet. "What is it?"

"Just a minute." He puts his hand over the mouthpiece. Turning to me, he says, "Could you give me a few minutes?" With a wave of his hand, he indicates I should go back outside. He's got his nerve, bossing me around in my own house.

It's a long phone call. He comes out to the deck, his face unreadable. "I have to run. I'll call you later. Something's come up."

What isn't he telling me? As I watch him pull out of the driveway, I'm curious to know what exactly came up and where exactly he's going without giving me a clue. Maybe there's a way I can figure out what he's up to. When I check the caller ID on the phone, I notice that Rebecca has called. Why did he tell me it was the duct cleaners?

Chapter Seventy-Six

Scott

"Hello, this is Rebecca. Is Cheryl there?" When she called, she must have assumed I was Cheryl's husband. I didn't tell her otherwise. I couldn't believe it when she told me she remembered the name of Julia's ex-boyfriend. When Officer Murphy told me drugs missing from lockup were seized from Terry Lawrence's car and apartment, I needed to think fast. The pieces were falling into place quickly.

I don't know how this is going to play out. But one thing I don't need is Cheryl tagging along with me.

My first stop is Lacey's house. She's expectant when she answers the door. "Where is he? Did you find him?"

"Not yet. But if you want him back, there's something I need from you." There's no way I'm taking no for an answer. "With the fires spreading, time's running out. If you love Christopher as much as you say you do, I know you'll do anything to make sure he's safe."

It doesn't take long for me to convince her. My next stop is the cabin in the woods. It's about a thirty-minute drive northeast to Kelly's Lake. The cabin is secluded, in an area where no one would ever look. It was built many decades ago as a hunting retreat. The access road is a narrow, dirt road that doesn't appear to go anywhere. You have to know where you're going in order to find it.

The sky's clouding up, so that could be a good sign. A good long downpour would aid firefighters in getting things under control. On the other hand, it might signal the possibility of more lightning strikes.

Like most back roads in the area, Fishbank Road is a two-lane winding gravel road through the middle of a dense forest. Not much to see. I'm not out for a scenic drive, though. My purpose is to get them out of there. Assuming I'm not too late.

Chapter Seventy-Seven

Cheryl

I know he's lied to me. He seems like a nice guy, a good cop, someone people would trust. But I should know better than anyone that you can't judge a book by its cover. As cliche as that sounds, it's true. People aren't always who or what they appear to be. Before I became Cheryl, I was Svjetlana, someone I no longer recognize myself. That seems like a whole lifetime ago.

What did Rebecca tell him? I asked her to call back if she remembered the name of Julia's old boyfriend. Is that why she called? Why did Scott hide that from me? Why did he run out of here in such a hurry? He said he was going to the station. I don't believe that for one minute. The secrecy around the phone calls and his rush to leave leads me to think he's got somewhere else to go.

Should I call the station and see if he's there? Maybe someone will tell me where he is or where he's going. He won't like me doing that, I'm sure. My nosiness isn't one of my better qualities. Even Jim doesn't care for it. Maybe I should respect Scott's wishes and stay out of whatever's going on. If he wanted me to know, he would have told me.

Just as I'm about to head back outside, I glance over at the fridge. A sheet has been torn off the magnetic notepad, leaving part of it stuck behind. On the page underneath, I see the faint imprint left by the pressure of a pen. With a pencil, I lightly rub over the imprint to bring it into focus. A map, doodled across the torn page.

Now I know where Scott is headed. I climb up to our bedroom, open my nightstand drawer, and remove my unloaded Glock 17 from beneath a pile of magazines. Then I open the safe in our closet to retrieve the locked metal box containing the ammunition. I hoped I would never have to use it again, but I *will* do whatever's necessary. I always have and always will. I'll protect Julia and the baby the same way I protected myself and my own baby.

Mavis doesn't mind watching the kids while I'm gone. Telling her exactly where I'm going, just in case Scott turns out to be a crazed killer, or I get trapped in the fire, or some other disaster befalls me, I grab my purse and set out to Kelly's Lake.

"I'm following Scott. If I don't call or come back in a few hours, phone the station and let them know where I went." Mavis looks at me like I've lost my mind and asks if it's about Julia. "Yes, I think Scott knows where she is. And I'm going to find her."

Chapter Seventy-Eight

Julia

July 5, Early Morning

Julia had a great night out with her friends. She enjoys letting loose a bit every now and then. Rarely does she have more than one drink. Tonight, she's had two. Although she wonders whether she should be driving herself home, she decides it's fine. There won't be much traffic this time of night. She'll take it slow, with the window rolled down for fresh air.

When she pulls into her driveway and shuts off the engine, she takes her house key out of her purse before exiting the car. The porch light has been left on, and she has only a few feet to walk to the front door. Although she feels safe in her neighborhood, living on the edge of town next to the forest can be a bit unsettling. And during the last few weeks, she has sensed someone following her. A noise, but no one's there by the time she looks. A shadow, a glimpse of someone. She could swear someone out there is watching her every move. It's happened in Lake Kipling, it's happened at work, it's happened at home. Could it be *him*? Maybe she's just being paranoid. Why would *he* be stalking her?

When she started bumping into him around town several months ago, they both acted as though they were old acquaintances, nothing more. They had a few casual conversations. Then he asked her out for dinner. She was impressed that he had turned his life around and was making something of himself. They broke up years ago; he said he wasn't ready to be saddled with a kid, so she got the abortion her parents pressured her into having. They went their separate ways. But he'd said he was going back to school, going to become a cop, a detective someday, and that she'd be proud of him.

And she is. Proud. Seeing him in his new role is heartwarming. He's a new man. A part of her wondered if there was any chance they could get back together and whether he was thinking the same thing. Seeing him again brought back all the old feelings. But she's with Danny now, and they've been discussing a future together. When she told him about Danny, his face remained neutral, and he wished her good luck. Then, he slipped out of her life as quickly as he had slipped back in.

She turns the key and is met by Cleo as soon as the door swings open. That puts her at ease immediately. Julia bends down to stroke Cleo's silky fur as she purrs around her legs. "I missed you, too. You're my guard cat. Good girl."

Locking the door, Julia sets down her purse and goes to the kitchen to boil the kettle. While it's heating, she changes out of her sundress and sweater into pajamas, scrubs off her makeup, brushes her teeth and her hair.

Ten minutes later, she's settled under the covers, with a cup of hot cocoa and a Twinkie. The radio plays music in the background for company; Julia opens her book, Cleo curled up beside her. "Shoot, I forgot! I'm supposed to call Danny." She thinks how sweet he is, worrying and checking up on her these last few weeks after she told him she suspected someone was stalking her. He never once made her feel like she was overreacting. Danny is such a nice guy. She knows her parents will learn to like him as much as she does once they get to know him better. When she picks up the phone to call him, the line is dead. "That's odd," she says to Cleo, who watches her through slitted eyes. "The phone lines must be down."

She's immersed in the middle of an exciting part of her mystery novel when the doorbell rings, making her jump. Who would be at her door this late? It's just past one o'clock. It rings again. Julia sets her book down on the bed and puts on her robe. She's not about to answer at this time of night. Peering through a tiny slit in the living room curtains, she checks out the driveway. There's a police car sitting behind her Sunfire. Her first thought is that she was spotted driving after being out drinking. Then it occurs to her that maybe something is wrong. Maybe something happened to her parents. Or Danny.

Without hesitation, she unlocks the front door and flings it open, stunned by who she sees. "Oh...! It's you!" Although she knew he was back in town, she certainly never expected him to show up on her doorstep, especially in the middle of the night, unannounced.

Now, here he is at her door. "Hi, Julia. Everything's fine, but I need you to come with me," he says when she asks why he's there. "There's been an accident a few minutes down the road. It's Danny. He's fine, but he asked for you to come. I'll take you to him."

"Oh no! Is he hurt? How bad is it?"

"He's fine. Rear-ended somebody. He's shaken up, but his truck's not in good shape."

"Is he in the hospital?"

"No, it's not that serious. He's staying with the guy in the other vehicle until the tow truck comes for them."

Julia slides on her new white sandals, grabs the spare keys from the entrance table, locks the door, and lets herself be escorted into the waiting police car. "Shouldn't I take my car?" This only occurs to her once she's buckled herself in. "It'll save you the trouble of coming back here."

"It's no trouble at all. I took a cruiser down the highway after someone called in a complaint about a black Ram speeding out of town. Lucky for Danny, I stumbled upon the scene right after it happened. I'll just let the speeding ticket slide this time, as he's your friend."

He cocks his ear to the right before closing Julia's door. "Just a sec. I thought I heard something out back. Stay here while I check it out."

He's back in a few minutes, saying it was just a raccoon. They head out of town. It's only when they have traveled about ten minutes toward Lake Kipling that Julia begins to wonder why they haven't come across the accident yet.

"Sorry, I guess it's a little farther than I thought," comes the answer. But when the car turns off the main highway toward the north, Julia starts to panic.

"Where are we going? Where are you taking me? Danny wouldn't be on this road!"

"Relax, everything's going to be okay."

Julia doesn't relax. Just the opposite, as realization hits. He's not taking her to Danny. Her pulse pounds as shivers course through her body. "Take me home! Turn the car around! Let me go!"

"I can't do that, Julia. You're meant to be with me, not Danny. You don't have all the facts about him. He's not who you think he is."

When Julia tries to open the door of the police car, she finds it locked. Screaming, she tries to roll down the window, but it won't budge. "Let me out of the car! Now!"

He doesn't speak the rest of the way, other than to tell her to calm down, everything's okay. When he parks the car in front of the cabin and unlocks her door, she makes a run for it. She doesn't get far. "Don't make me handcuff you." He pulls out a set of cuffs from his back pocket. "I'm not going to hurt you. I just want us to spend some alone time to get to know each other again. A mini vacation, you and me. That's all."

The sight of the handcuffs makes her more compliant. "No, don't. Please."

"Are you going to behave?"

"Yes, yes. I'll be good."

"That's my girl."

He tells her he's already ensured the cabin's ready for their arrival. Firewood is chopped and stacked for the cool nights, with an adequate supply of kindling and matches, and fans will keep her comfortable during the hot afternoons. The generator has a full tank of fuel. The cupboards and fridge are well stocked. Fresh linens are on the beds and fresh towels hang in the bathroom. There are books and magazines, along with a battery-powered radio to keep her entertained. If there's anything else she needs or desires, he'll get it for her. He plans to spend as much time here with her as possible. One thing he doesn't leave her—a phone.

* * *

In time, he hopes she will understand that he's doing this for them. Everything is for her. While staying in the abandoned house down the road to keep an eye out for Julia and following her at a distance, he put together his plan to get Julia back from Danny, her drug-dealing boyfriend. Knowing she was alone that night, he cut her phone wires so they would be undisturbed. The morning before, he had slipped into her house and stole Julia's cell phone from her purse while she showered for work. He didn't need Danny butting in while they worked on reconciling.

A quiet time for just the two of them is exactly what they need. Time away from her controlling parents and her drug-dealing obsessive boyfriend.

Once he has her settled down and promises he'll be back tomorrow, he kisses her and says he loves her, he always has, and always will. Then he gets back into his vehicle and embarks on the thirty-minute drive back to Lake Kipling, ready to play his role as a respected authority figure, no longer known as the guy who likes to party. No, that reckless behavior is all behind him now.

Chapter Seventy-Nine

H is car pulls up in front of the cabin. Julia is so excited to see him, she runs into his arms as he exits the vehicle. "I knew you'd come back for us," she cries, breathless.

"I'd never leave you. Why would you think that? It's just been hard to get away, with what's going on at the station and the fire. But we need to get out of here. It's not safe anymore."

"I've already packed everything." They look toward the fire on either side of them and realize there's no other option but to leave. What they don't agree on is where they're going. "I can't wait to get home."

His demeanor shows no indication that he's not planning on taking her home. It's simply not possible now. Even with the suicide note he'd typed on Danny's computer and the signature he'd copied the night he used Julia's key to enter the real estate office, there's going to be an official inquest into Danny's death. Terry Lawrence isn't likely to keep quiet about what he knows when he's pressured. Then there's the baby. They're not going to give him any kind of visitation rights now.

"Good. I'll pack up the car, while you make sure everything's left the way it was when we got here. I don't want to leave any sign that someone's been here." They go into the cabin and begin the process of evacuating.

Following one trip to the car and back, he hears a car engine in the distance. He tells her to take the baby and go out to the woods to wait until he calls her.

"Why? What's going on?"

"Just do as you're told." When she doesn't move, he shouts, "Now! Get

Christopher and head toward the south as far as you can get. I'll come find you. Go!"

* * *

From the tone of his voice, she knows something is terribly wrong. Julia gently picks up Christopher from his cot, leaves through the back door, and walks into the forest. She follows the path of least resistance through the dense growth, holding the baby tightly. As she moves farther from the cabin, she looks back to see him following, his arms overloaded with bags full of the clothing and essentials he brought from her house and the baby's stuff. He's trying to erase any trace of Julia and the baby having ever been at the cabin. Julia keeps walking farther, deep into the forest, as he told her to do. She doesn't want to disappoint him by disobeying. Especially after he's gone through so much effort to turn his life around to become a well-respected member of the force everyone looks up to. For her. So they could be together.

He's not the bad guy.

* * *

In the cabin, he gathers more of the items he brought and prepares to hide them in the forest when he hears the car pull up. It's too late to run. The only option now is to fight or surrender. He has no intention of surrendering.

When he peers out the front door and recognizes the vehicle, he realizes there's no way he's going to explain this to the intruder on his property. Gun drawn, he steps outside.

The shape standing beside the unwelcome car takes a slow, tentative step forward, arm raised, gun pointed. "It's over. I know what you've done. Put the gun down. You don't want to shoot me."

Chapter Eighty

Cheryl

C It's a bumpy ride down the dirt path. I have a hard time believing there's a cabin at the end of it. But I can see a set of tire tracks on the road. Someone's obviously been down this road recently. The fires burn on either side of me, black smoke in the sky, the smell of burnt wood in the air, but I need to get to the cabin. If there's any chance of Julia or Christopher being there, I'm sure they're going to need help. It's not about the story anymore. It's about getting them to safety.

I'm close enough to see part of the cabin through the trees now. Shutting down the engine, I exit my car and shuffle along the rest of the way. If I've been heard, I need to continue from another angle to ensure I catch him by surprise. Making my way through the forest as quickly as possible, considering my sore leg, a rustling startles me. I stop to listen, convinced someone or something is out here in the forest with me. If it's a wild animal, there's no way I can outrun it. And I don't want to use my gun and alert him. I inch cautiously toward the cabin, hoping whoever or whatever's out here doesn't hear me. The rustling sound fades.

A few minutes later, voices carry from the cabin.

"Where are they?"

"I don't know what you're talking about."

"What have you done with them?"

"Like I said, I don't know what you're talking about."

"Put the gun down, and we'll talk."

I'm close enough to see them now. Neither one is lowering their gun.

This isn't good. I have to do something. If I shoot from this distance, I'm going to miss. I haven't shot a gun for twelve years. And that was my first and only time. Searching the ground for another possible weapon, I pick up a rock and a fallen branch, then ease my way out of the woods toward the back of the cabin. I flatten myself against it, then slide along the exterior wall till I reach the back door. It's unlocked. Not making a sound, I slink through the cabin toward the front door, which has been left wide open. The two men are out front, one of them just outside the door with his back to me. If the other one, facing my way, notices me, he doesn't let on.

I can't bring myself to shoot him. It brings back too many memories. Using all my strength, I throw the rock as far as I can to the left of the cabin. It's enough to distract him for a second. He turns in that direction, and I bring the branch down hard across his shoulder, dislodging the gun from his hand.

"What the hell!" He lunges to the ground to retrieve it, but I kick him with my good leg, sending him sprawling forward. By the time he turns around, swearing, scrambling for his weapon, my Glock points directly down at his chest, finger on the trigger. His hand grips hold of his own gun, calling my bluff.

"Stop! Don't even think about it!" shouts the man across from us, his gun trained in our direction.

I'm not sure which one of us he's talking to, but I'm hoping I haven't made a mistake.

Am I pointing my gun at the wrong guy?

Chapter Eighty-One

Jim

July 26

The rain that started yesterday afternoon continued through the night and into today. With the wind settling down, conditions became more favorable for extinguishing the fires. Thanks to the donation of the mine equipment and the volunteer heavy equipment drivers, the fire break between Emery Park and the fires to the east and west was successful in stopping the spread.

The establishment of fire lines and the dousing of flames, along with the destruction of vegetation fueling the fire, brought the fires northwest of Lake Kipling under control. Jim is thankful to be returning home to his family three days after leaving.

* * *

Scott

Cheryl throws herself into her husband's arms when he walks through the door, nearly knocking him backwards. "You have no idea how worried I was. I'm so glad you're home." She kisses him for an unbelievably long time, despite the audience.

Brent jumps up and down shouting, "Dad! You did it! You beat the fire!"

Jamie runs circles around him, shouting, "Yay! Daddy's a hero!"

Cookie joins the reunion, jumping up on Jim's legs, yipping in excitement.

Mavis speaks up from the living room sofa. "Welcome back. Your wife and kids missed you."

Jim notices me standing off to the side, observing the happy family reunion. "So, what's been going on here?" His eyes move from me back to Mavis.

Mavis raises her eyebrows. "You won't believe it."

"Oh, nothing much." Cheryl shrugs her shoulders. "We found Julia. She's safe and sound. The baby's back with his mom. I'm afraid Danny won't be coming back." She explains that Danny's body was found over an embankment in Emery Park.

"That was Danny?" Jim looks stunned, his mouth open and wide eyes shifting from me to Cheryl now. "I should never have left you guys on your own. What exactly happened here?"

Cheryl repeats what she's said. "It's over. Officer Aaron Parker's been arrested for abducting Christopher. He's his biological father. And he's probably facing manslaughter charges for Danny's death. He tried to make it look like suicide by slipping a note in his car. Danny's super, Terry Lawrence, witnessed him pushing Danny over the cliff, and he's going to testify in exchange for a lighter sentence on blackmail and drug trafficking charges."

"Why would a police officer kill Danny?"

"Aaron is Julia's old boyfriend. He wanted to have her back for himself, but when he found out she was seeing Danny and it was getting serious, he took her off to his grandparents' cabin in the woods and kept her prisoner."

I speak up for the first time to clarify things. "She wasn't exactly unwilling. It seems she fell for Aaron all over again even though he abducted her. Stockholm Syndrome—I don't know if you've heard of it—is when a captive falls in love with their captor. It'll be hard to make charges stick for her abduction since she won't testify against him."

Once we're all seated in the family room, I tell Jim the whole story about how I found out it was Aaron who abducted Julia and the baby. "When Rebecca rang to return Cheryl's call, I was the one who picked up the phone. She said Aaron was the name of Julia's old boyfriend and that he wanted to be a cop someday; I called the station to speak to Aaron Parker and was told he called in sick for the day. Officer Murphy also informed me that drugs seized from Terry Lawrence's car came from lockup. Terry had lawyered up and was keeping quiet until he had a chance to talk to me. I said I'd deal with him later and asked Officer Murphy to get me any known addresses for Aaron Parker. Besides his apartment and his family's home, Officer Murphy remembered that Aaron's grandparents had a cabin in the woods. He'd been there with him on a couple of occasions. When Logan Murphy asked why I was inquiring about Aaron, I confided my suspicions to him and told him to keep that information to himself. Before heading out to the cabin, I talked to Lacey. Under pressure, she confirmed that Aaron was Christopher's father. She was afraid to say anything about him being the father because he threatened to tell social services about her drug addiction and take the baby away from her. She didn't want to lose Christopher. When I confronted Aaron at the cabin, he pulled his gun on me ."

Jim turns to Cheryl and rubs his forehead. "Please tell me you weren't there."

"I can't lie to you," she replies. "I saw what Scott had scrawled on the notepad by the phone. It was directions to the cabin. I followed him up there."

"You what?" Jim's voice rises, his brow furrowed.

"I'm glad she did," I interject. "She probably saved my life." I explain how I hadn't wanted Cheryl to come with me to the cabin because I didn't want to put her in danger. "Especially with her sore leg. That's why I left without telling her where I was going."

"What sore leg?" Jim looks back and forth between Cheryl and me, trying to follow what happened during his absence.

"She's okay. She hurt her leg when she fell running for the phone Friday when Scott called," Mavis explains. "And then he came over to spend the night. Luckily, he's a registered masseuse."

"He what?" Jim's eyes spring wider.

"It's okay." Mavis raises her hand to calm Jim. "He slept in the basement. I had my eyes on him the whole time he was here. Except when the power went out. Everything went dark, and we all went to bed."

Jim turns to Cheryl for an explanation. "Honey, why did Detective Evans spend the night?"

"Mavis was evacuated from her home, so I invited her to stay in our guest room. I invited Scott, too, because the highway was closed, and he couldn't get home very easily," Cheryl says, as though it's all perfectly fine and normal.

As a cat comes along and rubs against his legs, causing him to sneeze, Jim says, "I see. Are there any more evacuees here that I should know about?"

Brent speaks up. "Scott likes pizza and cool cars."

I'm positive Jim suspects there's something else I like, something that belongs to him. "Is that so?" His eyes bore into mine and I lose the staring battle. And if Cheryl hadn't made it clear enough already that she's taken, Jim certainly does.

"How about I order some pizza right now?" I take out my cell phone and step back, hoping to escape Jim's scrutiny. "Three meats and mushrooms for you?"

"That's right. How did you know that?"

"I'm a good detective. So's your wife."

"Detective Evans and I make a good team." Cheryl smiles at me while she slings her arm around Jim.

"That we do, partner. I'm so glad you showed up when you did." I move toward the kitchen to place the pizza order, still feeling Jim's suspicious eyes on my back.

"So am I," Cheryl says. "So am I."

"They're just friends," Mavis adds. "That's all."

Realizing that's all we'll ever be is bittersweet. I could never break up this happy family, regardless of my feelings. But I'd rather have Cheryl as my friend than to have never met her.

* * *

Cheryl

It seems like a good time to wrap both my arms around Jim's neck and give him another passionate kiss to remind him how much he means to me. "You're not jealous, are you?" I laugh when I break away. "You know there are only two men in my life. Only you and Brent." I muss the hair on our son's head, and a memory intrudes on my happiness.

It had been triggered yesterday afternoon when I held the gun pointed at Aaron Parker's chest and fought the compulsion to pull the trigger. As Scott shouted for Aaron not to make any sudden moves, Julia had come running out of the forest with the baby, yelling, "Stop! Don't! Don't shoot him! Please! Don't shoot him! Please!"

Aaron dropped his gun at the sight of Julia and his son.

Scott shouted, his revolver still drawn, "Where'd you get the gun, Cheryl? You can lower it now."

I kept it pointed at Aaron as I picked up his gun as well. "A woman needs to protect herself," I said. "By the way, you're welcome."

Love's a killer.

Poor Julia. In love with the wrong man. But you can't help who you fall for. I know what that's like. It's a lesson I learned early in life. Another lesson I learned is: Don't kill the only son of a Mafia godfather. And don't frame him for the murder.

I didn't want any part of that lifestyle for my unborn child. I wanted to leave it behind. Permanently. But I'm learning it's hard to outrun the Mafia. You have to keep running. It's been almost twelve years since I looked in the eyes of the man I loved, Brent's father, as I put a bullet through his heart. The image makes my blood run cold.

But there's no point in dwelling on the past. No good comes of that.

Acknowledgements

Thank you to my husband, Brian, who was instrumental in the creation of the Blue Water Mysteries series. In this second book, his insight helped me to provide the male point of view and create a distinct voice for Detective Scott Evans. My number one PR guy, Brian is by my side at every book event, never tiring of telling people all about my fictional worlds.

As well, I'd like to acknowledge our family for listening to my non-stop book talk. Thank you to my son, Bryant, for standing by me and ensuring my technology remains up and running; to my daughter, Brittany, son-in-law, Eric, and grandson, Rowan, for their encouragement and presence at book events; also to my brother, Joseph, and sister-in-law, Audrey, for supporting my writing and attending my book signing. Also thanks to my cousins Nancy and Peter Frankovic for their support and a surprise visit at the bookstore. I'm thankful for my nephews Evan and Reid, my step-nephew and step-niece, Max and Maia, my in-laws, Kim, Craig and Jody, and for T.C. and Scruffy, my loyal feline fans who never leave my side as I tap away on my laptop.

Thank you to my family and friends, both in real life and online, who have shown support for my books. I had the pleasure of meeting up with former classmates at our high school reunion this past fall and their interest in my books meant so much to me. To my friends from the post office, to friends in our small community, and to my former colleagues, thank you for your support. And to the other writers I've connected with, I'm grateful for the opportunity to share ideas and read each other's work.

Thank you to the beta readers who gave their opinions about Lost Like Me. A special thanks to my critique partner and friend, Norah Blakedon, for her expertise as a writer and her excellent insight into my characters.

To my agent, Cindy Bullard of Birch Literary, thank you so much! I wouldn't be in this position without your help. I am grateful for the opportunities you have provided and for your continued support of my writing.

To my editor, Shawn Reilly Simmons, thank you for your editing expertise and another perfect cover. Thanks to Verena Rose and the entire team at Level Best Books for putting this book into the hands of readers.

And to my readers, thanks for taking the time to be part of my Blue Water world. I appreciate every book purchase and each kind comment!

About the Author

Ivanka Fear is a Slovenian-born Canadian author. She lives in Ontario with her family and feline companions. Ivanka earned her B.A. and B.Ed. in English and French at Western University. After retiring from teaching, she wrote poetry and short stories for various literary journals. *The Dead Lie*, A Blue Water Mystery, was her debut novel. *Lost Like Me* is the second book in the Blue Water series. Ivanka is also the author of *Where is My Husband?*, A Jake and Mallory Thriller. She is a member of International Thriller Writers, Sisters in Crime, and Crime Writers of Canada. When not reading and writing, Ivanka enjoys watching mystery series and romance movies, gardening, going for walks, and watching the waves roll in at the lake.

SOCIAL MEDIA HANDLES:
  Facebook: https://www.facebook.com/ivankafearauthor/
  Twitter: https://twitter.com/FearIvanka
  Instagram: https://www.instagram.com/ivankawrites/

AUTHOR WEBSITE:
  https://www.ivankafear.com/

Also by Ivanka Fear

The Dead Lie, A Blue Water Mystery

Where is My Husband?, A Jake and Mallory Thriller

Milton Keynes UK
Ingram Content Group UK Ltd.
UKHW030946140324
439440UK00001B/92